TAB'S TERRIBLE THIRD EYE

ADVANCE PRAISE FOR TAB'S TERRIBLE THIRD EYE

"An engrossing horror yarn with a lot to say about the real-life challenges of OCD."

—*Kirkus Reviews*

"Colorful possession narrative spin with a relatable human heart beating at its center."

—Booklife Review by *Publishers Weekly*

"Thorne seduces us to the point where nothing is outlandish or impossible."

—Drew Rowsome, *My Gay Toronto*

TAB'S TERRIBLE THIRD EYE

ISAAC THORNE

Lost Hollow Books
Spring Hill, Tennessee

Copyright © 2025 by Isaac Thorne

All rights reserved. No part of this book may be used or reproduced in any form or by any electronic or mechanical means, including information storage and retrieval systems, without permission in writing from the publisher, except by reviewers, who may quote brief passages in a review.

You may not use this work for training AI, large language models (LLMs), or any other generative algorithms or software without permission in writing from the publisher.

ISBN 978-1-938271-60-1 (Hardback Edition)
ISBN 978-1-938271-59-5 (Paperback Edition)
ISBN 978-1-938271-62-5 (eBook Edition)

Library of Congress Control Number: 2024906553

This is a work of fiction. The characters, events, locations, and dialogue are either products of the author's imagination or are used fictitiously. Any resemblance to actual events or persons, living or dead, is entirely coincidental and not intended by the author.

Cover design by Paula Rozelle Hanback
www.paulahanback.com

Published in the United States of America by Lost Hollow Books
223 Town Center Pkwy #309
Spring Hill, TN 37174

www.isaacthorne.com
www.losthollowbooks.com

For the traumatized and the anxious.
You are safe right now.

Information about the tropes and other contents of this story can be found at the author's website:

www.isaacthorne.com/tabs-terrible-third-eye

Those who dream by day
are cognizant of many things
which escape those
who dream only by night.
—Edgar Allan Poe, "Eleonora"

Tis the eye of childhood
that fears a painted devil.
—William Shakespeare, *Macbeth*

Rule your mind or it will rule you.
—Horace

MAY 1, 2010

CHAPTER ONE

Someone was shaking him, rattling his teeth inside his skull. Rough, sandpapery hands gripped his shoulders, snagging on the soft cotton of his pajamas. The tugging sensation ripped him, without consent, from the sticky web of sleep. Awareness inevitable, Tab Beard opened his eyes. Senses snapped to attention. The burly silhouette of his father, Tim, loomed over him in the dark. Worry sat heavy on his features, visible even in the low light filtering in from the hall. A bright flash, a crack of thunder, and sleep was relegated to a distant memory.

"Wake up, son." The older man's voice resonated with remnants of dreams interrupted. Its texture mirrored the scent of his breath, tinged with the stale odor of Marlboro cigarettes. The taste of it along with a day's fade of Old Spice burned the back of Tab's throat. "Come on. Storm's here. We got to go. You're too old for me to have to carry you. Come on."

"Just leave him, Dad!" said a voice from somewhere outside his room. His older brother, Jeremy. The jerk.

In the next instant, he heard his dad grunt. Pressure invaded his armpits as his body launched into the air and snuggled the man's torso. Tab allowed his chin to rest on his father's broad shoulder. He wrapped his arms around his neck on instinct. Cheek stubble tickled his left temple, prompting a giggle despite the urgency of the situation. Nine years *was* too old to be carried, probably. Then again, he was too sleepy to care. And there was something comforting about not having to be in charge of his own body when the urge to remain asleep was this powerful.

Together, father and son bounded down the flight of stairs leading from the second-story bedrooms to the front door. A severe wind slapped the half of his face not pressed against his dad when they dashed outside. He turned away from it, glimpsing his mother, Sandra, running ahead of them as he did.

The gale whipped at her, peeling her nightgown away from her shins as she moved. Alongside, Jeremy ran like the devil was after him. He towed his homemade Sta-Puft Marshmallow Man pillow by one fluffy arm. It had been a birthday gift cut and sewn by his mom before Tab could even remember. At twelve, Jeremy claimed to be too old for toys. Yet the Marshmallow Man remained his buddy. At bedtime, anyway. Tab silently vowed to remember this image and use it the next time Jeremy called him a name. His brother's sleep-styled dark brown hair parted in a combover as he ran thanks to the force of the wind.

The four rounded the corner of the house when a brilliant bolt of bluish-white lightning struck the giant old walnut tree. Chopping it down had been on his dad's weekly to-do list for years because of how sick it grew. Somehow, he never seemed to get around to it. If the electricity in the air had its way, he might be too late.

The accompanying clap of thunder arrived a short time after. The explosion startled Jeremy, who bumped into his mom, knocking her off her feet. In his attempt to recover, Tab's brother slipped and fell into the mud himself. Dad stayed upright in spite of Mom bumping him on her way down but had to stumble backward a few paces to achieve it. Tab braced for impact, but his dad righted himself and set him down.

"Stay here," he said, pressing Tab against the side of the house. He next scurried to his wife and eldest son, helping them regain their footing, making certain there were no injuries.

Another *crack* echoed through the air, followed by a sharp metallic thud. A new odor permeated the environment: burning wood. Tab associated this aroma most with winter months. In this late spring thunderstorm, the scent created an otherworldly sensation, a stark contrast to the events around them. Dad wouldn't need to cut the tree down anymore. Creaking, swaying, and seconds later toppling, the beast crashed on its own. A thick, heavy branch now rested atop the door to the storm cellar.

"Fuck!"

"Tim!" his mom exclaimed. But at his dad. Not him. Everyone called him Tab because that's what his initials spelled: Timothy Aaron Beard, Jr. TAB. At school, he was only "Tim" until new teachers grew accustomed to calling him by his nickname.

Jeremy once tried to grate on him by telling him "Tab" could be short for "Tabitha," a girl's moniker. His brother went by "Jeremy" most of the time, although Tab had spent much of his toddler and up years pronouncing it *Jermy*, skipping the second *e*. Germs were gross things that made people sick. Tab thought *Jermy* could be a good comeback insult. Technically. But it had become too familiar among the family to offend his brother now. He once tried nicknaming the older boy "Jab" on account of his middle name, Alan, also started with the letter A, but that didn't stick.

Rain cascading off his head, Tab's dad swiped at his eyes to clear his vision. "Sorry." He motioned to Jeremy. "Come here. We can slide it far enough to get it off the door."

Tab offered no assistance. There were lots of things around the farm he wanted to help with. Like changing the tractor's tires or swinging the axe the way Dad does when he chops wood. Or stacking the hay bales in the barn loft. "When you're older," Dad would say. This seemed like one of those "when you're older" times.

Movement out of the corner of his eye caught his attention. Turning in that direction, he saw two tiny red dots of light glaring back at him from the darkness. Eyes. Animal eyes. Some animals' eyes glowed in the dark when they lurked on the sides of roads at night. When Dad's headlights struck them right. Cats and opossums and deer all had glowing eyes. He remembered seeing green ones. They used to scare him, but they were only wild creatures camouflaging themselves away from the noise and lights of passing cars. That's what Mom and Dad said.

An icy sliver of panic pierced his heart. *Alfie!* he thought. *Oh no! Alfie!*

Tab surveyed from a safe distance as his parents and brother, still in their nightclothes, wrestled with the unwieldy limb of the walnut tree. The family's orange tabby cat, who Jeremy named Alfie in honor of Batman's butler Alfred, had wandered up to the house a year before as a feral kitten. Tab had not objected to the name because Batman was the only thing he and his brother enjoyed together. Soon after, the cat adopted the Beards as his own. Now he could not be found.

"Alfie! Alfie, where are you?" He swiveled his head in every direction and settled again on the pair of red eyes at the edge of the lawn. They had not moved.

It has to be him, he thought. *The red must be a trick of the light. He ran out with us and got scared by the lightning and thunder. He's hiding in the woods. That's all.*

"Alfie!" he mimicked the singsong voice his mom used to call the family to dinner every night. "Alfie! *Psh psh psh*! C'mere, boy! C'mon!"

The eyes crouched lower to the ground, the way Alfie did when he prepared to launch attacks on unsuspecting toys that contained jingle bells. Or human toes.

"It *is* him!" Tab leaned forward, adopting his own crouch. The ground water soaked through his pajama pants and dampened his right knee. He bet he'd gotten them muddy, too, but chose not to care. Like Gramma always said, it would all come out in the wash. They couldn't allow the cat to stay outdoors all night in the storm.

"*Psh psh psh*." Tab stretched his right hand out and rubbed the thumb, forefinger, and middle finger together as further incentive for the beast to approach. He'd seen the tactic work when his dad and mom used it. He had no idea why. Dumb cat must have thought they had food. Whatever lay in the woods did not buy it.

For one anxious second, he thought he'd scared Alfie away. The twin dots of reflected light disappeared beyond the curtain of rain falling between him and them. Then they were there again, revealed by the branches of a small tree returned to its resting state after a fresh gust of high wind. Alfie had not moved.

Guess I'm gonna have to go get him.

He stole a glance at the rest of the family. They'd shoved the gigantic walnut limb most of the way off the cellar door. Not enough to swing it open. Only his brother's Sta-Puft Marshmallow Man, propped against the side of the house and near a mud puddle so Jeremy could help move the limb, had eyes on him. He could grab the cat and race back to the cellar before anyone knew. Mud sucked at his bare feet, lapping at them as if the earth wanted to swallow him whole. He hated the sensation. Rescuing the cat would be a welcome distraction.

Inching forward, careful to not frighten Alfie, Tab fought the urgency to pry himself free of the ground so he could secure the cat in his arms. The poor beast stood closer to the ground than him. If the rain and mud were going to drown anyone, it would be Alfie first. Halfway to the edge of the yard, where the tree line began, the eyes disappeared again. Tab stopped dead, terrified the cat had run off. Soon enough, they reappeared, closer to him than before.

He sighed. *Stay still!*

A menacing growl emerged from the maelstrom. Angry. Threatening. Tab's knees gave when its vibrations traveled through his ears and down his spine. The creature in the woods was not Alfie, and was *not* friendly. Before the little boy's brain could command his legs to flee, it was upon him.

Small branches obscuring the thing rustled and moved apart. The creature dashed from the woods on limbs made from springs. It closed more than half the distance to Tab in one ferocious leap. Trails of foaming saliva dripped from bared fangs. Canid lips peeled back to reveal blackened gums stacked with yellow rows of pointed teeth. A pale red tongue lolled from the left side of its mouth. It was as if the organ had died. Black fur hid the rest of the creature, save for the pink inside the bat-like ears at its temples.

The thing reared on its hind legs. In the next second, it transformed into something resembling a man, or a woman, with a mane of hair flowing over its entire body. A ferocious wolf's head capped these features, too big for the frame it sat atop. Triple-knuckled fingers dangled from the ends of extended hands. Crescent-shaped yellow-gray claws adorned each digit. Its human-like shoulders were broad, meaty, and muscular. As it stretched and straightened itself in the beams of the floodlights, Tab glimpsed pink rippling flesh in its armpits. The creature howled a lonesome, broken note that hung long in the air.

Tab's paralysis broke. He backpedaled, incapable of tearing his gaze away. Matching his backward steps with forward ones, the creature closed in with alarming strides. It towered over him. He froze, his terror-struck mind unable to process the scene. A strand of mucous snapped off the creature's lower lip, oozing onto the boy's upturned forehead. The glob ran down his left temple and lodged there, dammed by Tab's curly blond "rock star hair." His dad's description. Something sizzled in his left ear. A searing sensation accompanied it. Tab clapped his hand to it, trying in vain to massage it away. Two fingers smeared the goop on his temple. It was thick and gross and...burning? The tips of his fingers felt like they were on fire. Without thinking, he stuffed them in his mouth, then immediately pulled them free and spat toward the creature. Now his tongue and the back of his throat felt hot and sore as well.

Thunderheads opened, dropping a fresh deluge of fat raindrops akin to the force from the end of a garden hose when you press your thumb against it. Only, it poured everywhere. The creature in front of Tab yowled in agony and, he would swear, began to melt right before his eyes. Its snout drooped and ran from its skull like candle wax. Its gleaming red eyes went dark and caved into their sockets. Fur molted from its withering shoulders and fell to the ground in great heaping clumps.

By the time his dad's rough hand snatched Tab's left one, the creature had disappeared into the orangey black muck of Tennessee mud and clay. After a few thudding sprints—with Tab struggling both to remain upright and keep up this father's pace over the soft ground—the family huddled inside the storm cellar as the heaviest of the night's tempest thundered and crackled in the sky. It hammered nonstop at the steel cellar door over their heads.

Tim deposited his son alongside the boy's mother on the cellar floor, then strode back up the stairs long enough to latch the door. He knelt in front of his young namesake after, eyeing him in earnest.

"What have we told you about wandering off?" he asked, his voice firm but not unkind. "We heard you scream and thought something had happened to you."

"I—I didn't scream," Tab said. His voice sounded small and trembling to his own ears.

His dad smirked. "Well, *somebody* screamed. Sounded like someone was sawing your leg off." He glanced at their mother. "Mom here thought there was another man in the storm with us. You howled like a full-grown man."

"I didn't howl," Tab said, stronger this time.

His dad scoffed. "Okay. Whatever. The point is when I tell you stay somewhere, you stay. We're all safe in the storm cellar now, so it's fine. But in the future, I expect you to do what I tell you. Especially in an emergency, and this is an emergency. Got it?"

Tab stared at his feet. "Got it." He thought a moment and added, "Dad? Are there wolves in these woods?"

His father eyed him, confused. "Wolves? More likely to be coyotes. I don't think we need to worry about wolf attacks tonight, though. Any wild dogs are gonna hunker down in their dens, same as you and me."

"Baby Tabitha is afraid of the Big Bad Wolf!" Jeremy said from beside their mother. His almond eyes gleamed with big brother malice. Tab's mom elbowed him sharply in the ribs. "Ow!"

"Mind your business, kiddo," she said.

Jeremy returned to kneading smudges of dirty rainwater off the Sta-Puft Marshmallow Man with his thumbs.

Tab ignored him. He'd wanted to say something about the Marshmallow Man doll but couldn't seem to think of it fast enough. Besides, Gramma always said that ignoring a monster was the best way to make it slink away on its own. It was never easy, though.

"It's just that I saw one. A big one. I thought it was Alfie hiding in the woods. But it walked out and stood up on its back legs. I got some of its spit on me. Then the rain came and melted the wolf away."

Jeremy guffawed. "Oh, wow! Are you sure you're not still asleep and having a nightmare?"

"Quiet!" Tab's mom said.

Tab glared at his brother. "I'm sure. The place he spit on me hurts, too. It stings." He turned his head so his dad could take in his left temple, indicating the spot with his finger. An angry red lump had arisen there. Tab pressed it by accident, wincing at the sting of his own touch.

"It hurts to touch it?" his mom asked.

"Yeah."

His dad scratched his chin and examined the bump but did not poke at it himself. "It's a big old pimple. That's all. The kind we used to grow when we were teenagers. Could be a mosquito bite or something, I guess. 'Tis the season for those things. Does it itch?"

Tab shook his head. "No. It burns and hurts."

"Well, I don't think it's anything we need to worry about tonight. We'll put something on it after the storm passes. I'm sure it's a pimple or a bug bite."

"He's a little young for acne, Tim," the boy's mother said. She sounded exasperated, the way she sometimes did when she'd had a long day and the boys were "getting on her last nerve."

Tim nodded. "I know, Sandra," he said through teeth clamped tight together. Tab recognized that tone and expression. It set his stomach to knots. Mom had disagreed with him in front of their sons, an aggravation all-too familiar to the family unit. He didn't say so. Not this time. But he had before. Although Tab thought his mom should be allowed to speak her mind, he was also afraid of the humiliated rage he saw behind his father's eyes whenever she did. He wished his mom wouldn't try to talk to his dad when he was in those moods.

Sandra Beard's hair, which other than its length was a match for Jeremy's, hung limp and wet on her head and hid her eyes from her youngest son. He recognized the shape of her mouth, though. She was either worried or angry. Or both. She and Jeremy looked almost the same when they were angry, and Jeremy was always angry. A woman of slight build, the two of them seated together were like twins more than mother and son.

Tab didn't think he favored either parent. His dad had a round, friendly face and a brawny build. Tab's Gramma and Grampa always said each parent had their own child: Jeremy matched his mom, and the younger boy resembled his dad. Sometimes he saw the resemblance, but not right now. Right now, his dad's anger created pinchy lines along the sides of his nose. His warm blue eyes narrowed to ice-cold slits.

Jeremy had been right, he supposed. Mom and Dad were fighting again. Tab had not wanted to believe his brother because he lied. A lot. Once, he'd scared Tab half to death with nasty tales about their house. He said he'd heard the hauntings by noisy ghosts who banged on walls when everyone but Jeremy was asleep. The same night, Jeremy had knocked on the adjoining wall between their rooms. Tab bolted screaming from the bed, terrifying both his parents. He'd also scared the cat. Poor Alfie found cover between the refrigerator and kitchen cabinets. Hours passed before the fraidy feline dared show himself again.

The cat. Alfie. *Oh, no! Alfie!*

He searched the cellar but saw no sign of the cat. "Alfie!" He startled both his parents. "Where is Alfie?"

Tim placed a hand on his son's shoulder, no doubt intending for it to be comforting. Tab fought the urge to shrink away.

"I'm sure he's okay," Tim said. "We'll only be down here until the storm passes. He'll find a place to hide."

"But he's all by himself! He's all by himself and if a tornado comes, he'll be hurt! We need to go get him!"

Tab rose and padded toward the cellar stairs. His father tucked a finger into his shirt collar as he brushed past and stayed him. His voice deepened. He'd pushed Dad too far, and this would be his last warning. "Son, I told you we can't go back out right now. Alfie's smart. He'll go in the bathroom and hide. That's where people go in these storms if they don't have a cellar like we do."

"But he's *not* smart! He's an orange cat and—"

"Sit. Down," Tim growled at him, pointing a thick, cracked finger at a long wooden bench on which the rest of the family had settled. "Or I'll make you."

He tugged Tab backward, guiding him back to his seat. The boy crumpled. A tear rolled down his left cheek. He shoved his elbows into his knees and sobbed. His dad's reassurances were not. Impatience inundated the older man's voice. How did he know where Alfie hid? For all they knew, the cat had followed them outside unseen. Alfie might have been devoured by a dog like the one Tab encountered. Or maybe he was lurking in the rain, pawing at the door, trying to find his way into the locked cellar. Tab sobbed but shut his mouth when he spied his dad's third-warning glare.

"Let's all just be patient," Tim said, the scowl on his face betraying his own lack of it. "This will all be over before morning."

Tim plucked his iPhone from his back pocket and launched the iTunes app. He scrolled for a moment, then tapped. An old Eagles song, "The Last Resort," started playing. It was from their *Hotel California* album, Tab recalled. He only knew this because it was one of his father's favorites. Dad played it endlessly on car trips, short or long. Mom had once pointed out that Dad seemed to play it mostly when he was stressed. Tab enjoyed the song, too, although he couldn't make heads or tails of the meaning of the lyrics. When he asked, his dad dismissed his questions with something like "it was a different time."

"I hate that song," a gruff voice with a gravelly edge announced from the darkness along the opposite wall of the cellar. "Your cat is fine, though. Alfie is hiding under the couch in the living room."

Tab trained his eyes in the direction from which the voice had come. Leaning against the cinder block sat a mammoth man wearing beige coveralls and a red baseball cap. From beneath the cap's band, strands of yellow-blond hair hung in short waves. Enormous chapped hands stained with oil or black dirt rested on his knees. His cheeks, chin, and neck sported at least a day's worth of salty stubble. The shadow of the cap's visor obscured his eyes. He grinned. It was a broad smirk that flared his nostrils and crinkled most of the musculature of his lower face.

None of the rest of the family appeared to be aware of the new voice in the room.

"Dad?" Tab said, tugging on his father's sleeve with one hand and pointing at the stranger with the other. "Who is that man?"

CHAPTER TWO

In the next instant, Tab splintered the bonds of unconsciousness to discover himself in his own bed. He did not remember what happened after the man in the cellar told him Alfie was safe. His feet had warmed and felt clean. His skin beneath his pajamas was dry. He could smell the lavender-scented soap his mom bought that one time at Kroger, the stuff no one wanted to use so she had to find uses for it until it was gone. He also had to pee.

Had the night before happened or had he been dreaming? He supposed the latter was possible. It had been only a week since Jeremy had filled his head with stories about a demonic dog infestation in Lost Hollow. The two boys had "camped" on the floor in front of the family's television set the previous weekend. Tab's older brother, flashlight on and tucked beneath his chin, had regaled the younger with folktale after folktale, all set in their own little hometown. He'd told a story about the mysterious hitchhiking woman who was really a ghost. She caught rides with young men who were driving in the wee hours and then asked them to drop her off in front of Lost Hollow Cemetery where she promptly disappeared. He'd told a story about the spirit of a headless engineer who wandered the train tracks down by the old depot, apparently looking for the head he'd lost in a freak derailment on a crisp and moonless October night.

But the scariest stories Jeremy told during their sleepless escapade involved the hellhounds of Lost Hollow: enormous doglike creatures with glowing red eyes and black fur that could walk on two legs like a human and run on all fours like a wolf. These creatures, Jeremy said, were responsible for the disappearances of many their hometown's residents over the years, especially bad children. They emerged straight from a hidden portal connecting the town to the bowels of Hell, claiming sinful souls that they'd then drag kicking and screaming into the fiery depths.

His voice deepening, sounding as gravelly as the earth shoveled over a fresh corpse, Jeremy explained that seeing such a hound but not being dragged into Hell presages earthly (and fatal) disaster for the witness. Just like the poor souls who sheltered in their great aunt Kathy's old general store during the hundred-year flood of 1955. One by one they had entered the safety of that building, never to be seen or heard from again.

That explains last night, Tab thought. *It must have been a dream.*

Rain slapped against the glass of his bedroom window, streaking the fog of humidity condensed there. His curtain was half drawn. Based on the halo of gray haze filtering around the edges of the fabric, he figured it must be sunup.

How long can it rain? He sat up, threw back his bed covers, and slid off the edge of the bed. At the foot, Alfie the orange cat yawned, revealing sharp yellow fangs and a curled pink tongue. He stretched his toes, nestling his right cheek into the velvety fur atop his paws. Tab smiled. Alfie turned out to be fine, after all. The strange man in the cellar had been right.

He peeled back the curtain and glanced out the window. *Dad said it would all be over by the morning*, he thought. *But it's still raining* hard!

Then it dawned on him. He didn't remember returning to bed from the cellar the night before. He didn't remember finding Alfie. Nor did he remember cleaning up before pulling on fresh pajamas and climbing back into bed. The last thing he remembered was asking his dad about the man who was in the cellar with them. If he'd received an answer, he had no memory of it.

He checked the first two fingers of his left hand. They were uninjured. No burns. No scrapes or scars. His throat felt a little sore, but that could have been from the cold rain and night air. Not a speck of mud or dirt from the evening's adventure marked his feet. The only thing peeking out from under the hem of his Spider-Man jammies were clean, pinkish toes with neat, trimmed nails. He'd been wearing his Incredible Hulk PJs in the cellar. He was sure. Someone else had clothed him in Spider-Man, and that was creepy. No one had changed his clothes for him since he was little.

He wiggled his toes, almost forgetting he had to pee. His feet fell in fleshy slaps against the bedroom floor as he danced the dance of urgency, trying to not dampen his fresh nightclothes. He dashed out of his room and past the entryway to his parents' bedroom. From within came the faint sound of the television, on already. On most days, they didn't switch it on until after supper. The voice coming from it sounded like one of the Bad News Guys his dad watched every night while Mom tried not to listen.

He made it to the bathroom. After peeing, he stopped to wash his hands. Mom would be able to tell if he didn't. In the mirror, he caught sight of his left temple. A square of folded gauze had been fastened to his head with four pieces of sterile white cloth tape. A strip pasted each edge of the square to his skin. The cloth covered the pimple or bug bite or whatever the bump was they'd discovered last night. There was no pain when he touched it now, thankfully.

Pinching a layered corner of the tape between two fingers, he peeled away the edge. There, big as life, sat the bump. Except it was not a bump. It was more of an oblong crater, like the pictures of the moon on the wall of his third grade classroom at school. The interior pulsed a deep, angry red. Swirling within the crimson were blotches of bulky, ichorish goop with a scab-like, chitinous texture. But they weren't like any scabs Tab had ever seen. He poked at one with a fingernail, sending fiery pain in a flare through his skull. He winced, seething.

Peeling the bandage farther back, he leaned toward the mirror. The "scab" disappeared into the swirling mess. A long red line broken by spidery branches wended across the center of the wound. It rolled backward, shortened, reeling the thickest part of itself into the wall of surrounding flesh. Dead center, a shiny black dot emerged from its depths. It glistened in the light of the bathroom fixture. Without warning, it moved, rotating like an eye rolling in its socket. When it stabilized, it seemed to focus. An iris narrowed in its center, staring back at him from his own reflection.

Tab screamed.

From elsewhere in the house came the thudding sounds of his mom and dad racing to locate him. They burst into the bathroom without knocking and collapsed to their knees, one on each side. His mother's hands landed on his shoulder, her eyes enlarged, alarmed. His dad looked sleepy. A double-layered set of purple baggage accessorized each of his eyes.

"It's okay," his mom said. "It's okay, hon. It's okay. You're okay."

"What is this?" Tab asked, indicating his bandaged temple. "It looks like a mad eyeball. And it's moving!"

"Shh, shh, shh. Let me look, honey." She pried the bandage the rest of the way off his temple and chucked it aside. "Go get a fresh one, please."

Both Tim the younger and the elder understood she intended the command for Dad. He grunted, pressing his hands against his knees to help himself to his feet, and left the room. Sandra selected a clean washcloth from a short stack of them she kept in a basket by the sink. She dampened it, then dabbed it against the open wound.

"You fell asleep in the cellar last night," she said. Her voice was tender, soothing. "That's all. You're not awake yet. Your dad carried you up here after the storm died down. We cleaned you up and put you back in bed." She smiled, wistful. "You didn't know, did you?"

"No."

"We saw the bump on your head had opened up when Dad picked you up. He thinks you must've scratched it open in your sleep or something. We need to keep it clean so you don't get an infection. If it doesn't get any better, we'll have a doctor examine it, okay?"

"Why does it move around?" Tab asked. A second lump lodged in his throat. The thought that it might be a twin of the one on his head occurred to him. He flitted it away, not wanting to follow it to the nightmare conclusion that his entire body might transform overnight into a bag of eyeballs. It was getting hard to stand still while his mother worked. "I thought it was looking at me!"

His mom scoffed. "Well, sometimes, when we're young, things look scarier than they are," she said. "That's more true when something is new or strange. Here." She produced a hand mirror from a drawer under the sink. "Watch in the big mirror while I hold this up to the bump." She combed his blond curls away from his temple with one hand and held up the mirror with the other. "See, honey? Just a bump that's been scratched open. That's all."

She was right. Now that he was able to glimpse the wound without turning his head and cutting his eyes, he saw no black swirls or shining pupil-like dots careening through the redness within. What's more, the redness was now not so red to him. It was pink. Tab breathed a relieved sigh as his dad rejoined them.

"Got some fresh gauze and tape," he said. "Also grabbed the Neosporin while I was at it. Figured it couldn't hurt."

"Thanks." She accepted the bandage and tube of triple antibiotic from him without looking. "Tab, we all had a bad scare last night with the storm and everything. It's natural to be a little nervous and hypervigilant after something like this."

"What's hypervigilant?"

Sandra smiled. There was sweetness in it. "Hypervigilant means being more on the lookout for problems than you need to be."

"Oh."

"Being hypervigilant can make us think we have problems that don't exist. You can double that if you're tired. With young folks like you, the imagination runs amok sometimes. You've only experienced the world through your home life, your school, and I guess a little from TV and the internet. So the problems you're hypervigilant about are still fantastic and monstrous."

"When'd you get a psych degree?" Tim asked, chuckling. The grogginess had departed from his voice. Sandra ignored him.

"I've read a lot about psychology, Tab. You're gifted with a vivid imagination. It's evident in your drawings. I noticed Dad didn't bring your sketchbook to the cellar with us last night, by the way. He probably should have. Would have been a good way to keep your head occupied."

Tim sighed and performed an exaggerated shrug. "Sorry. Jesus."

"If things aren't better tomorrow, we'll go to a doctor, okay?"

"We can't go today?"

"It's Sunday," Tim said. "Doc's not open. Plus, a lot of the roads are flooded. The news is calling this a 1,000-year flood." He chuckled. "One of those temporary metal school buildings went floating down I-24 up in Nashville this morning! We'll be lucky if we can go buy groceries this weekend."

"Tim!"

Tab's eyes had grown wide, alarmed. Sandra cut her eyes to Tim and nodded in the boy's direction.

"Oh," Tim said. "Sorry. We'll be fine, Tab. It's just bad weather. It'll pass soon. We're not going to run out of food."

From elsewhere in the house there was a loud moan followed by a series of staccato farts and an irritable snort. Soon after, Tab's brother Jeremy settled into a snoring rhythm. The trio in the bathroom looked at each other and grinned.

"He's your son," Tim said, laughing.

"No, he only favors me. When it comes to his digestive system and sinuses, he's you made over."

Tab stopped mid-giggle and peered at his mother in earnest. "Do *I* have digestive and sinus issues, Mom?"

"No, son, but you're going to have sleep deprivation issues if you don't get back to bed."

"But the sun's out!"

"Yes, and most of the time I'd say it's way past the hour both of you were out of bed. But we had a long night. The weather guy thinks we might be in for another one tonight. The more rested you two are, the better. Don't you agree, Dad?"

She considered Tim for the first time since he'd returned to the bathroom.

"Sure," he said. "I think we could all use as much extra rest as we can get. We'll feel better when this has all blown over."

With a fresh coat of antibiotic ointment and a new bandage applied, Tab did as he was told. His bare feet had grown ice cold again from being out from under the covers too long. They welcomed the return of bed warmth with a funny tingling sensation once he slid in and settled down. Tab grinned, allowing his eyes to close. *The human body is weird*, he thought.

"Yours is weirder than you imagine," came a reply.

Tab's eyelids fluttered open again. He sat up. The voice was coarse, masculine. The same voice from the night before in the cellar: *Your cat is fine.* Tab glanced around his bedroom. No one sat in the little rocking chair in the back corner beside the bed. No one stood or sat near his chest of drawers, nor at the desk where he spent hours at a time drawing. No one stood in the bedroom's open doorway.

It took a moment for him to summon the courage, but he bent down from the bed, raised its skirt, and glanced underneath. No one. A shape in the gray light of the morning through the skirt somewhat resembled a rat or a mouse. After some focus, Tab realized it was a bunny. One of the dust variety.

He clambered topside. The folding doors of his closet caught his eye. The closet was lengthy but not deep. It lay behind a pair of bifold doors, each disguising its contents with slats his mom called louvers. He used to rely on the closet often back when he and Jeremy played hide-and-seek, when Jeremy was still fun. It was a great spot. Tab could cover himself with fallen clothes but also see through the spaces between the louvers. He always knew when it was safe to leap from his hiding spot and run for base.

If the man he'd seen in the cellar last night was in his room, he might also choose a great spot like the closet in which to conceal himself. As if in answer to these thoughts, one of the bifold doors cracked open at its hinge. It made the tiniest of noises, the sound of the roller along its track as the hinges spread apart. The gap where the sets of doors met grew wider, menacing, like a mouth intent on swallowing him whole.

Tab leaned back against his headboard, drawing his covers to his chin, over his mouth, over his nose. His unblinking eyes stung, but he could not avert his gaze. He tried to call for his mom and his dad. The sounds emerged as only squeaking non-words, as if there was no breath left in his lungs to force them over his lips.

The door widened to its limit. The ambient light of the room fell direct on the man from the cellar the night before, who now sat on the floor of Tab's closet. His beige coveralls were unmarred by the previous night's events. No dirt. No dried mud. No dampness. His red baseball cap was likewise clean and dry. He stroked the stubble on his chin and grinned at Tab. A distinct absence of warmth and familiarity contaminated the gesture.

Tab's heart pounded in his chest, filling his ears with pulsing bass. His head throbbed with the rhythm. The wound on his left temple itched and burned under its new bandage and against the rapid flow of hot blood. He resisted the urge to tear the gauze away and scratch it.

"There it is," the man said aloud to him. "Your weird thing. That new third eye you have is gonna come in real handy for you, Timbo. For *us*."

"My name is Tab. Everyone calls me that." The words were out before he could stop them.

"Heh. Yeah. You'll see, Tab. Been following you since you got slapped with the demon spit. You're gonna be a huge help to me. You got three eyes now. Me? I got none."

The man shoved the bill of his cap backward, allowing light to fall on the parts of his face hidden in shadow. Below his prominent forehead ridge were two deep, black eye sockets. No eyeballs occupied them. The lids were there, but ragged and split. It was as if someone had stuck a finger in his sockets and plucked out the eyeballs, mangling the thin membrane of eyelid skin in the process.

"Boo!" he said, flailing jazz hands beside his face. He followed the performance with an endless, thunderous roar of insane laughter.

Tab yanked his bed covers the rest of the way over his head. There, he found the breath to scream again.

CHAPTER THREE

Tab did not go to the doctor on Monday. Nor were Tim and Sandra able to take him on Tuesday, Wednesday, or Thursday of the week following the flood. Roads remained impassable. Schools, which had been only two weeks from dismissal, had not yet reopened. Businesses remained shuttered while merchants clashed with insurance companies and volunteers cleaned up. Small business owners dedicated days and nights to pushing broomfuls of brown sludge water from their buildings. They disposed of ruined stock, mitigated mold, and evaluated salvageable items, all in the service of rebuilding and moving on.

Sandra changed Tab's bandage each morning. She never mentioned the bump, but Tab knew it wasn't healing. To make matters worse, the soreness in his throat had become unbearable to the point that he fought swallowing. When he did, it felt like someone had mashed crushed glass into his tonsils and uvula. The concern on his mother's face while she worked was unmistakable. Her forehead wrinkled and eyes drooped at the edges. Her lips stretched into a grimace. Tab sometimes peeked at the wound but saw no more evidence of the blackened swirls or the pupil he thought he'd seen on Sunday. It wasn't healing, but at least it hadn't worsened. He considered that a win.

At his mom's behest on the worst day of his throat pain, Tab opened his mouth baby bird-style so she could examine his throat. "Oh no," she said. "I can see white streaks on your tonsils, kiddo. I'll bet you have strep again."

Again. So close to the end of the school year, too. Was it his third or fourth bout with the infection since he started third grade? He couldn't remember. Tab closed his mouth and sneered at his own reflection. Why did this keep happening? He didn't use the school's water fountains. He washed his hands after using the bathroom. Usually. For him to keep getting strep while the other kids remained free of it seemed unfair.

Lucky for him, their pediatrician, Dr. Patel, knew about his strep proclivity. All it took was a phone call from his mom for her to call in a scrip for amoxicillin to a pharmacy that was within easy reach. His dad picked it up, careful to avoid any flood zones, and Tab's throat began to feel better that same day.

Too bad the bump isn't strep, he thought.

Each night during Tab's recovery, his dad searched his son's room for evidence of the man living in his closet. The man who wore "tan work clothes," had no eyes, and spoke to him from the depths of the closet regardless of their efforts to stop him. Frustrated after three nights of nothing, Tim bent a wire hanger tightly around the door to prevent it from opening on its own.

"My guess is it's not hung square," he told his son. "The house gets cooler at night and things contract. Enough for gravity to pull the door open." When Tab protested, pointing out his father's theory didn't explain the presence of the man, he was met with dismissive silence.

The hanger wire didn't work, so on the fifth day, Tim tried removing the bifold from its track. He reinstalled it with spare hardware he'd discovered in the cellar. That didn't solve anything, either. He finally suggested Jeremy might be playing pranks on his younger brother. Or, in an angrier moment, that Tab was causing his own problems to get attention. On night six, he screamed at the boy to "man up" and go to bed. Tab spent the rest of that night in suffocating silence, afraid both of the man in his closet and his father. Tim's outbursts could be explosive, a pressure cooker full of shrapnel shredding anyone in his path.

"You read them psychology books," he overheard his father say to his mother on the morning after he'd reinstalled the door. "Don't kids do this kind of acting out when they know their parents are fighting?"

Tab didn't wait for his mother's answer. He dashed to Jeremy's room, sensing no safety in his own, even in the daytime. He threw himself face-first onto the empty bed. The covers were taut and clean smelling. Not at all like his brother. Jeremy had of late disappeared into the internet. That, and a series of old horror comedy DVDs their father had collected. He kept falling asleep on the couch instead of going to bed. Tab envied him. He buried his face in his brother's pillow, thrusting his fists into the soft mattress.

"I'm going crazy," he mumbled. "I'm going crazy. No one believes me and I'm going crazy." He lay like that for a few minutes before anyone discovered him. When the light touch of another's hand settled between his shoulder blades, his breath caught in his throat. He rolled with a start.

"Hon," his mom said. "I'm sorry you overheard. You're frustrated. Your father and I are...struggling, too. Listen, you're a sensitive, imaginative boy. There's nothing wrong with that. But sometimes sensitive boys, especially the creative ones, take a little longer to grow out of phases than other kids. That's what I think you're going through: just a scary, scary phase."

"Jesus, Sandra," Tim interrupted. "He's nearly a preteen at this point and still all over the goddamn map developmentally, at least according to his teachers. He's small for his age, but that doesn't mean he's a mental baby. You still talk to him that way, though, don't you?" He gestured open-palmed at Tab. "Third grader reads at a fifth grade level, draws like he's some kind of fucking Mozart, but is still afraid of monsters and needs his mom to comfort him like a preschooler." This last he said in a mocking childlike voice that Tab knew was directed at him, not his mother.

"He can hear you, Tim," Sandra said, although her eyes remained locked on her son's. "And Mozart was a composer, not an artist." To Tab, "Hon, if you're convinced that you're not pretending or imagining things when you see the man in your closet, we're going to need some help to figure out what's going on. What if your dad sleeps on the floor of your room tonight?"

"What?"

"Tim! Shh!" Sandra hissed. "Would it help you feel better? If anything happens, you can wake your dad up when it does. He'll figure out what's going on. Then we can all work together to fix it."

"Sandra, my back—"

"Tim!" she snapped.

His dad sighed. "Okay. Okay. Let me go see if I can find those air mattresses we bought for camping and never used because you were too scared of bugs and the dark to go. We live on a farm, for Chrissakes, Sandra. How can you be afraid of bugs?" The question escaped his lips with a growl, the intensity behind it palpable. It wasn't meant to be answered. His mother would poke the tiger anyway.

"You wanted to go camping for a whole week!" Sandra shot back. "All I said was I don't think I could last that long without some light and a proper bed. I would've been happy to do a weekend."

"Oh, please," Tim sneered. "I offered to start with a weekend and do a long trip later, but you said you were too busy."

"I never said—"

"STOP FIGHTING!" Tab rolled onto his back, facing them. His cheeks glowed a bright red. Tears rolled from the corners of his eyes, one of them washing over the bump on his temple. "WHY CAN'T YOU BOTH STOP FIGHTING?" A tickle irritated his throat. The words broke off with a violent coughing fit, forcing him to sit up. Sandra embraced him, pulling him snug.

"Sorry," she said. "We're sorry, honey. You're right. We shouldn't fight in front of you."

He wiped his mouth and nose with his pajama sleeve, smearing a blend of tears and snot there. "You shouldn't be doing it at all!"

"Sometimes moms and dads fight, Tab," Tim said. "It's okay. It's all going to be okay. We promise. Right, Mom?"

There was a noticeable pause before she answered, but she did answer. "Right."

"I'm going to go find the mattress," Tim said. His back to them, he punctuated his exit with a scoff and a sad, slow shake of his head. Sandra and Tab watched him go. Once the echoes of his footsteps had faded away, Sandra again attended to Tab. She bore a doleful expression, her eyes downcast.

"Look, whatever problems your dad and I are having right now are not because of you or your brother, okay? I promise. Grownups—well, grownups are selfish and silly about some things. That can make it hard to get along for a while. Your dad's a hard-head and has a temper, but I can handle him. We're doing our best to work things out. You know?"

She smiled. "If our problems are causing you problems, you put us out of your mind right now. We're not going to let anything happen to you or your brother."

Tab returned her smile.

"Okay?" she said.

"Okay."

"Awesome. Now, let's bail on your brother's room before he finds out we're in here. He's at that age now. He doesn't like other people poking around in his things."

"I wasn't poking."

"That won't stop him from thinking it. Come on." She grasped his hand and helped him slide off the bed. "Your dad might need your help setting up the air mattress. I need to find some sheets and a pillow for it, I guess."

"Dad doesn't believe me at all," Tab said.

"Well, Dad's one of those people who has to see things for himself," Sandra said. "Some people just need to see."

"Even if I already know what I saw?"

"Yes, even if you're sure about what you saw." She rubbed her forehead with three fingers of her left hand. "Please, Tab. I have things I have got to do. Can you go help your dad? Let's put this on the back burner until bedtime."

CHAPTER FOUR

"Told ya they were fighting again," Jeremy taunted when Tab strolled into the family room. He'd evidently overheard the snappishness between their parents while Tab was seeking refuge in his room. The older boy sat in front of the family's iMac, surfing the web as fast as their satellite service would allow. Which wasn't fast at all compared to the cable service their school had somehow been able to obtain. Jeremy had a bad habit of using up all the month's high-speed data allowance in the first week of the new billing cycle, dragging the rest of the month to a nearly unusable crawl because their father refused to buy more data or a higher tier.

"They're always fighting," Tab said, a hitch in his voice left over from his earlier fit.

"Yeah. They're probably gonna get divorced. I'm guessing I'll go with Dad and you'll have to stay with Mom. Maybe even Gramma and Grandpa when everything goes tits up."

Tab clapped his hands to his ears. "Don't say things like that!"

Jeremy shrugged, not looking away from the Wikipedia article he was perusing. "Listen, I'm just being honest. I don't think Mom loves him anymore. She spends all her time on

Facebook now and Dad barely knows how to turn a computer on. She's probably having an online affair or something."

"STOP IT!" Tab cried.

From elsewhere in the house came an irritable bellow. "JEREMY ALAN, LEAVE YOUR BROTHER ALONE!" He'd managed to piss off Dad again. That was his warning shot. If Tab cried out a second time, they'd both hear the elephantine stomp of Tim Beard's boots toward the family room. That would most likely be followed by a ten-minute session of screaming. Not at Jeremy specifically, but at both boys in general. And not because Jeremy had been mean to Tab, but because Tab's outcry had interrupted whatever their dad happened to be doing at that moment.

No apology nor acknowledgement escaped the older brother. Only silence. His eyes remained glued to the Wikipedia article on the iMac's screen. They neither spoke nor looked at each other, but Tab understood exactly what Jeremy was thinking and feeling at that moment. He had accidentally poked the tiger in their father again. And for all his bravado, poking the tiger was never an intentional act. So, instead of getting upset, apologizing, or crying, Jeremy simply shut down, becoming invisible until the storm passed.

From over Jeremy's shoulder, Tab recognized the featured image in the Wikipedia article. It was the title screen for *Ghost Adventures*. "Dammit!" Jeremy stage-whispered, presumably so his mother and father wouldn't hear. "They moved the new season premiere to September." He slapped the palm of his hand down hard on the iMac's keyboard, accidentally causing the page to scroll to the "Cast and Crew" section of the article. He spun the swivel chair around to face Tab, his face still red from their dad's chiding. "What do you want, twerp?"

The younger boy ignored the slight. "You're into ghost stuff," he said. "You told me some stories about demon dogs. I want to know if you were making it up."

"Nope."

Tab waited, expecting more, but Jeremy only stared back at him, seemingly annoyed although there was something else there as well. A hint of a smile? A gleam in his gaze? It was like he wanted to share some secret that only he knew. "So you think there really are demon dogs in the woods who drag people to Hell?"

"Doesn't matter what I think. It matters what the evidence says. Right now, we only have stuff people said they saw, but there's enough of it that you can't ignore it or chalk it up to mass delusion."

"What's *delusion*?"

Jeremy sighed, exasperated. "I'm not a dictionary. It means believing that something is real when it's not. Like Santa Claus. Santa Claus is a mass delusion parents force on their kids."

This again. Tab had not quite forgiven Jeremy for spilling the beans on the man in red last Christmas. Now it was his turn to sigh. "Can't you just give me a straight answer for once? I keep seeing a man in my closet at night. He doesn't have any eyes. I want to know if it has anything to do with the demon dogs you told me about when we were playing campout." He paused, then added, "Or am I having a *delusion*?"

"I wasn't *playing*. And I'm not your encyclopedia, either. Look, I've never heard any stories about eyeless men in closets. It's probably your imagination. Maybe Mom and Dad let you sleep with them too long when you were little or something. Don't be such a pussy, *Tabitha*. You're too old to think there are monsters in your closet."

"I'm three years younger than you."

"Yeah, well, that's still too old. Preschoolers think there are monsters in their closet, dude. But you're all 'Oh, no! Mom! Dad! There's a monster in my closet!' Grow up."

"But *you* believe in ghosts!" Tab countered. "And why do you have to be so mean?" When he'd first walked into the room, Tab was debating whether to tell his brother the full details about the dog or wolf he thought he'd seen before the family had locked themselves in the cellar to wait out the storm. Now he was relieved that he hadn't followed through on that plan. It would've only made Jeremy's teasing worse.

"I believe in collecting evidence." Jeremy spun his chair so that his back was to his brother again. "Why do *you* have to be so annoying and dumb? Look, you're too old to be worried about stuff like that. I don't care what Mom says about your *sensitivity* or your *imagination*. It's time for you to start acting like a man. Like me and Dad."

Tab noted some chocolate smeared on the iMac's mouse when Jeremy grabbed it. An empty Snickers wrapper lay to the right of the device. He considered pointing it out, but decided it might be better to keep the parting shot to himself: *You sleep with the Sta-Puft Marshmallow Man and you think* I'm *the one acting like a little kid?*

✳✳✳

Bedtime arrived too soon for Tab, who now dreaded it every night. It arrived too soon for his dad, too. Tim made no secret of his resentment at being forced from the comfort of his normal bed for the night.

"Just pretend it's camping!" his mom said, mocking the grown man, before she kissed Tab goodnight. She'd reserved no such well wishes or warmth for Dad.

This was scarier than camping, as far as Tab was concerned. His room was supposed to be a safe place. With the closet on one side and his father grunting, snoring, and farting on the other, he longed to abandon his room for the safety of the sofa. The glow of a warm television set might help him relax. Mom would not approve. And without Tab to wake him, Dad might miss seeing the eyeless stranger who lives in the closet.

Following an hour of wakefulness, Tab's eyelids began to weigh on him. He closed them, prepared to slip into the fuzz of dreamlessness that begins every slumber. Before his lashes fell, he heard it: the familiar but terrifying sound of the roller gliding along the closet door's track. Tab remained still. He opened his eyes and held his breath. As on the previous few nights, the closet door at first swung open to what appeared to be empty darkness. Tab identified only a row of his school clothes hanging neatly from the wooden rod that spanned the width of the closet.

The figure didn't materialize so much as he was just *there*, the personification of an epiphany. Tab was reminded of Magic Eye hidden picture puzzles. His drawings worked the same way. You had to look at the paper a certain way before the image revealed itself. Then *blam!* he'd created something by adding graphite to a field of blankness. Creating art was Tab's talent. Mom, Dad, and all his teachers said so. Un-creating it was not something he understood. And now that Tab spied the man in the closet, he couldn't *un*see him.

"Dad?" Tab squeaked. It came out almost too small for his own ears. He steeled himself and tried again. "Dad? He's here."

On the floor, Tim grumbled something. It might have been "go back to sleep," but sounded more like a mumbling concoction of syllables strung together without spaces.

"DAD!"

That kickstarted everything. His father sat up and barely missed slicing open his own left temple on the corner of

Tab's nightstand. "Whu—?" he groaned. "What's wrong? What's going on?" He crawled to his knees, using the edge of Tab's mattress for support. His back popped, prompting a moan and a wince of pain.

Down the hall, a light in the master bedroom flickered on. It cast a polygon of brightness onto the dingy beige carpet mapping the way to every room on this level.

"Dad! Mom! He's here!"

Tab's father rubbed his swollen eyes and peered blearily at the space to which Tab pointed. Still tying her bathrobe, his mother arrived in his doorway and likewise followed his gaze. Tab glanced from one adult to the other, his disappointment evident.

"There!" he said. Then, weakly, "Don't you see him?"

They did not. His mother squinted into the darkness of his closet, using her left hand to block the light from the hall. His father wore an expression identical to hers. Neither of them could distinguish the ghastly visage who sat in the bottom of his closet. As if to underscore this fact, his father crawled to the enclosure on his hands and knees. He threw open the remaining bifold door and passed his hand through the open closet space under Tab's dangling clothes.

"Hee hee," said the man with no eyes. It was laughter without mirth. "That tickles."

"You—you don't see him?" Tab's gaze darted from his father to his mother and back again.

Tim shook his head, irritable. "No, son. Ain't nothing here."

"Please," said the man in the closet. "You know I'm here, kid." He jerked a thumb at Tim. "This guy can't see me because he's an idiot. Hell, he don't even know his wife's a cheat. Look at him. Trying to touch me. Clueless."

Tab pulled his covers over his head. "Shut up!"

"Tab!" his mom said.

"He's talking to me, Mom! He won't stop!"

"Jesus Christ." That was Tab's dad, the tiger lurking just under the hoarseness of his awakened-from-sleep voice. "Nobody's here but us. Go to sleep. You're too old to believe in monsters."

"I'm no monster," the man said. "I'm here to help you, Tab. Your dad's something else, ain't he? Taking out all his weakness on you and your big brother."

Tab peeked out from under his covers. His father was leading his mother out of his room. The man had emerged from the closet and was closing in on the left side of the bed.

"You know what you should do, son?" the ghost said, adopting a conspiratorial whisper as he leaned in close to Tab's ear. The boy shivered, whimpering involuntarily as the thing drew closer. "You should kill him."

CHAPTER FIVE

Sandra made two appointments for Tab the next morning. The first was with his pediatrician. The second, with a counselor who also authored Sandra's latest read, *Anxiety, Depression, and Your Child*. The back cover of the book showcased a striking photograph of a smiling man with a brown complexion. He was thin and bald with attention-grabbing cheeks and dimples. A pair of square glasses sat on the bridge of his nose. Their Zyl frames swirled with every color of the rainbow. The bio beneath the picture informed her that Clark Clifford, PhD, "lives and works in Hollow River, Tennessee."

Hollow River was the same town in which Tab's pediatrician worked. Sandra loathed driving so far for medical care, but she didn't trust Lost Hollow's pediatric center. It was a double-wide trailer consisting of two pasty, angry-sounding men with hair sprouting from their ear canals. To Sandra, they looked like bipedal Persian cats with nasty tempers. Dr. Susan Patel, on the other hand, was no more than forty years old. She was patient, had a kind face, smiling brown eyes, and a compassionate demeanor. All must-haves for those Beard boys.

Tim hated doctors. He had spent the entire morning on the family's landline arguing with a developer who had asked about buying his great-aunt's old farm. The plan was to develop the massive acreage into a live, work, shop development. With luck, it would bring money and infrastructure to their backward little hometown. "We might subscribe to cable TV and internet instead of this shitty, expensive satellite crap," Tim had surmised one evening after a couple of beers.

The flood from the previous weekend might have ruined that plan. A large area of the acreage was surrounded by Hollow Creek. And Hollow Creek had flooded the night of May 1, much like the old-timers said it had way back in 1955 when Aunt Kathy and a number of other folks got washed away, never to be seen again.

So the stories went. Some rumors were circulating that one of those people had turned up in Lost Hollow the day before the latest flood. Tim said he'd seen a doddering old stranger with some memory problems wandering the decrepit general store on Aunt Kathy's old property. "Coulda hurt himself," he'd said. "I took him home. It was weird, though. He didn't seem to know his own last name."

The flood made travel into Hollow River treacherous while creeks and rivers ran high. The day before his phone call, those levels dropped. At least according to Tim. Not that he knew much about waterways. Or anything, except how to drive a tractor and thud heavy bass in his titanic Dodge Ram. While Tim played farmer and real estate mogul, Sandra cared for the kids and made ends meet. She was grateful farmers in Lost Hollow had little interest in handling their own accounting.

Except for today. Today she took yet more time off work to uncover why her youngest kid had a marble lodged in his temple and was seeing eyeless ghosts. Were the problems related? If Dr. Patel believed they were, Sandra might cancel Tab's appointment with Dr. Clifford. She had hesitated to schedule it for that reason, although she longed to meet the man to whom she had devoted her bedtime reading of late. This might be her only opportunity.

She considered carrying one of Dr. Clifford's other books, *Soothing the OCD Beast*, with her so she could ask for his autograph. Of all the volumes, it was the one in the best shape. She'd plucked it from its place on the study bookshelf, but replaced it, thinking that asking him to sign it might make her too fan-girly. This appointment was for Tab, not her.

By the time the trio of Beards arrived at Dr. Patel's, Jeremy was already obnoxious and bored. In typical fashion, he took it out on Tab. Both boys sat in the back seat of Sandra's pearl-colored Honda Accord. By state law, Jeremy long ago qualified to ride up front but chose not to for reasons known only to him. In the last fifteen minutes of the trip, Tab grew weary of Jeremy's handsiness. The elder jammed a finger into the younger's shoulder, causing him to squeal "STOP TOUCHING ME!" Startled, Sandra nearly slammed the Accord into the back of a Wal-Mart semi.

In the doc's parking lot, she paused to center herself, then admonished both boys. "Tab, you stay with me the whole time, okay? Don't wander off to the play area." She lowered her voice an octave. "Jeremy. Stay in the waiting room and occupy yourself while we're in with the doctor."

"But I'm boooooored," Jeremy whined.

"Take your iPod Touch with you and play a game or something. Sheesh."

"Y'all won't let me get any *good* games." He pushed his lower lip out in a mock pout. Sandra hated it when he did that. Everyone, including Jeremy, knew that he was far too old to throw tantrums. His toddler-like reactions were just attempts to needle his folks. He couldn't poke them physically like he could Tab, so he schemed psychological ways to frustrate them instead.

Sandra seethed. "Please do what I say and stop acting like a child."

"Why do *I* have to stay in the waiting room with all the sickies?"

"God, son, do what I ask. Okay?"

The truth was Sandra didn't trust Jeremy to keep his brother's diagnosis quiet. Tab already had trouble getting along with the other kids. Jeremy's big mouth would be no help there, in particular if the man in the closet was a hallucination. Tab lived in his own head most of the time. His teachers confirmed that, telling Sandra they often caught him drawing, daydreaming, or staring out the window instead of sitting at attention or doing his class assignments.

"Fine, then. Let's go," Jeremy said.

The older Beard brother didn't speak to either Sandra or Tab for the rest of the walk to the waiting room. Nor did he acknowledge them after they pushed through the door. He found a row of empty chairs and stretched out across three of them. His iPod Touch, held landscape in two hands, floated over his face. Sandra was grateful for the short period of peace. Not so much for Dr. Patel's assessment.

✳✳✳

"I think it's a dilated pore of Winer," the doctor said. She had peeled away Tab's latest bandage and set it aside. As Tab entertained himself by swinging his legs back and forth on the edge of the exam table, Dr. Patel had spent the past fifteen seconds mashing on the borders of his temple wound with her thumbs. She had already examined his throat and pronounced him cured of that affliction. There were no visible signs of strep, although she said he should finish the course of antibiotics she'd prescribed just in case. His bump, on the other hand, remained a mystery. "Not like anything I've seen before, but I'm not a dermatologist."

"What's a dilated pore-of-whatever?" Sandra asked.

Dr. Patel turned to face her, a pleasant smile on her lips. Sandra could not help but return it. "Really, it's an oversized pimple. A big blackhead. They happen when a pore clogs. Lots of people have them, but it's more common in adults and the elderly.

"Right here, you can see an enlarged pore right in the middle of it. The edges are a bit inflamed, too." She indicated the spot with one gloved finger. "When I press on the sides, no plug comes out, so it's empty right now. They usually fill up again, though."

Sandra closed in to examine Tab's bump. She hadn't paid its appearance much mind after Tab's first freak-out. She'd only changed the bandage and applied more antibiotic ointment from time to time. Dr. Patel was right, though. The bump now resembled a tiny volcano on the side of Tab's head, more pimple than injury.

"It didn't used to look that way," Sandra said. "I mean, when we first became aware of it the night of the storm it was *more* like that, but I don't remember seeing the enlarged pore. The next morning, he had this open, festering hole in his head."

"You said before you thought Tab had scratched it in his sleep?"

Sandra nodded, not taking her eyes from Tab's bump.

"Well, that's one explanation for the way it might have appeared. If it was somehow traumatized." She turned to Tab. "Did you hit the bump on something? When you were trying to get down to the cellar?"

Tab shrugged. "I don't know."

"Mmm-hmm." She backed away from the exam table and leaned against the counter lining the opposite wall. "Well, I'm more concerned about the man you say you're seeing in your closet at night than I am about your bump. Like I said, it's more common in older people, but it's not impossible for children to get them if they enter puberty early."

Tab shuddered at the mention of his nightly visitor.

"If he hit his head on something and doesn't remember it, that might explain some of the—" Dr. Patel paused, seeking the right word, "—stranger stuff you've been dealing with. A conk on the head can have some unpredictable results. Sometimes they include psychiatric issues like hallucinations.

"Since he says he doesn't know if he hit his head that night, I'd like to do some tests. Let's see if we can find evidence of a concussion." She retrieved a penlight from her coat pocket, flicked the switch, and crouched to meet Tab at eye level. "Stare straight ahead for me." She directed the light from the outer edges of each of Tab's eyes towards the pupil. After a satisfied nod, she switched it off again. Some memory experiments, reflexes, balance, coordination, hearing, and other tests followed. When the work was done, she returned to her place against the counter.

"There are no obvious signs, so that's good. It's nothing to worry about, but I'd like to schedule a CT scan just to be safe. If we're quick, we might be able to get him over to our imaging partner this afternoon."

"No!" Sandra said. It came out louder, more emphatic than she had intended. "I mean, we can't do it this afternoon. We have other appointments we can't reschedule."

"Uh huh," Dr. Patel said. She plucked her laptop from its spot on the stool beside her and pressed a few keys. Was there judgement in her posture? Sandra thought there might be.

"It would be better if we schedule it for first thing in the morning. I can leave my other son with his father tomorrow and spend all day in Hollow River, if we need to."

"It's whatever works for you. But, Tab? If you start getting bad headaches, or feeling off balance, or throwing up a lot, you need to tell your parents right away, okay?"

Tab nodded.

"If the headaches start, it would be wise to have him scanned as soon as possible," she continued, turning to Sandra. "Head injuries can cause blood clots in the brain." She peered over the laptop, her eyes dark, her lips unsmiling now.

And if there's a blood clot in his brain and it's not operated on, her expression read, *he'll die.*

CHAPTER SIX

"It's a dilated pore of Winer," Dr. Clark Clifford said upon examining the bump. Dr. Patel hadn't seen a need to continue bandaging. There was no open bleeding or scab tissue, so there was no point. It was the single relief both Sandra and Tab had taken away from Dr. Patel's. Now, Sandra was beginning to think the appointment with Clark Clifford, PhD, and renowned author of a dozen psychology books, might have been a mistake. So far, events had unfolded the same way they had in Tab's visit with Dr. Patel.

Dr. Clifford crouched on one knee beside Tab. The boy sat on a dark faux leather couch. He seemed more comfortable than he had on Dr. Patel's exam table. After being introduced to the bump, Dr. Clifford resumed his seat across from them. Sandra sat in a small chair to the right of the couch, not wanting to crowd Tab in case he needed to lie down like patients in the movies.

"I assume Dr. Patel did tests for concussion?" Dr. Clifford asked Sandra, who nodded. "So, we're reasonably certain you don't have a concussion. I agree with your family doctor, though. You should get a CT scan. It can be expensive, but better safe than sorry."

"We'll schedule it as soon as we're home," Sandra said. Both times the scan had been mentioned, her mind had automatically drifted to the family's savings account. Their health insurance plan was basically a legal scam. "But what we're here about isn't—"

Dr. Clifford raised a palm. "I understand," he said. "Let's talk about the man you're seeing in your closet at night, Tab. Can I call you Tab? Or do you like Tim better?"

"Tab's fine."

"Okay. Tell me, Tab, when was the first time you saw this man?"

"In the cellar the night of the big storm." He rubbed his left eye with the tips of his fingers. Sandra and the boys had been away from home for nearly four hours, much of it spent in the car or in waiting rooms. It must be exhausting for him. Not to mention Jeremy, who remained in Dr. Clifford's waiting room, away from his beloved internet.

"You could see him clearly? Like he was in the room with you? Or was he kind of there, but not all the time? Like a shape in a fog?"

When Tab did not answer, the doctor continued, "Did you ever look at the sun too long? You know how when you blink afterward you can still kind of see the sun's shape if you look in another direction? Did he look like that?"

Tab shook his head, fervent.

"You're going to need to describe him," Sandra prodded.

He sighed. "I mean, I didn't know he was in the cellar at first," he said. "I only saw him later. He looked real to me. He was wearing this tan uh, jumpsuit, I guess? With a zipper going all the way up to your neck?"

"Coveralls? Like your dad wears sometimes?"

"Yeah! Coveralls. Not blue like Dad's, though. And he was rounder than Dad is."

"Okay. What did his face look like?"

"Kind of big around here." Tab stroked his chin with his thumb and forefinger. "Wide, I mean. He needed to shave.

I remember he had a red baseball cap on, but he had it pulled down over his eyes, so I couldn't see them."

"He has eyes?" Dr. Clifford asked. "It was my understanding when your mom told me about him that he doesn't. Did you mean you couldn't see them?"

"No! I mean he doesn't have any. He didn't hide them under his cap on the other nights I saw him. One night he said *I* was going to be his eyes, and he showed them to me. He had empty holes where his eyes were supposed to be." He shuddered.

Sandra stretched a hand to him and squeezed his forearm. "It's okay, Tab," she said. "Remember as much as you can."

"He told you that *you* were going to be his eyes?" Dr. Clifford asked. He scribbled on a legal pad propped in his lap.

"Yeah."

"What do you think he meant?"

"How should *I* know?" Irritability had found its way into his voice, a precursor to frustrated tears in Sandra's experience. "How should *I* know what he means by anything? I just want him to go away."

"Of course," Dr. Clifford said, softening. "Of course. I understand. Has the man ever told you his name or anything else about himself?"

Tab shook his head. He crammed the palms of his hands into his eyes and rubbed at them.

"Does he remind you of anyone? Someone from school or anywhere else?"

Again, Tab gestured negative.

"What about talking to you? Has the man in your closet said anything other than what you and your mother told me today?"

"Not much," Tab said. "He said my cat Alfie was fine even though he wasn't with us in the cellar." His breath slowed. His eyes cleared.

"*Is* the cat fine?"

Tab nodded.

A smile curled Sandra's lips, unbidden. "He'd do anything for that cat," she said, and regretted it as soon as the words were out. Dr. Clifford seemed to be making progress with Tab. Distracting the boy with her thoughts and insights might cause him to clam up.

"Okay," Dr. Clifford said. "Is there anything else? Has the man in the closet said anything scary to you? I mean, he sounds scary, but has he said anything upsetting?"

Tab considered this. "The thing about me being his eyes," he said.

"Right. How about besides that?"

"No. Nothing I can think of."

Dr. Clifford leaned back in his chair and, for the first time in what felt like hours, turned his attention to Sandra. Those eyes! Empathetic. Understanding. She became aware of every muscle in her face, struggling to control them so her expression didn't give away her thoughts. She'd seen *The Silence of the Lambs*. Tim had coerced her into it. She didn't know whether all psychiatrists had high-powered perception like Hannibal Lecter's, but it couldn't hurt to keep herself in check.

"It's far too early to make a diagnosis, but I do have some thoughts about what's going on," the doctor said. "Tab? I'd like to talk to your mom alone for a few minutes, if that's okay with you. But first, when you get home, I want you to try something for me. If the man appears in your closet again—"

"He will!"

Dr. Clifford smiled, patient. "Yes. *When* he appears in your closet again tonight, I want you to talk back to him. Ask him for his name. If he doesn't give it, you give him one. If he says anything upsetting to you, argue with him. Okay? Talk back to him. Find out how he reacts."

Tab's eyes swelled in their sockets. "What if it makes him mad?"

"It might make him mad," Dr. Clifford said. "But if I understand the situation, this man who stays in your closet lives there. Except for the one time you saw him in the cellar during a scary storm. Right?"

"Yeah."

"Good. I think if he was going to hurt you, he would have already. It's possible *he's* scared of *you*, Tab. You're a bright boy and your mom tells me you're an artist. You have a potent imagination."

"What's potent?"

"It means strong, honey," Sandra said.

"Right. It means strong. You're stronger than this man in your closet. Now, I'm not saying it will be easy to talk back to him. But I think if you can do it, and you can *keep* doing it, he'll leave. Do you think you can try talking back?"

Tab thought for a bit, then nodded. "I'll try."

"Good!" Dr. Clifford smiled, the broadness of it building mounds atop his cheeks. Sandra couldn't help but regard his teeth, all straight and a brilliant white. Perfection. Tim refused to go to dentists. "Now, give me a couple of minutes to chat with your mom and we'll be done."

Tab slid off the couch and bolted for the door. He glanced over his shoulder to acknowledge Sandra only when she called after him to catch up with his brother in the waiting room. When the boy was gone, Dr. Clifford set his pen and legal pad aside. He crossed his legs and rested his hands one atop the other on his left knee.

"What's wrong with him?" Sandra asked.

He chuckled. "'Wrong?' Absolutely nothing. I want to continue seeing him, though. Tell me, does Tab do certain things with repetition, like washing his hands when he shouldn't need to? Anything?"

"No. Not that I've noticed."

"Does he need a lot of reassurance or comfort? I mean, more so than any other kid his age?"

Sandra shook her head. "No."

Dr. Clifford scratched his chin. "I have some homework for you, too," he said. "I want you to pay special attention to his behavior over the next couple of weeks. Regardless of how things go with the man in the closet, I'd like you to watch him for any signs of compulsion."

"You think he has OCD?"

"Well, it's possible, but OCD-type behavior can be a symptom of other anxiety disorders. The hallmarks of OCD are the obsessions and the compulsions that are used to relieve them. Repetitive handwashing because of a fear of contamination, chronic confessing to things he thinks he might have done wrong whether he did those things or not. Being overly scrupulous, in other words.

"Tab seems to be going through a fearful phase right now, seeing someone who isn't there. It doesn't necessarily mean he has an anxiety disorder or personality disorder or anything. It might be a natural response to something going on in his life. You said you and your husband have been arguing. Then there was the flood. Maybe this 'man in the closet' is how Tab's mind presents things he doesn't yet know how to cope with. When he learns coping, they'll go away. That's one of the reasons I asked him to try talking back, to name the man. Whatever the outcome is might tell us more about what we're dealing with."

He cupped his right knee in both hands. "No physical test can determine whether it's OCD or generalized anxiety or something else, not in the way medical doctors test for things. There are a few things to watch for, though. If Tab is prone to strep infections—"

Sandra sat up straight. "He is! He gets them all the time. He's just getting over one, as a matter of fact."

"Uh huh. Have you ever heard of PANDAS?"

"The bears?"

"No, it's an acronym. It stands for," he paused, eyeing the ceiling in recollection, "Pediatric Autoimmune Neuropsychiatric Disorders Associated with Streptococcal Infections. Believe it or not, strep infections can cause the sudden appearance of OCD-type disorders or even tics. Practically overnight. Ages three through twelve is when kids are most susceptible."

"So how do we know for sure?"

"For now, I'd like to see Tab a couple of times a month. Let me keep chatting with him. If he presents in ways other than the man in the closet, it will help guide us in the right direction. He probably won't have every symptom, but be on the lookout for OCD-type things like we discussed. Look for ADHD symptoms, too, like fidgeting or an inability to pay attention. Trouble sleeping. Mood changes. Separation anxiety. Frequent urination. All of those could be indicators that we're dealing with PANDAS.

"I should add that one instance of strep and the onset of OCD symptoms does not make a PANDAS diagnosis. Most kids get strep multiple times per year. If the anxiety symptoms worsen in close relationship with future infections, Tab might have PANDAS."

"Do people with OCD hallucinate, too?"

"Well, not typically in a visual way. Sometimes OCD can cause some sensory or tactile—well, *hallucinations*, for lack of a better word. I prefer *sensations*. These sensations reflect the individual's specific obsessions. It's a little like when someone coughs and sniffles near you in a public place and there's a sudden tickle in your throat. Not the same, but close. And a lot stronger.

"You mentioned Tab's powerful imagination. People who have OCD and vivid imaginations are most often the people who experience hallucinations associated with the condition."

A lightbulb switched on above her head. "Tab said he saw the bump turn into an eyeball," she said. "The man in the closet has no eyes!"

Dr. Clifford nodded, thoughtful. "Right. So if Tab does have OCD, his obsession might be related to his eyes or his eyesight somehow. I can't say I've had other patients with ocular obsessions, but it's not out of the question. He's an artist. His eyesight is important to him."

Dr. Clifford leaned forward, elbows on his knees. "When you're watching him, find out if he's doing things he thinks protect his eyes. Find out if he has a classmate that's going blind or needs glasses. Something mundane for us can be triggering for a child his age. Now, do you have any questions for me?"

"You said there was more than one reason you asked him to talk back to the man in the closet."

"Ah," Dr. Clifford said, leaning back again. "Yes. OCD can cause voices—again, for lack of a better term—inside your head to say nasty things to you. These nasty things can be harsh criticisms of themselves or extreme stuff, like trying to convince them they want to hurt themselves or someone else. The man in the closet could be a manifestation of this symptom. Many times, just learning to talk back to these *voices* can minimize them. It doesn't make them go away, but it can help diminish them to a point. Either way, talking back to this man and naming him won't hurt Tab."

He stood, picking up his legal pad and pen as he did, and returned to the desk he'd been sitting at when Sandra and Tab arrived. Sandra got the message. The session was over. She beamed. "Oh, thank you!" she said, rising from her seat. "This has been so helpful."

"Absolutely. Check with Beth on your way out and schedule another visit. No more than two weeks from now. It was nice meeting you. I hope both you and Tab get a restful night tonight, free of eyeless men in closets."

He grinned.

CHAPTER SEVEN

The analog touch-tone protested with an irritable *ting* when Tim slammed the handset into its cradle. He wanted to kill the landline, but cell signals in Lost Hollow were spotty. The carrier? Not important. Hell, a tower jutted out of the landscape only a mile or so away, but it made no difference. It was as if someone had enshrouded the mud-hole of a town in a Faraday cage. So he conducted business on the landline in the family's makeshift study, although he wished he'd used his cell today. It might've cut out on him before Chuck Derryberry dropped his bomb.

"Fuckers," he said. "Backstabbing fuckers."

His disappeared great-aunt Kathy's farm remained in his possession. Chuck's company had failed to account for the credit bubble burst and the collapse of the housing market two years before. None of the places they'd bought and developed were selling. They'd also failed to hire qualified engineers. Now they were stuck with a half-dozen investment properties submerged in mud and water. There was no spare money to buy new land. The Derryberrys also now seemed gun-shy about land so near a body of water like Hollow Creek.

"There's tons of stable developers eyeballing your area right now," Chuck had tried to reassure him. "I'm sure you'll find someone else who wants to take a chance on your farm. It's not a bad spot. It's just not for us."

His speech came off more patronizing than he'd likely intended, as if Tim was an adolescent rejected by a first crush. That only infuriated him more. Worse, the rejection had come after The Derryberry Group had courted *him* about the property, not the other way around. How long might it be before another developer discovered the land and approached him about it? He supposed he could start reaching out to developers himself or hire someone who worked in real estate as an agent. But he had no idea where to start.

Similar to his aunt's place, Tim's farm had been handed down by his father. He'd paid a hefty inheritance tax, but that was the extent of the burden. Kathy's place, on the other hand, had been nothing but trouble. Keeping vandals and vagrants away from the ramshackle general store was a full-time job. *And* there was the problem of paying the property taxes when the property wasn't creating income. Well, Sandra handled the taxes, but Tim often woke with night sweats over the county foreclosing and selling the property out from under him.

Not that he didn't trust Sandra, but...well, these days he wasn't sure he *did* trust Sandra. She seemed unhappy with him so farm focused. It was as if his being home more often had put him in her way. At first, he'd thought nothing of it, figuring the situation was new and they'd grow into it. However, when he'd sat down at the computer in their study, he noticed Sandra had left Firefox open. Her Facebook messages were loaded in one tab and a Wikipedia article about a small town in Massachusetts sat open in another.

It was a violation, but Tim couldn't help himself. He eyed the highlighted name in her messages: Seb Tanner. The minuscule profile picture accompanying Seb's messages depicted a man who appeared to be around Tim's age, except with a chiseled jaw and sparkling blue eyes, his full head of boyish black hair swept to one side by an ocean breeze. Without scrolling, Tim parsed the lines of text.

> **Seb:** Anytime! I'd love to see you again.
> **Sandra:** I can't imagine being able to do it right now. After Tim sells that old place, maybe. I can't believe I'm thinking about this.
> **Seb:** He doesn't deserve you.

He doesn't deserve you.

An invisible dagger stabbed Tim's chest, twisted, and carved its way up into his throat. He tried to swallow the lump but couldn't. His eyes burned.

He doesn't deserve you.

Beside the last word was a tiny thumb's up. He wanted to believe Seb himself had added the emoji to punctuate his final thought in the chat. A closer examination revealed no. It was a Like. Seb hadn't added it. Sandra had.

He doesn't deserve you.

After everything I've done for her, he thought. *After everything I've sacrificed.*

He stood, forgetting for the moment about the Derryberry call. He was willing to give his wife the benefit of the doubt. Seb could be a lonely old friend she'd become entangled with online and now couldn't calculate her way out. It might explain why she'd handed Seb the sale of Aunt Kathy's place as an excuse instead of considering the kids. But she'd reacted to *He doesn't deserve you* with a Like. There was no defense for staying—for her, for the kids, or for himself—in the Like. It was an acknowledgment by her of Seb's statement as fact.

That hurt.

And there was that Wikipedia page open in the other tab. Tim resisted the urge to click on the About section of Seb's account to see where he lived. He wasn't sure he'd like what he found. Instead, he pulled his John Deere cap low on his forehead. Having spent hours on the old tractor in recent days, tooling around Aunt Kathy's property, he decided to occupy himself by continuing to search for ways to monetize it. Before Chuck Derryberry reached out to him, he'd explored maybe a third of the place. Might as well take another tour. Maybe he'd have an epiphany. Hell, he could develop the land himself. Become a famous real estate mogul with his own reality show like Trump.

He snatched his pickup keys from his pocket and strode out.

✲✲✲

By the time he arrived at his Aunt Kathy's old farmhouse, Sandra and the kids would be at their first doctor appointment. He considered himself lucky he'd been busy with the Derryberry call. Otherwise, she might've forced him to tag along. He hated doctors. More, he hated the time it took them to drive the distance.

Her mistrust of the locals remained a sore spot between them. Tim was fine seeing Dr. Reinhold in his office just a few blocks off Lost Hollow's Public Square. Well, *office* was a stretch. Still, there was nothing wrong with the place. Sandra insisted on going all the way to Hollow River. She'd made the appointments and dashed out with both kids in tow. On her way, she'd handed Tim a yellow Post-it reading, *Taking Tab to doctor and counselor. Back this afternoon.* He'd stuck it to the computer monitor while he sat and forgot to grab it when he left. He'd need to remember to grab it before she got back with the kids. Otherwise, she might guess that he'd seen her Facebook. Angry as he was, Tim was not ready to have that conversation. Not yet.

A sensation of power came with climbing aboard the old John Deere. It doubled when he started the engine, sensing the vibrations along his feet, legs, and ass. Sandra, who seemed to think he was an idiot, might scold him for taking it out without someone else around to watch after him. You know, in case he did something stupid and had an accident.

"You haven't met every cave, rock, or hole on that property like you have ours," she'd say. "You might be hurt or killed, and no one would be the wiser." Her voice prompted momentary doubt, causing him to retrieve his iPhone from his bib pocket, to verify his tether to help in case something *did* happen. Barely a bar.

Whatever.

Sandra was not here now, and he was fine with it. He glanced at the sky, contrasting its blue with the green of the overgrown old fields. They were long bereft of livestock to graze them or crops to flourish on them. A light breeze combed the tops of the weeds and scrub in front of him, beckoning him into their waves. It was a beautiful day for a tractor tour. He smiled, turning his face to the sun.

Fuck Sandra.

The tractor trundled off its trailer. Tim aimed it for the northwest corner of the farm.

CHAPTER EIGHT

Tab's eyes drifted closed. The smooth roll along a deserted stretch of highway home and the warm hug of the afternoon sun against his skin made him sleepy. That, and the dumping of the entire past week of his history and each associated emotion and sensation to two total strangers. He loved the heat of the oncoming summer against his eyelids. The light through the thin skin created a red filter over his retinas.

His mom had convinced Jeremy to sit in the front seat, distracting him from incessant picking on his younger brother. Without the chronic threat, Tab could relax, allow his mind to drift. To calm. To sleep. Imagination took over consciousness.

His Strathmore sketchbook slid off his lap. The page to which it was open contained an image of his dad, clad in denim overalls and his green John Deere cap. The figure was seated on a tractor among a field of tall fescue. Tab imagined it green, although he'd drawn the field in No. 2 pencil, so it was really only soft, thin strokes of gray. His dad had carried him from the bed to the cellar the night of the storm. His dad had slept on the floor of his bedroom to protect him. Resentfully, yes, but he *had* done those things. What was so important to his dad that he couldn't come along to doctor appointments?

Land. Always wanting to sell the land. Tab loved his mom, but it was his dad who protected him from the external world: a world full of men and women who held themselves at a distance from others, who spoke in flat and emotionless voices, and who sometimes judged him for being himself. His dad's refusal to tag along felt like a betrayal.

Before he drifted into unconsciousness, Tab had added another character to the image. A wider man stood in front and to the viewer's left of the tractor as his dad closed in on the frame. This man also wore a cap but was otherwise clad in coveralls. His back was to Tab, because he did not want to draw the man's gory eye sockets. This was Tab's new protector, or helper. So he claimed.

In his sleep, an enormous field of green spread out before Tab. Shoulder-height grass and weeds obscured much of the view. A pleasant breeze pulled them apart, caressing his face and allowing brief glimpses further afield. The sweet aroma of fresh-cut straw rode on the air. The scene reminded him of an old episode of his mom's favorite TV show, *Unexplained Phenomena*. She and Jeremy usually watched it together, although Jeremy preferred *Ghost Adventures*.

Unexplained Phenomena had once aired an episode about people who had died and returned to talk about it. He hadn't paid much attention to the show because thoughts of death and dying filled him with dread that was difficult to stuff at bedtime. He'd glanced up from a *Peanuts* coloring book long enough to catch a woman who described flying over a beautiful field of flowers and grass after she had supposedly died.

Was he dead now? He didn't think so. From somewhere in the back of his head, he heard a buzzing sound. Not a bee buzz. More like someone running a chainsaw in the distance. As he concentrated on the sound, it grew louder. In his dream, he spun on the balls of his feet to see his father's John Deere tractor. His grinning dad sat atop it, bearing straight down on him at high speed. The shadow of the bill of his cap obscured his eyes, forcing Tab to wonder whether his dad still *had* eyes in his head. He tried to scream, *Dad! I'm here, Dad! Stop!*

Nothing came out.

He glanced to his left and his right, seeking a path to run. In both directions, the overgrowth obscured escape. He chose to go right because it was his "strong side," but his feet refused to obey the command to move. He couldn't bend at his knees, either. He couldn't swivel his hips, seemingly frozen from the waist down. No, not *just* from the waist down. When his eyes locked again on the approaching tractor, he could neither move his head nor shut his eyelids. His arms stuck to his torso as if bound by rope.

What's happening to me?

The tractor closed in enough for him to smell its belches of diesel fumes, loud enough to drown his thoughts. Without warning, the grille of the beast lurched into the air at a slant. Tab could see half the tractor's right front tire over the tops of the weeds growing in the shrinking expanse between him and the machine. Dad, whose cap had blown off his head, was in midair on the tractor's left. His eyes bulged from their sockets, engorged with terror. His jaw spread open in a scream Tab could not hear.

Dad!

The flailing body dipped below the tops of the weeds and scrub, after which the earth finally turned loose of Tab's feet. His knees wobbled, but he was able to remain upright. He broke into a run through the green wilderness, toward the spot he saw his father fall. The tractor completed its roll, landing on its right side. Two tires flattened horizontally on the ground. The others slowed to a stop while suspended in the air on their axles. A choking, sputtering death silenced the engine.

From the emptiness, a guttural wail emerged. It sounded like his dad did in the mornings when he gargled the green stuff that burns your mouth and tongue, except louder and more terrible.

"DAD!"

He dashed forward, stretching his arms into a wedge to deflect the overgrowth. Just as he began to fear that he was lost, a clearing opened. There he found the shattered body of his father. The man's right leg was broken, bent in a nine o'clock right angle at the knee. His left forearm rested above his head. His right lay at his side, the forefinger extended as if pointing at his injured leg.

His eyes were open, blank, staring at the sky. Thick, brownish-red blood drooled from his right nostril and the right side of his mouth. The latter gaped, but his teeth and tongue were invisible behind the pool of blood and bile filling the cavity. An enormous crimson welt arose on the right side of his face. Beside him, a jagged gray stone coated in a thin film of blood protruded from the earth.

Tab knelt beside his father, tried to talk to him, reached out to shake him. The welt on his dad's face reminded him bitterly of the thing on the side of his own head. His bump began to itch and burn, as if someone had squeezed lemon juice into it, sending thousands of mites living inside into panicky flights. The world around him went fuzzy. Gritty laughter echoed from a distance. Something jarred him.

Then he was awake in the back seat of his mom's car, staring at the back of his brother's head.

"Oh, I'm sorry, hon," his mom cooed from the driver's seat. She eyed him in the rearview mirror. "I didn't see the pothole in time to miss it. Are you okay?"

Her words buzzed in his ears, part dream and part reality. The remaining tendrils of the other dimension from which he'd been extracted had not yet shaken free. Reality still felt somehow *less* real than his dream. "Okay," he said. He rubbed at his eyes and fingered his bump. It throbbed, hot to his touch. "Where's Dad?" he asked.

"Still at home, I suppose. We're on our way from our doctor visits. Remember?"

"Yeah."

"Yeah," Jeremy said, mocking the grogginess in his younger brother's voice.

"Jeremy!" their mom scolded.

The boy grumbled a reply under his breath and returned to the dopamine provided by the screen of his iPod Touch. He was probably still playing Angry Birds, a game he'd been obsessed with since Christmas.

"Is Dad okay?" Tab asked. "Can we call him?"

His mom glanced at him again from the rearview, her forehead creased. "I don't see why he wouldn't be? I don't like to use the phone while I'm driving. Why?"

Tab squirmed. "I don't know. I had a dream—"

"Aww, poor widdle baby had a bad dream!" Jeremy heckled.

Their mother sighed. "Jeremy, I swear. If there's one more peep out of you for the rest of this ride, I'm taking away your iPod and your computer privileges for the rest of the week. Do you understand me?"

Jeremy glared at his mother, gauging her seriousness. She did not falter. He nodded, reluctant but willing to obey in order to protect his leisure time. And almost *all* his time was leisure time.

"Now, what were you saying, Tab?"

"I had a dream that Dad's...hurt," he said. He almost said "dead," but changed his mind as the words came out of his mouth. It wasn't that he thought he'd scare his mom by saying he'd dreamed about his dad dying. It was more fear that saying it out loud would somehow make the nightmare a reality.

Mom smiled at him. "Oh, honey, we all have bad dreams sometimes. They don't mean anything. Except you're worried about your dad and me. But, listen, everything's going to be fine. I used to have bad dreams all the time when I was a kid. I mean, they were *scary*. Sometimes I'd wake up not knowing if they'd happened or if it was all in my head. But I've been walking the earth for thirty-five years now, and not one time have any of my bad dreams come true."

"Never?"

"Nope. Never."

His tummy loosened under the elastic waistband of his jeans. The muscles in his neck and shoulders relaxed as well. Mom sounded certain, and that was a comfort. "Good," he said.

"Yep. If I know your dad, he's been on the phone all day trying to get somebody to buy his Aunt Kathy's old place. More power to him. You saw it when we drove by on the way to Hollow River. It's almost nothing but mush after those floods. They'd have to deal with knocking down the broken-down old store, too. Seems like a lot of work for something that's just going to turn into a swamp every time it rains."

"It'll sell," Jeremy said. There was a hint of defensiveness in his voice. "Dad said so." He cringed then, having apparently forgotten about their mom's threat to take away his iPod and computer time. Mom only nodded, not taking her eyes off the road.

"Yeah. That's what he says, alright."

The rest of their drive was in silence. When they passed the dilapidated old building that was Beard's General store perched on its tiny Hollow Creek peninsula on the outskirts of Lost Hollow, neither Tab's mom nor his brother gave it a second glance.

Tab, however, took note of the height of the weeds and dense scrub populating the surrounding field. It triggered a feeling in him he couldn't place, a recent memory he couldn't quite retrieve. He bore down on it, struggling to recall. But it was as if a veil had been draped in front of it he could neither part nor tear down.

CHAPTER NINE

Pain slashed Tim Beard's head, neck, shoulders, and legs. A second jagged field rock pointed out of the earth beneath him, stabbing him in the back when he tried to move. It was as if the earth itself sprouted fangs in order to chew him up and swallow him. Drawing breath strained his lungs to exhaustion. He tried to scream, but all that came out was a raspy whisper, audible through his nose. His mouth filled with blood. He squeezed his jaw closed, the hot stuff running down his cheeks from each corner of his lips.

The thing Sandra had always lectured him about had happened. The thing he had believed never could or never would. He was careful, after all. He examined the paths ahead of him when they were visible through the overgrowth. He plodded along them when they weren't, feeling his way with the front tires of his now-wrecked John Deere.

The man from nowhere had intercepted him, causing him to yank the tractor to the left. He must've hit the rock at a wrong angle, because the tractor had flipped onto its side and thrown him through the air like a javelin. When he landed, he'd struck the side of his head on a sharp, brittle piece of flint. He'd rolled and come to rest on his back on top of another.

Where was the man now? Tim had managed only a glimpse of him, but it was enough to note the dirty beige coveralls and bright red baseball cap. The cap shaded his eyes, so as far as Tim could tell, the man hadn't reacted at all when the tractor bore down with him dead in its sights. There was no way to determine whether his eyes had been open or closed. His hands had dangled at his sides. There'd been no expression on his lips. Something about him felt familiar, but Tim couldn't place it.

"El—*uk*," he gurgled, intending to scream *help*, but the word would not come. Blood trickled down his throat, convulsing him into a coughing fit that thrummed through every organ of his body. From his periphery, he thought he saw the overgrowth part on his left. The stalks bent in a V shape as if someone (*or some thing?*) had peeled them back like curtains. Human or animal? He couldn't tell. The grass returned to its height a moment later, sealing the gap.

Tim's life ebbed away, each breath drawn shallower and further from the last. Darkness clouded the edges of his vision, obscuring more of the weed curtain. The end of the tunnel of blue sky above him shrank in his vision. With it came the sensation of falling. Tim knew, with his rational mind, he remained broken on the dirt and rocks. He could feel it beneath him. Poking. Prodding. Angry. Yet the tunnel seemed familiar, too. Welcoming.

The end of the tunnel went dark. No. Not dark. Obscured. Someone (*or some thing?*) stood in the way of the light. The silhouette of a figure monitored him from the other end of the tunnel.

Jesus? he thought. *Momma?*

No, not unless one or both of them had adopted a modern farmer persona in the afterlife. As if to clarify its own identity, the figure became illuminated from within his tunnel vision. It stepped out of the shadow of its silhouette, allowing Tim to obtain more detail. It was the man he'd nearly run down. Red baseball cap. Beige coveralls, the collar of the latter turned up in a gust of western wind, flapping against his cheek. With one gritty and calloused finger, the man pushed the bill of his cap up so Tim could look him in the eye.

Except he had no eyes.

None.

Help me, Tim thought. He could not say it. *Help*.

"Tab is mine now," the man said. His voice skewered Tim's brain. The words reverberated in his ears, causing a sharp, stabbing sensation that traveled straight to the base of his skull. "I will protect him from now on. You are free to go."

Jeremy. Sandra. He could not form the words, but it didn't matter. The man at the tunnel's edge heard them anyway. And answered.

"They are none of my concern," he said. "Or of yours. Anymore, anyway."

Why? Tim asked. But before he'd completed the thought, he recognized the man and remembered, understood why he'd been haunting Tab. *You. You? NOT YOU!*

The thing smiled at him with a gap-toothed grin. The gums where a couple of his lower front chompers should have been were charred, black. It was as if he'd clamped them on a burnt-up stick of wood instead of the archetypal Southern farmer's long yellow strand of straw. The same muscles that stretched his mouth also pulled at the corners of his eye sockets, allowing Tim a glimpse of the gleaming white bone of the man's skull.

"Me," he said. "Good old Roy. Reckon they should call me Blind Roy now, though, on account of these here festering wounds." He indicated his empty eye sockets with one grimy finger.

Tim choked on another thick gulp of blood. *What do you want from me?*

Roy chuckled. "Well, now, what makes you think I want something from *you*? I got what I wanted from you. You're dead now. Or, you will be soon.

"Besides, I tend to operate on what you call a need-to-know basis. Right now, I don't think you need to know. Or ever. See, you're dying here in this old field, Beard. That much is obvious. But just because you're dying don't mean you're gonna stay quiet. So, I gotta make sure I play my cards close to my coveralls as long as you're still hanging around."

Roy glanced around, then leaned in as if to whisper a secret to a fellow conspirator. "Hey, you know what? If you was to promise to let go and let God, I might leave be. But if you're gonna stick around here on this plane after you're dead, I can't move on, neither. You might blab to your boy too soon. Or find some way to send a message to that cheating wife of yours."

Tim's eyes widened. Roy laughed, uproarious. "Yeah, I've been watching y'all a long time. A *long* time." He sniffled, wiping his mouth and nose with his left hand. "I told you back then your wife was a cheater, didn't I? Didn't believe me, though. She wants that Seb dude bad. She also wants to fuck that doctor fella what writes all them head books." He tapped his temple for emphasis.

"So, what do you say? If you promise to let the Lord or the Devil or whoever's on the other side of the veil have you as soon as you're gone from your old shell, I'll let the boy alone.

"I can tell you one thing right now, though. I kinda hope you don't leave." He shuffled closer from the end of the tunnel, leaning into the light so Tim could see his entire face. He could smell the thing's rancid breath.

"That boy and me? We got a lot to catch up on."

CHAPTER TEN

Four days passed before Tab remembered to try the technique Dr. Clifford suggested for talking back to the closet man with no eyes. Had the man whose name he'd never learned gone away on his own? He hoped so but didn't know.

The day of his dad's funeral arrived. They conducted Tim Beard's service outdoors at two o'clock in the afternoon on a Thursday. Tim had loathed the idea of being buried underground. Instead, they were supposed to entomb him in a vault drawer that sat among a stack of vault drawers with a view of the highway about forty yards away. Unfortunately, the vaults were full, so Dad would be buried in a casket in the ground after all.

Tab only knew about his dad's fear because he'd once overheard his parents talking about a scene in a movie from the Eighties, something about a snake and a rainbow. Tab didn't like snakes, but he couldn't understand why a movie about rainbows would be scary. Unless it was *The Wonderful Wizard of Oz*. That was a scary movie. Well, it had been when he saw it at six years old, anyway. He wasn't sure he would feel the same about it if he saw it today. Briefly, he imagined his father alive in his casket, pounding on its padded ceiling from six feet beneath the earth, screaming in vain that he was not dead yet. Sleep tonight would be hard to find.

Cars raced by the cemetery at a harrowing pace. They made the preacher—a squat man sprouting tall, dyed black televangelist hair who had been hired by Thompson Funeral Home—challenging to hear. Tab sat with one leg tucked under the other, his right shin dangling off the edge of a metal folding chair. He tried not to rock, because his rocking resulted in long, annoyed sighs from the folks who sat behind him. There was comfort in the motion when he was forced to sit. But often, his feeling that he was inconveniencing someone else outweighed his own desire to be comfortable.

His attention turned to his thumbs, which were at war with each other in his lap. Now and again, as the preacher droned on, Tab thought he could sense the familiar, comforting baritone of his father's voice on the wind. It was inconceivable that the man wouldn't walk up to them after the service and demand to go home. At times, the wind sounded like it whispered Tab's name.

The funeral director, a tall woman with a solemn face and world-weary eyes, pinned a white flower on the lapel of Tab's suit jacket before the service. Jeremy got one, too. She instructed them to place their flowers on their dad's casket after the pallbearers carried it to the gravesite. Tab protested. He wanted only to be invisible among the strangers who had come to see his father laid to rest. His mom had said he and Jeremy were "honorary pallbearers" and therefore had to help.

He'd only known it was time for him to play the part when his brother stood up and unpinned his own flower from his suit. Tab followed, shaking off the daydreams into which he'd disappeared during the eulogy. He mimicked his brother to the letter, standing behind him in a short line as the other pallbearers, all grown men who were either friends or coworkers of the adult Beards, tossed their flowers onto the casket. Tab was last in line.

He didn't look at the casket when he tossed the flower. It was too much. He had intended to cast it among the others, watch to ensure it didn't slide off, and walk away. But just as his hand returned to his side, the frigid fingers of another wrapped around his wrist. He glanced backward, thinking his mother had taken hold of him. She was not there. No one was. He glanced at his wrist and recoiled in horror. The fingers ensnaring him were farm-hardened and freezing. They had emerged from the wall of his dad's casket.

He saw no hole in the side of the box. It was as if the mortician had lobbed off the arm below the wrist and fastened it to the side of the casket as some sort of morbid, post-mortem prank. Caked-on rolls of makeup covered wormlike scars from his dad's accident. The cold and hard palm and fingers gripped his hand like the clutches of a stone sculpture.

Startled, Tab swiveled his head toward the crowd. No one seemed to notice what was happening to him. They waited patiently—or impatiently, it was hard to tell—for him to walk away. Then they could shake their heads sadly, offer the family condolences, and go about the rest of their day. Tab yanked on his arm, struggling to break free. His feet slid out from under him. He stared with longing at his mom, wanting to run to her side, pleading for her help. She only stared at his predicament from melancholic, unseeing eyes.

He pulled once more, hearing the body give and slide across the casket floor with the effort. When he looked at the box again, the corpse's full arm, shoulder, and half its head had emerged from the wall. Its eyes fluttered open. The stitches that held them closed made wet *pop* sounds as they cut through the eyelids. His dead father's right eye rolled in its socket, trained on Tab. The right side of its face curled into a familiar paternal grin. Its mouth never opened, yet it spoke.

Hey, son, it said. A gravelly gargle was embedded within the voice, along with an unnatural echo that made it sound like three or four dads speaking in chorus. *I'm sorry I had to leave.*

"Please let go," Tab cried. A tear rolled down his left cheek. He strained against the corpse's grip. The effort only caused the dead man to slide farther out of the casket wall. "Please."

I can't do that yet, Tab. I need to tell you something. Well, I need to warn you about something. Your mother, Tab. Your mother is a cheater. She cheated on me and it made me commit murder.

Tab's heart raced, its rapid beats reverberating in his chest, leaving him struggling to breathe. He plucked at the fingers with his free hand, frantic.

"I don't wanna know," he said. "Let me go!"

Listen to me, son. I don't remember a whole lot right now. The void is messing with my memories. But I do know a few things I have to tell you. The man in your closet? His name is Roy. He's here because of what we—what I—did to him.

The earnestness in his dead father's voice broke through his panic. Tab relaxed his arm. The dead hand's grip on him loosened in response.

"What did you do to him?"

We're the reason he's dead, son. And he's the reason I'm in this casket today. I was riding the John Deere and he was there. It was like you said it is when you see him in your closet. He's not there, and then he is. I thought he was a real person, so I swerved. Then the tractor threw me.

The memory of his nightmare in the back seat of his mother's car swam to the front of Tab's mind. "I was there, too," he said. His father's eyebrows shot upward, questioning. The makeup the mortician had applied to his face cracked in the folds of his forehead. Tab had a crazy moment when he considered making suggestions for correcting the work. He was no makeup expert, but his art experience had taught him that a lighter touch often created better results. The horror of the situation caught up with him, dispensing with the thought in short order.

"I was there in a dream," he added. "I saw you wreck. Didn't remember it until now, but I saw it happen. Didn't see *him*, though."

Roy.

"Yeah. Roy." Tab's father released his wrist. It fell limp at Tab's side. "What does he want?"

Tim eyed his son with sadness. *He says he wants to protect you. From your cheating mother, I guess. He doesn't have the same feelings for your mom and brother as he does for you, though. He made me promise I would leave Earth in death. That he would leave if I left. I can't do it right now, Tab. I waited too long. Stayed so I could watch over you and Mom and Jeremy. But my time will come again, and I'll be gone. He'll take care of you, though. You watch out for your mom. I don't want her hooking up with that Seb guy from Facebook. Or that handsome head-shrinker she's taking you to see nowadays.*

His dad's corpse began to recede into the casket wall again. *Strength is fading*, he said. *I should go.*

Tab cried in the open now, sniffling as tears ran from the corner of each eye. "I miss you, Dad," he said. "I love you."

I love you, too, son. However, something in the words rang hollow, lifeless. As if they had been spoken by someone who resembled his dad but wasn't. Tab thought maybe that was just how you sounded in death.

Then he was gone.

Tab turned his back to the casket. His gaze landed on his mom, who stood in front of her chair with her hands clasped together. She stared at Tab, her eyes soft and shining, her lower lip turned down in a sympathetic pout. She drifted up to him, produced the clean handkerchief she'd had folded between her palms, and dabbed at the snot and salty water streaming down his face.

"I know, Tab. I know."

But she didn't know. How could she? How could anyone gathered around him and his father's casket comprehend what he'd just seen and heard? No one else reacted to it. Most folks stared at the sky or at their feet. Some stared ahead, seemingly seeing nothing at all. Waiting.

His mom took his hand, leading him back to his seat. Together with Jeremy, they observed the strange men in business suits crank a handle on the odd device on which his dad's casket sat. A platform of nylon straps lowered the casket into the ground at a snail's pace. When it reached bottom, two men on either side pulled the straps away, rolled up the green astroturfing they'd used to cover the spoils, and began to shovel loose dirt on top of his dad. The clods made unpleasant *thud* sounds when they hit.

Tab twisted away as they went about their work and the crowd began to disperse. A lump rose in his throat. His belly hitched. He was about to blubber again. Jeremy would pester him about it later, no doubt. His brother hadn't shed a single tear for their dad except on the day they found his body in the field.

Tab transitioned his gaze away from the grave, toward the grass leading to the noisy highway at the cemetery border. Amid a scattering of gleaming modern gravestones stood the man whose name his dad had said was *Roy*. The man with gross, gory holes for eyes. Tab bet those eye sockets smelled, too. Literal stinkeye. Even without eyes, he sensed the man's stare. A gigantic shit-eating grin marked the lower half of his stubbly face. One thick, crusty finger beckoned to him. The man bent at the knees as he gestured, almost as if he was calling a dog.

Tab squeezed his eyes shut tight. He waited, then flung them open again, hoping the vision would be gone. Instead, Roy had closed the distance between them seemingly without moving a muscle. He stood in front of Tab's mother now. She did not appear to see him. He knelt, resting his hands on one knee, staring at Tab nose-to-nose from his empty eye sockets.

"Sad day for you, huh, boy? Happy one for me, though! I seen you talking to your old man." He indicated the space where the casket had been with a sideways nod of his head. "Couldn't hear him, though. What'd he say to you? I reckon he was filling you in on some stuff, huh? Reckon he was telling you why I'm hanging around?"

Tab sat silent, allowing his eyes to drift away from the visage before him. The man seemed able to read his thoughts, respond to them. So Tab would not speak. In spite of what his dad said, Roy—*Stinkeye Roy*—had done nothing to gain his trust. Well, except for telling him Alfie was safe.

He focused his mind elsewhere, wanting to protect the conversation he'd had with his dad's dead body. He replaced his thoughts about it with memories of Alfie sleeping at the end of his bed. Watching Jeremy play his video games. His mother beaming while he played with toys on the living room floor.

His mom. A pang of guilt stabbed his chest at the thought of her. His dad had said some vile things about her, nasty things. Things Tab was not ready to believe. Think on something else. Like visiting Dr. Clifford and Dr. Patel on the same afternoon.

Dr. Clifford!

"You're not here," he said to Roy. "I name you Stinkeye Roy, and you're not here. You can't hurt me."

Roy glowered at him. "Don't call me that," he said. "I don't want to hurt you. I'm here to help you, like your dad said."

"How do you know what my dad said? You said you didn't hear. And call you what? Stinkeye? Stinkeye Roy?"

"Shut up. I'm your elder. You need to show me some respect."

"No, you shut up. You're dead. You are not welcome in my life, Stinkeye Roy. You are not welcome in my closet. You are not welcome in my room. You are not welcome in my house."

"I can go wherever I want, kid. I'm here to protect you."

"You are not welcome on my family property. You are not welcome anywhere I am. You killed my dad, so I'm taking away your power."

Roy chuckled. There was a sinister echo to it. "You think I killed your dad? Sure, I was there. But so were you."

Tab paused in his litany, unable to conjure any other places he could list where Stinkeye Roy was not welcome. He was right, though. Tab had been there, too. His dad had been driving straight at him until the second the tractor careened onto its side and threw him into the air. But he hadn't been there in person, at least as far as he knew. It had only been a dream in the back of his mom's Accord.

Tab glared at the dead man. "What are you trying to say? My dad said he saw you standing in the field. He had his accident because he swerved to try to miss you."

"That so?" Roy answered. "Well, you're the only living person able to see me. Your dad saw me when he was already in between planes, I think. He might as well have already been dead. I talked to him.

"Then again, he was alive when he was on the tractor, boy. So it wasn't me who caused him to die all alone in the field. It wasn't me he saw. It was all you."

A hot bolt of electricity ran down Tab's spine. What if he hadn't been dreaming in the back of the car that day?

His mind wandered back to another episode of *Unexplained Phenomena* that had been on in the background one night. That one had been about something called an out-of-body experience. One segment was about a mother whose son had gone to war. While she was reading one night, her son appeared to her. He stood in front of her and stretched out a hand but said nothing. At the same time, halfway across the world, the young soldier in reality lay dying on the battlefield.

Had his dad misremembered? Tab thought it was possible. If the last face he had seen was Stinkeye Roy's, his dying brain might've replaced Tab's translucent, out-of-body form with the man's image in his memory. But Tab was skeptical.

"You're trying to confuse me," he said. "I said you're not welcome here. Now go away."

Roy raised a palm in front of him, smiling. "Alright. I'm going, but I ain't gone. You think about what I said, boy. Ain't no way your dad saw me standing there. You killed your dad with the little drawing you made. If I was there, it was only on account of you putting me there. Your bad wishes did it, not me."

He remained for one more second, long enough to drop his hand to his side. Then he wasn't.

Tab fingered the bump on his temple. It was hot to the touch, throbbing in time with his adrenaline-addled heart.

CHAPTER ELEVEN

Clark Clifford scratched his chin, eyeing Tab with curiosity. The ink pen he balanced in the crook of his index and middle finger had gone unused throughout most of Tab's appointment. The room had fallen quiet. Tab glanced at his mother, who silently wept, and then at his own hands. He searched for something to say that would fill the unbearable void. After what seemed like an eternity, Dr. Clifford broke the silence.

"Let me see if I have this right," he said. "The last time you saw me, you had a dream about your dad having an accident on his tractor after you drew a picture of him riding on that same tractor. This was the same day he had the accident?"

Tab nodded but did not look up from his hands.

"You saw the man from your closet at your dad's service? He told you it was your fault?"

Another nod.

Tab's sketchbook was stretched open across Dr. Clifford's lap. He picked it up and folded it on the spiral, holding it up so the boy could take in the drawing of his father on the tractor. Tab winced. He'd shown the drawing to Dr. Clifford on his mom's insistence. He'd wanted to throw it away, but she'd told him it might be important.

"I'm looking at your drawing here. I don't see anything at all that looks like an accident. This is your dad?" He tapped the image of the man on the tractor with the trigger of his pen.

"Yeah."

"And this figure. This is the man you've seen in your closet?"

Again, Tab replied in the affirmative.

"Well, I have to say I don't see you in this drawing at all. Nor do I see any accidents or sabotage. I think you drew this because you knew your dad would be on his tractor. And the other man? He's been on your mind a lot. For very good reasons. It feels normal to me you might combine the two things most on your mind into one drawing like this."

"I didn't make Dad die?" There was some desperation behind the question.

Dr. Clifford closed the sketchbook and handed it back to Tab. "Okay, let's talk about it. It's only been a couple of weeks since the accident. It's early in your grieving process. Do you understand grief?"

Tab shrugged. "It's sadness when something bad happens?"

"Mostly, yes," Dr. Clifford said. "But it's also a process that has five different emotional stages, more or less. There's no order to them, despite what people say online or in the movies. Some people cycle through all of them. Some people get stuck on one stage for a while. But the five major stages are common enough that someone once thought about writing them down."

"Okay."

"The five stages are denial, anger, bargaining, depression, and acceptance. What you're going through right now—seeing your dad lifelike at his own funeral and everything—is part of your denial stage. That's what it's called when we don't want to accept the reality of what's happened. When we can't believe something is true.

"I want to underline this next part." He mimed drawing a horizontal line in the air. "You won't go through every stage and come out all smiles and rainbows on the other side. I want to make sure you are prepared. People go through the stages out of the order I listed them. And the stages can repeat. So, one day you might think you've accepted what happened. The next day or hour or minute, you might end up in denial all over again.

"It's normal. Everyone goes through it. Most of the time, we as a society try to prevent young people like you from encountering it too soon. But that's not always possible." He leaned back and steepled his fingers, the ink pen bobbing between them. "I can't say I've met anyone who manifested it in the way you have. Have you considered your sadness combined with your imagination might be you trying to explain to yourself what happened?"

Tab sighed, curling his upper lip into a sneer as he did. "I don't know."

"Mr. Beard often went out on the tractor by himself, although he knew you didn't like for him to. Didn't he?" Dr. Clifford addressed this to Tab's mother.

"Yes," she said. "I begged him to wait until we could find times for us to both go so I could be there to make sure nothing bad happened. Tim isn't—*wasn't*—stupid, but he could be careless on the farm equipment." She scoffed. "I can't tell you the number of times I bandaged that man."

Tab allowed himself a ghost of a nostalgic grin. Memories of times when his dad had gotten cut or scraped or otherwise injured bubbled to the surface of his mind. The first aid always came with a feather-light lecture from Mom about not being so careless. She and Dad often laughed together about his predicaments in those days. Dad was hurt, but they still felt like happier times. Less angry times.

"So," Dr. Clifford said, "I want you, Tab, to understand you had no power over what your dad did that day. Even if you drew it and you dreamed about it, there's no way on Earth you could have caused it. Even if you had *wished for it* instead of only dreaming about it, you could not have caused it."

Tab stared at the doctor. "So why did I dream it?"

"That's a good question," Dr. Clifford said. "It's something we'll want to explore. For now, I suggest it's possible you could predict your father would go out on the tractor that day because it's what he would have done anyway. You knew that, right?"

Tab absorbed Dr. Clifford's words but made no signs of agreement. He wasn't sure he did agree. The doctor pressed on without his acknowledgment.

"You also understood your mom and dad were not getting along as well as they used to, I think?" He glanced from son to mother and back. Tab nodded and then regretted it when his mom sniffled.

"I *told* him we needed to be careful about when and where we fought!" She banged a fist that was wrapped around a Kleenex on the arm of her chair for emphasis. "I *told* him we were hurting the kids!"

Dr. Clifford nodded but did not affirm the outburst. "I want to reassure you both. Couples arguing is normal," he said. "If you want to spin it in a positive way, it demonstrates that communication channels are open between them even if they're not quite on the same frequency about everything. Make sense?"

"I guess so," Tab's mom said. She dabbed at her eyes with the Kleenex. A black smudge of liner appeared beneath her left eye.

"The arguments only become a problem when they become everything," Dr. Clifford said. "By that, I mean if you're arguing *most* the time, and nothing ever resolves—or at least *evolves*—you want to be in counseling. I'm sure there are things you haven't told me, but it doesn't sound to me like you two were there yet.

"The important thing is you, Tab, realize your parents were not arguing because of *you*. Grownups argue about all kinds of things that seem silly to kids. Money, work hours, divisions of household labor. There are many. Yes, sometimes they fight about children. But it is *never* the child's fault."

He glanced at the clock hanging on the wall over Tab's head. "We're almost out of time. But let me finish by telling you that you did the right thing by talking back to...Roy? Right?"

"Stinkeye Roy," Tab corrected. It prompted a chuckle from the doctor.

"Right. *Stinkeye* Roy. He went away when you talked back to him. I'm glad you have a name for him now. Naming your demon helps it become more like another human being instead of a monster. In time, it'll be easier not only to talk back to Roy, but also to dismiss the bad things he says to you."

Tab's eyebrows shot up, hope kindling behind his eyes. *Dismiss* was the word teachers used when they were ending a class. To Tab, it meant *go away*. "Dismiss?"

"I mean ignore them," Dr. Clifford amended.

"Oh." Tab sank back into the couch again, his head hanging lower atop his neck.

"I don't want to discourage you," Dr. Clifford said. "But most people are never entirely rid of their anxiety disorders. A combination of physiology, environment, and life events causes them, so there's not a single source we can point to and say 'Aha! If we just fix this, it'll all be okay!'

"Someday medicine will cure anxiety disorders, but for now we're stuck with medication and mitigation. It's similar to the common cold. There's no cure. We can only treat the symptoms. The symptoms are what cause us the most misery."

"I get it," Tab said, although he was not sure he did. He was unable to hide the disappointment in his voice.

"You keep working on making Stinkeye Roy less of a presence in your life. That's your homework. Together, we'll keep working on ways you can make it happen. How does that sound?"

"Mmm-hmm."

Dr. Clifford grinned at him. "Now, our time is up. I'd like to see you both back here in a couple of weeks, though. If it's okay with you, Sandra, I'd like to talk to Tab alone next time."

Sandra furrowed her brows. "Okay. I guess. Why?"

"Children are more comfortable talking about the things in their heads when it's just them and me. With no possibility of parental disapproval in the room."

"Yeah, I understand." She sniffled and dabbed at her eyes again.

"Meantime, Tab, I'd like to speak with your mother in private for a couple of minutes. Would you mind going back to the waiting room?"

Tab glanced at her in time to notice something pass between Dr. Clifford and his mom. He couldn't tell what, but the knowing expressions on both of their faces made him uncomfortable—the pleading or longing he saw in his mother's eyes in particular. A burning sensation flared in the core of his bump. It itched, too. He scratched at it unaware as he rose from the couch and headed for the door.

"Next time," Dr. Clifford said after him.

CHAPTER TWELVE

Except he wouldn't want a next time. Tab wandered to the waiting room and flung himself into a beanbag chair in the corner. Beside him stood a small shelf of children's books. He selected a copy of Mary Pope Osbourne's *Mummies in the Morning*, ready to escape into a fantasy world after spending the past hour in his own head. But he couldn't read the book. The words swam and blurred into a rainbow smear of text and colors.

He set his Strathmore on top of the book and began to draw. Dr. Clifford emerged first on the page, smiling eyes ready to receive any problems Tab lobbed. Next, he drew his mom. She sat across from Dr. Clifford. The expression on her face came out wrong. She looked like a puppy longing for a tennis ball. Tab erased and redrew it, but with a similar result. Frustrated, he tossed the sketchbook aside. Its clatter startled an older woman and a young girl on the other side of the waiting room.

Squeezing his eyes shut, Tab blinked away the irritation behind his eyelids caused by the intense concentration. When he opened them again, he sat not on the bean bag in the waiting room, but cross-legged in a corner of Dr. Clifford's office. On the couch, which might be still warm from where Tab had spent the previous hour of his life, Dr.

Clifford and his mom sat together, eyeing each other. The doctor held both of his mother's hands in his. Behind his glasses, his eyes were large and gleaming. Puppy dog eyes.

He couldn't see his mom's face from this angle. But he didn't like the way her shoulders heaved. She was breathing hard. He could hear it, in fact. She inhaled through her nose and then exhaled with the same depth through her mouth. The forceful breeze of it fluttered the point of the collar on Dr. Clifford's crisp white button-down shirt.

"Oh," his mom said. "Sorry. I didn't mean to blow on you."

Dr. Clifford smiled at her, open-mouthed, baring his perfect teeth. "No worries," he said. He pried his right hand away from her left and stroked a strand of stray hairs off her forehead. "You're very beautiful."

"And you're a genius," his mom said. "I have all of your books. I can't believe I'm here, talking with you in your office."

The backs of Dr. Clifford's fingers traveled from her hair to her cheek. They lingered for a second. Then they proceeded down her neck and towards the V of her blouse. Tab launched himself from his spot in the corner and aimed an accusatory forefinger at the doctor.

"STOP IT!" he said. "STOP IT! You are not my dad!"

Neither Dr. Clifford nor his mom acknowledged him. Nor did they stop. Dr. Clifford leaned in, closing the gap between himself and Tab's mom. He planted a tenuous, trembling kiss on her lips.

Tab raced toward them, his arms outstretched, palms forward. He meant to shove himself between the two grownups, putting an end to them physically if they wouldn't listen to him and stop on their own. His hands went through both of them. His knees and shins vanished, melting into the couch on which the two adults sat. Tab had expected to smash his knees into the space of cushion between them. Instead, he plummeted into the furniture.

It was as if he were a ghost or a hologram, an observer in a room where no one sensed his presence.

There was a horrifying moment when it seemed like Dr. Clifford and his mom were leaning in to press impassioned kisses into Tab's cheeks. Just before they closed, he snapped to in the waiting room. Someone was shaking him. Someone else was screaming, their words indistinguishable from the white noise of his liminal space. Consciousness and awareness sank ragged gnashers into his brain. His mother's face hovered above him. She had him by the shoulders jiggling them, making his neck ache. It wasn't until he closed his mouth that the screaming ceased. The piercing wails of panic had been his own.

"Tab!" his mother said. "You fell asleep at Dr. Clifford's. You're having a bad dream. Hush now! It's time to go."

Silence followed. Tab crammed knuckles into both his eyes, wiping away the nightmare. A glance around the room revealed the remainder of the patients waiting to see the psychiatric professionals with whom Dr. Clifford shared his office space. Every eye stared at him. Some of the patients sat open-mouthed. Others assessed him with narrow suspicion. Or fear.

"What's wrong with him?" a little girl with a mocking voice he thought he recognized asked, loud enough for everyone in the waiting room to hear. He looked at her and immediately put name to face. She was Ashley Reardon, a lanky blonde girl with limp straight hair falling to her armpits. Among the knife-edged features under her hair were a pair of ice-blue eyes glinting with malice. Ashley was also from Lost Hollow, older than Tab but not by much. She went to his school. Embarrassing. His face remained hot, but the itching and burning in the bump on the side of his head had subsided. For now, at least.

Ashley's mother, who was identical to her daughter except for having survived puberty and the inevitable transition into adulthood, slapped the girl's knee. "Shh! Hush! It's not your business. You have problems, too!" The knowing in her eyes, however, signaled that Mrs. Reardon also recognized the Beards. And she very much wanted to make it her business. The school's business, maybe. Tab was grateful Jeremy had been allowed to remain home in front of the computer this time. At least he had been spared *that* humiliation.

From behind Tab's mom, the gently smiling face of Dr. Clifford appeared, dawning like the sun over the horizon of her shoulder. "Let me through, if you don't mind," he said.

Tab's mother slid out of the way, allowing the doctor to kneel in front of Tab.

"Sounds like you had a bad scare in there." He indicated Tab's forehead with one well-manicured forefinger. "Do you want to come back to my office and talk about it?"

"Excuse me, but we're here *waiting*," said Mrs. Reardon. "He's already had his appointment. We've been sitting here for fifteen minutes!"

Annoyance overshadowed the doctor's good-natured resting face for a moment. In a blink, it was gone. He spoke again to Tab without acknowledging the impatient woman's outburst. "Do you want some water or anything?"

Tab shook his head. "No. I want to go home."

The doctor offered a hand to Tab, who used it to pull himself up from the beanbag chair. The copy of *Mummies in the Morning* that laid open in his lap plummeted to the floor. Dr. Clifford scooped it up and placed it on the shelf without a word. A smear of makeup slashed Dr. Clifford's neck, above his shirt collar. It looked like the napkins his mom used to "blot her lips." It might be the same color.

"Nude." Tab thought "nude" was a hilarious name for a color. Yet in his head now, it sounded ominous.

"I tried to tell you!" shouted a gleeful, watery voice from elsewhere across the room. Tab looked about for its source and landed on the tight space between the two chairs in which the Reardon girl and her mother sat. There stood Stinkeye Roy. The wall of the waiting room was visible behind him, which was a new thing. Every other time Tab had seen him, the man had appeared solid. A hopeful spark ignited within Tab. Regardless of his vision about the good doctor and his mother, Dr. Clifford's advice might already be working, poisoning the monster's well of power.

"I tried to tell you, boy!" Roy's voice was weak. More distant, as if he were speaking from the bottom of a deep well. "You can't get rid of me. You're my eyes now, and my eyes only bear witness to the truth. Your momma wants that doctor to pork her! Your momma's a whore!"

Pork was another funny word. Tab smirked at the sound of it. He understood it to refer to pig meat. The other connotation, the one Stinkeye Roy meant, he knew because his brother went on and on about such things when their parents were out of earshot. Jeremy didn't have many friends, at least many Tab knew about. Tab figured he was learning things like the other meaning of *pork* off the internet. Still, the fact he could laugh at words Roy was using to intimidate him emboldened Tab. His heart pounded hard in his chest. His fists readied themselves at his sides.

"Go away!" he said. "You're not welcome here! I don't want you in my life!"

Mrs. Reardon rose from her chair. Her right hand passed through Roy's hip when she did. "How dare you!" Her voice was shrill, trembling. "Come on, Ashley!" She grabbed the girl by the hand and pulled her from her seat. "Clark, we're going to your office *right now*. We've been waiting forever and that, that, that *boy* is beyond help." She glared at Tab's mom. "You should cut his hair. He might as well be a little girl." She sneered at him when she said this last, ensuring her insult was unmistakable. In a clip, the angry woman and Ashley disappeared through the door to the treatment rooms. The floor trembled when the door slammed behind them.

Tab combed his mane away from his face with his right hand. Little girl hair or no, he enjoyed the feel of it through his fingers. It made him feel strong, like that old Bible story Gramma told him about the man with the long hair who fought a lion and tore a temple down. He'd had a buzzcut once, at his dad's insistence when he was little. All he remembered about it was how embarrassed he'd felt arriving at school the next morning.

Dr. Clifford raised a hand to the remainder of the patients in the waiting room. There were two couples left, each member of whom stared at the trio of Tab, his mom, and Dr. Clifford with enlarged eyes and mouths ajar. They appeared to hold their collective breath, waiting for a hidden camera crew to tell them they were on a prank show and it had all been a joke.

"It's okay, folks," the doctor said, adopting a soothing timbre. "The young man is fine and the, uh—" he jerked a thumb at the closed door to the treatment rooms "—well, they'll be fine, too. I'm sure Dr. Aziz or Dr. Weissman will be with you soon." He turned his attention back to Tab's mother. "I'll see you in a couple of weeks. In the meantime, why don't you and your boys take some time off? Go on a mini-vacation or something and bond a little. They need you right now. Hollow River has a wonderful zoo." Without another word and without looking back, he vanished into the depths beyond the waiting room.

Tab hung his head. His cheeks stung. The surge of strength he'd enjoyed when confronting Roy had departed. The eyes of the other living people in the room burned him still. It made him wish he could sink again into the beanbag chair, sink through it and into the floor below.

Mercifully, the door to the treatment rooms opened again, dragging their attention away from him. Dr. Aziz, smiling, motioned for one of the couples to follow her. The other couple, who Tab presumed was waiting for Dr. Weissman, turned their attention to each other.

Across the room, where the Reardons had previously sat, the remaining wisps of Stinkeye Roy laughed.

And laughed.

And laughed.

CHAPTER THIRTEEN

Stinkeye Roy kept his distance all that night and the following day. As the weekend rolled around, Tab's mom informed him and Jeremy she planned to take Dr. Clifford's advice. She organized a day trip for all three of them to the Hollow River Zoo. Euphoria washed over Tab. He loved the animal shows on the National Geographic channel. Even better were all the animal-themed videos Jeremy sometimes found for him on the internet. He could be a nice brother when he wanted to be. Panda bears rolling down hills and cats saying funny things in flawed English made Tab laugh hard enough to hurt his belly. Jeremy, who had already seen the videos, laughed with him anyway.

Tab's dad hated the crowds at zoos. His mom always refused to go without his dad. Until now. Aside from the absence of bickering in the house, it was the first thing Tab discovered himself grateful for with regard to his father's passing.

What he most wanted to see was the river otters. Hollow River Zoo's otter habitat included all kinds of ways for the little water puppies to entertain themselves and their visitors. A winding otter slide constructed from mud and rock emerged from the middle of the back of the habitat. An ever-flowing trickle of water ran from the slide into the false river below. A selection of bouncy balls of various colors and sizes enabled the critters to play toss to their hearts' content. Bubble-shaped glass portals along the higher walls allowed visitors to watch the otters swim underwater.

The blistering sun baked the back of his neck. His mother's warm, damp palm rested on his right shoulder. Tab perceived neither of these things. He stood mesmerized in front of one of those portals. Otter after otter glided by like furry brown clouds in a high wind. Nose to the glass and hands firmly against the wall, all awareness of the group of people gathered behind him was lost. They waited their turns from another lifetime. Another planet. The otters knifed through the blue-green depths, blissful. Happy. How Tab wished he could be a carefree river otter.

Soon enough, the otters became background. In his head, Tab pondered what life without care must feel like. No mean older brother. No mean girls saying mean things to him in a doctor's waiting room. No brusque ghost of a gore-eyed redneck harassing him every day. If life could be that, with all his needs provided for and without hurt—. Well, he didn't know what. But it had to be better than dead dads. Or moms who spend their son's counseling appointments porking the rich and famous doctor.

His daydream shattered and awareness filled the void it left behind. He couldn't remember the last time he'd seen an otter pass by the little window. Likewise, the sunlight that had been so warm on his back was now baking his shoulders in a painful way. His mother's hand was gone.

"Mom?" He turned around to seek her and found instead a semicircle of other grownups, some of them with toddlers in their arms, scowling at him.

"You done, kid?" one of them asked. He was a rail-thin man hauling a purple bag under each of his weary eyes. In his arms, a toddler boy squirmed and fussed and demanded, "Down! Down!"

Tab nodded at the man, then searched the crowd for a gap through which he could escape. He saw only a forest of arms, legs, and trunks.

"Mom!" No one beyond the giant wall of cargo shorts, polo shirts, and sundresses replied.

Tab located one small spot of brightness he might squeeze through: at the rightmost edge of the semicircle, where a bleary-eyed man smoking a cigarette stood apart from the others. It was a small open space, smaller than Tab, but he thought he might squirm through if he made himself as small as possible. Surely the throng of spectators would allow him to pass.

"Excuse me," he said, raising both arms high in the air. One strap of the camouflage tank he was wearing rubbed against the side of his neck when he did. Pain prickled the spot, raising gooseflesh. They'd forgotten his sunscreen. He'd have a burn when they got home, but he couldn't worry about it right now. He inched along the exterior wall of the otter habitat, sucking in his tummy to further reduce his girth. "Excuse me! Excuse me!"

His distance from the void felt agonizing. Just as he arrived there, the bleary-eyed stranger leaned against the wall in front of him, shutting off his escape. Tab peered up at him, frustrated tears welling in his eyes.

"Excuse me?" he said. The presence of the unfamiliar adults created a tinny, timid quality to his voice as he spoke. "Can I get through, please?"

Without looking at him, the stranger returned to his upright position. The gap was restored, but it didn't seem as wide as Tab had thought when he saw it from the portal. He held his breath, stood on his tiptoes, and tried to squeeze through. The coarse, sweat-oiled hair of the stranger's left leg rubbed against his exposed armpit. Then came the sting.

"Ow!" Tab squealed. He stopped moving, wedged between the smoking man and the otter habitat. He'd been stung by a sweat bee only once before in his life. The pinching, stabbing pain in his temple, on his bump, felt a little like that. It also felt like he was on fire. He patted at the bump as if to snuff the flames, batting the stranger's cigarette out of his hand in the process. "You burned me!"

For the first time, the man with the bleary eyes took note of him. He lolled his head in Tab's direction and, with slurred speech, half-lidded eyes, and a broad grin absent of intellect, said, "Oh. Sorry." Tab sensed snideness in the man's tone, leading him to suspect the burn might have been deliberate. But there was no way to prove it.

"What the hell is that thing on your head, kid?" The man narrowed his eyes and leaned in. Tab could smell his breath. It reminded him of the overpowering odor of chlorine, urine, and urinal cakes in the zoo's men's rooms. "It keeps *looking* at me." He squeezed his left eye shut, as if doing so might make his vision clearer. "It's like you got a third eyeball." He raised the hand that had held his cigarette and attempted to poke at Tab's bump.

"You're not supposed to smoke here," Tab shrieked in the man's face.

The drunk man recoiled, stumbling into two other men standing near him, enabling Tab to shove himself the rest of the way through the gap. The two other men propped up the stranger, their mouths twisted into grimaces of disgust.

Tab ran. He ran so hard that a sliver of mucus trickled from his right nostril and onto his lower lip. He tasted salt, smeared it away with a swipe of his wrist.

He didn't know where he was going. He only knew he needed to escape. After a quick glance around, he spied a bench and ran for it. From the back pocket of his cargo shorts, he produced a small spiral notebook. His mom would not allow him to bring his Strathmore to the zoo because he might lose it. Tab retrieved his pencil from where it was tucked in the spiral and began to draw the man with the cigarette. In time, the man on the page stood on the side of a road. A gigantic pickup truck barreled down on him, about to knock him into oblivion.

Tab's eyelids grew heavy while he worked. His eyeballs rolled backward, revealing the whites. He blinked and glanced toward the drunk man for reference, but the otter habitat was gone. Before him stretched a long, narrow segment of city intersection. Tab recognized it. Mom had driven through it before making the right turn into the zoo. Cars and pickup trucks too large for such a narrow section of town sped by.

Across the street, the bleary-eyed man stood at the crosswalk, facing Tab. He did not appear to notice him. He did not appear to be capable of noticing anything. He couldn't stand upright and keep his hands still at the same time. His shoulders hunched and his hands swayed just above his knees. His mouth hung slack from his jaw, eyes unfocused.

Behind him stood two other men. Among them was one man who had held the smoker upright. He was gripping the bleary-eyed man by his shirttail to keep him from falling into a passing car before the Walk light appeared. Tab recognized the third man right away.

It was Stinkeye Roy.

He grinned when Tab spied him. It was a Chesire grin, taking up his entire face, squeezing his eye sockets into hollowed slits. In a blink, he shoved the palm of his ethereal right hand into the bleary-eyed man's back. The man's friend lost his grip on the shirttail. The stranger who had only a moment before burned him with a lit cigarette went sprawling face-first off the curb and into the street. A thick maroon pool of blood oozed onto the pavement from his forehead.

But the bleary-eyed man did not die. Not yet, at least. After flailing his arms and kicking his feet like a turtle turned on its back, the stranger managed to get his hands under his shoulders. Just as he was about to push himself onto his knees, a black Ford F-150 struck him dead-on.

The man shot forward from the truck's bumper, tumbling through the air like a child's doll flung across the room. His arms and legs flailed about him mid-arc. When he landed, his left shoulder hit first. The arm connected to the hand that had burned Tab's bump crunched against the asphalt. His shoulder came loose from its socket. The arm twisted around backward, making it seem like the man had two right hands, one turned inward and one turned outward.

Soon, sirens wailed in the distance. The F-150 sped off, slowing only to circumvent the body. Lot of good that did now. Its right rear tire managed to roll over one of the stranger's ankles in the process. The pickup's windows were tinted so dark Tab could not see any details about the driver. Nor could he make out the numbers on the license tag as it fled the scene. As other drivers prevented traffic behind them from entering the area, the crowd from the sidewalks began to tend to the man. Tab's eyes darted back to Stinkeye Roy.

He cocked his head to the left and shot the boy a thumbs-up. Then, without so much as a *pop*, he was gone.

"No," Tab said. Louder, "No. No! *NO!*"

Suddenly, he was seated on the bench and staring at the otter habitat again. Tab glanced up in time to glimpse the backs of his mom and Jeremy as they strolled in the opposite direction. Dashing toward them, wheezing and out of breath, he caught up and tugged at the hem of his mother's pink V-neck tee.

"Where were you?" Tab asked. "I was stuck at the otter window. The people wouldn't let me through. *Where WERE you?*"

Tab's mom knelt and dabbed at the tears rolling down his cheeks. "What do you mean, hon?" she asked. "We were right there." She pointed to the small crowd gathered around the otter habitat. "I thought you were with us." Her sweet, thin smile turned downward. Concern darkened her eyes.

"What happened to your bump?" she asked. "Did you hit your head on something?"

Tab pivoted, extending his right hand to point out the man who had burned him, then remembered the street scene that had unfolded there moments before. He lowered his hand.

"Tab?" his mom said. "Tab, what's wrong with you?"

He glanced back at his mother, gesturing at where the scene should have been in front of them. "Mom, did you not see what happened over there?"

"See what, hon?"

"The—"

But she hadn't. And it was gone. The crowd of people who had gathered around the otter habitat when Tab stood at the portal had mostly dispersed. One person, who from the back looked like he might have been the bleary-eyed man, shuffled away in the direction opposite of Tab. A second later, he was joined by another man, who grabbed the stranger under one armpit, as if to help him remain upright.

"See what?" Tab's mom asked again.

"N—Nothing. I thought one of the animals got out. I guess it didn't. That's all." It might have been the first time he had ever lied to his mother. It felt wrong. A lump lodged in Tab's throat, which he swallowed with effort.

His mom examined the bump on his temple. Tab could smell her body lotion when she leaned near. It was an aroma he associated with her and was of some comfort most times. Not today.

"I don't like this," Sandra said. "Let's stop by the first aid office and have a closer look at it. Can't you tell me what happened?"

"I don't know," Tab said, his voice flat. "I must have hit it on the wall at the otters."

CHAPTER FOURTEEN

While his mom navigated the drive home and Jeremy remained glued to a screen, Tab kept watch from the back seat. They drove through the intersection in which he'd witnessed the bleary-eyed stranger's demise without incident. Tab perceived no tire marks, no blood, no shocked eyewitnesses milling about. There were no flashing lights and no sirens. No sign of the stranger and his cigarette, either.

"Maybe I *am* crazy," he murmured.

"What?" Jeremy asked, not looking up from his device.

"Nothing. Thinking."

"Well, think quiet. I'm trying to talk to my friends here." He had abandoned his iPod Touch for their mom's iPhone, because the Touch had no way to connect to the internet without WiFi. Tab didn't understand the difference between WiFi and cellular, but Jeremy complained about it often.

"Jeremy, leave your brother alone. Please? You spend too much time looking at screens anyway."

His brother harrumphed and disappeared again into his digital void.

Tab allowed himself to relax after they passed the intersection and veered onto the stretch of highway that became Hollow Creek Road into Lost Hollow. His eyelids felt like automatic garage doors on which someone kept pressing the remote. They fluttered down, to half-mast, then down again. But he did not sleep. He could not sleep. The otter incident and the scenes Roy had shown him both in Dr. Clifford's office and outside the zoo surfaced on repeat in his mind.

"Mom?" he asked through a yawn. "When do we see Dr. Clifford again?"

"In a couple of weeks," she said. "Why?"

"I think—"

Jeremy interrupted them. "Holy shit! Oh, man!"

"Jeremy. Alan. Beard!"

"Oh. Sorry, Mom. It's just Chris Wilson's family went to the zoo today, too. They're stuck in traffic right now because some asshole—"

"Jeremy!"

"—ran over a guy right outside the gates. Chris says blood is all over the road and the cops aren't letting anyone through."

"Wow. I guess we're lucky we left when we did."

"Yeah, Chris says they've been sitting for fifteen minutes already and there's no way around. He's pissed about it."

Sandra sighed. "Jeremy, please. Watch your language. I can't scream at you about it like your dad used to do. But just because he's gone doesn't mean the house rules don't apply."

"We're not at home," Jeremy retorted.

Sandra rolled her eyes. "Ugh. Then stop being such an asshole."

They laughed together. Tab couldn't remember the last time they had. He didn't join them. The image of Stinkeye Roy shoving the bleary-eyed man into the street haunted him. Yes, the man had burned him with a cigarette. Sure, he was angry. But it should not have amounted to a death sentence.

The nurse at the First Aid Office had applied some Neosporin and said it would hurt for a while but was *su-*

perficial. Tab asked his mom what *superficial* meant. She'd told him it meant it was no big deal.

"Are you sure you hit it on something?" the nurse had asked. "It looks more like a burn."

"I must've hit it on something hot," Tab said.

The nurse nodded. "Zoo has some hot surfaces. Balmy summery days like this make everything hot." The doubt in her eyes betrayed her, though. She didn't buy his story.

He ran the first two fingers of his left hand over the bump. The drunk stranger said it looked like an eye. Tab didn't think that was true, at least not at the moment. It was more like a small flesh-colored knot under his skin. He saw no slot or hole through which an eyeball might emerge. Not anymore. Not since his first visit to Dr. Patel. At times the bump appeared red and inflamed. During those moments, Tab thought he sensed something moving around. When he pressed on it, it hurt like hell. Once, it moved while he was pressing his finger against it, as if whatever lurked there was trying to orbit away.

Oddly, Tab was beginning to feel a small amount of gratitude for the bump. And for Stinkeye Roy. He imagined telling his mom or his dad about the stranger burning him with a cigarette. Their response would have been much milder than Roy's. He imagined his mom telling him in her lilting Mom voice, "The man didn't mean to hurt you, hon. It was an accident." Never mind that smoking in the zoo was against the rules.

His dad would've gotten angry, but at Tab instead of the man who burned him. Their dad tended to blame them when Tab or Jeremy got hurt, regardless of the actual circumstances. Tab's impression was that his dad wanted to be by himself those days, was too busy to deal with them. His sons were an inconvenience, especially when one of them made noise about getting hurt.

Roy seemed to take Tab's side, sticking up for him when he couldn't stick up for himself. Warmth enveloped his heart at that thought, followed by a stab of guilt over thinking of Roy as *Stinkeye* Roy. After all, Tab himself had been bullied and called names before. He wouldn't wish it on anyone. Even his worst enemy. He forced himself to try thinking of Stinkeye Roy as just *Roy*. It wasn't easy. But, with time, he was sure he'd be capable of thinking about his ghostly friend without including the pejorative.

With that idea in mind, his remaining tension melted away, allowing him to drift. He bowed his head, his shoulders and torso slumping against the security of the seatbelt, and nodded off. Vaguely, he became aware of a figure sitting in the back seat beside him. He cracked open his right eye a hair and recognized Stinkeye—no, *Roy's*—work boots and beige work pants. A faint smile curled up Tab's lips. His right eyelid closed again. Soon, he slept.

※※※

By the time Sandra's Accord jerked to a halt in the driveway, Tab's nap had plunged into a full-blown sleep of dreamless, snoring exhaustion. He had a moment of panic when he felt his mother's hands on his shoulders, shaking him. Was it storming again?

"Wake up, hon. We're home." Then the switch flipped on his consciousness and light dawned inside his head. He examined the seat to his right while he unbuckled his seatbelt. Roy was nowhere to be seen. Nor could Tab detect any evidence he had been there.

His bump ached a little. He resisted the urge to touch it again. It would be warm. There might be something moving underneath the skin. Or it might send a sharp, stabbing pain into his temple. In any case, he wasn't keen to revisit the discomfort.

Full awareness took some time. Tab spent much of the rest of the afternoon on the couch in front of syndicated network television. By the time he felt human again, his mom was well into preparing dinner for the three of them. The scent of stewed potatoes and pinto beans wafted into the room from the family's adjacent kitchen. Tab's tummy grumbled. *Feed me!* He stood up, intending to check on his mother's progress as a *Jeopardy!* rerun ended and one of the local news anchors appeared in a split screen to tease the evening's stories.

"A man is dead and police need your help in the search for suspects after a hit-and-run in front of Hollow River Zoo today," the brunette with the grave expression intoned. The summery floral print she wore diminished the drama in her expression. Why did news people, who rarely talk about anything but politics, crime, and disasters, dress colorfully like that? They should wear black suits, like for a funeral. Because what did they talk about more than death? "Details next on *News at 5*."

Tab collapsed to the couch. Hearing the story teased on the news made the day's events more real. A heaviness settled in his chest as the *Jeopardy!* end credits disappeared and the news began.

"Good evening and welcome to Channel 6 *News at 5*," the brunette said. "We'll get to the latest information about the flood damage and recovery in a moment, but first, Hollow River Police want you to be on the lookout for this vehicle." An image from a security camera mounted on the Zoo's entry gates appeared on the screen. Within, a two-ton black pickup sped away from a scene partially obscured by a heavy waterfall of gray pixelation. "Channel 6 reporter Afia Afton is at the scene with more information."

The image transitioned to a younger woman in a dark, short-sleeve blouse and matching slacks. Her severe expression forecast the story she was about to tell.

"Thanks, Lisa," Afia said. "Police and witnesses tell me the driver of a late-model black Ford F-150 hit a man who had fallen into the street at this intersection in front of the Hollow River Zoo. Eyewitnesses report the driver stopped at the scene but sped away before authorities arrived. By the time help was available, the man identified as 36-year-old Hollow River resident Michael Robbins had already succumbed to his injuries.

"Another man, who accompanied Robbins to the zoo and who did not want to be interviewed on camera, says he tried to catch Robbins when he stumbled, but was unable to reach him in time.

"Investigators have so far been unable to obtain license tag information on the vehicle or a description of the suspect," she said. "They have few leads. Again, the truck appears to be a late model black Ford F-150 and most likely has front grille damage. If you have any information on the whereabouts of the vehicle or the driver, you are asked to contact the Hollow River Police Department at the number on your screen. For Channel 6 *News at 5*, I'm Afia Afton.

"Back to you, Lisa."

Tab regained his feet and switched off the television. His ears were hot, on fire. A tiny hammer and chisel tapped at the back of his mind, carving out the certainty that somehow the whole thing would be traced back to him because he had seen it before it happened.

He scraped a palm across the back of his neck. If he stopped thinking about it, the likelihood he would telegraph what he knew to others would decrease. But his sense of responsibility remained, along with the guilt.

I didn't do anything, Tab reminded himself.

Isn't that the problem? his conscience shot back. *You could have* stopped it.

How?

Silence.

Tab's tummy growled again, but he had lost interest in dinner. He strode to his room, curling himself into a fetal position around his pillow. The toddler in him wanted to pop his thumb in his mouth. Instead, he allowed a single tear to creep from the corner of his right eye. Spying his sketch pad and pencils on his desk, the urge to draw struck him. He bounded off the bed and opened the Strathmore to a blank page. The eraser side of the pencil tapped against his bump seven times before he pressed lead to paper.

He lightly rocked as he drew. The first image to emerge from the pencil clutched between the thumb and fingers of his right hand was of an angry looking eyeball. It was a cornea in profile, and not much else, but Tab thought it appeared angry anyway. Above and touching the upper swell of the eyeball, he scribbled another dark circle. This, in his mind, represented the cigarette burn he'd endured courtesy of the (*dead*) bleary-eyed man.

To the right of the eyeball, he sketched what he remembered about the black pickup truck he'd watched mow the man down. The first line became a rectangle, which transformed into the pickup's tailgate as he continued to draw. Sure enough, the word FORD soon appeared inside a small oval positioned dead center in the rectangle. To the left of the oval, Tab crafted the word F-150 in italicized block letters with rounded corners. Below the logo, in a script he didn't recognize because he hadn't mastered cursive, he wrote the words RORY SANDS FORD. In smaller type farther down: HOLLOW RIVER, TENNESSEE.

Beneath the tailgate, the rectangular space for the license tag sat empty. Tab waited, pencil hovering over the page, but nothing came. He tapped his bump with the eraser three times and touched the graphite to the paper, hoping to prompt a memory that might reveal the pickup's tag number. He surrendered when his fingers began to cramp, dropping the pencil into the jar on his desk with a thin *clink*.

"Tab!" his mom yelled from the kitchen. "Dinner's ready, hon. Go find your brother."

"I'm on the computer, Mom," Jeremy shouted.

Tab sighed, shoving the sketch pad away. He tried to remember the telephone number the news had flashed on the screen for the Hollow River Police Department, but it escaped him. That was okay. He'd find it on the internet if he could pry the iMac away from Jeremy's sticky fingers for a few minutes. He thought about asking his brother to Google it for him. Jeremy was always better at stuff like that. But Jeremy would ask questions and might tell.

For now, he thought it best if he kept what he knew to himself, at least until his next appointment with Dr. Clifford. Assuming, of course, there *would be* a next appointment with Dr. Clifford.

CHAPTER FIFTEEN

Lost Hollow's lone school reopened for one week after water and mold mitigation had been completed and before the county's schedule closed it for the summer. When their mother dropped them before the bank of reinforced glass front doors, Jeremy slinked away toward the stairs leading to the middle school classrooms. He didn't bother to acknowledge either his mother or his brother as he did. Tab snatched his backpack off the seat and propelled himself out the door after Jeremy. "Bye, Mom!" he said before slamming the door.

"Bye, hon. Have a good day. Oh, wait! Come back!" He returned to the car as his mother leaned over the passenger's seat, dangling his sketchbook out the window on that side. "You forgot something!"

Tab rescued the pad from his mother's grip and tucked it under his right arm. His mom beamed.

"I'm so proud of you and your art," she said. "But try not to draw during class again. Okay?"

"We're not doing anything important. It's just going to be busywork so they can say we went for the whole year."

"Well, mind your teachers."

He nodded, waving goodbye again as he turned and headed for the doors. His heart sank when he saw who stood in front of them. Ashley Reardon, the girl who had taunted and insulted him in Dr. Clifford's waiting room, glared at him. Her hands rested on her hips. Her bottom lip turned downward in a mocking pout when their eyes met.

"Mind your teachers, Tabitha," she said, pitching her voice in a lecturing tone meant to mimic his mom. "Don't draw during class again!" Her derisive eyes gleamed, as if expecting him to well up any second. Tab shoved past her without looking, pretending she wasn't there. Her stare burned the back of his neck when he pried open the heavy glass doors. His efforts prompted an involuntary grunt. Embarrassing. Unmanly, his dad and Jeremy might say. But the doors were heavy.

A year ago, he would've had to use two hands to open them. Now he could do so one-handed, at least enough to squeeze between the door and the frame. Seemed manly enough to him. The door whooshed closed behind him. He inhaled, relieved to be inside, and coughed it out in surprise when Ashley breezed up on his left.

"What do you draw?" she asked. Her pace was brisk. She was about same height as him, but her strides were shorter. Most girls around his age were taller, yet something about Ashley felt more intimidating. Maybe because she was focusing so much attention on him. Other girls ignored him completely. "You draw cars and trucks, I bet."

He did not respond.

"Hmmm, not cars and trucks?" She pressed a finger to her lips, considering. "Monsters? Or boobs! I bet you draw boobs all over every page, you nasty little pre-vert! Just like a boy. I have a brother. I know how y'all are."

He rolled his eyes and plodded onward. "It's *per*vert. And I'm not one."

"Hmm. Not boobs, either? Pee-pees? Are you telling me you like pee-pees?"

"I'm not telling you anything. Leave me alone, Ashley, or I'll tell *on you*." The familiar ache had begun to throb in his temple. He rubbed at it and soon regretted doing so because it drew her attention.

"What *is* that?" she asked, wrinkling her nose in disgust. "You got a VD from all the pee-pees, *purrr*-vert?"

"It's a bump. Everybody gets them sometimes."

"You mean a pimple?" She laughed. "My big brother gets pimples, but he's fifteen. You don't get them at our age, doofus. I think you have a VD. You should have the nurse look at it. I mean, you're out sick from school a lot. Kind of suspicious, if you ask me."

"I'm get strep throat a lot."

Sharp as The Joker's chin, "I think you mean VD."

Tab reached his classroom door, which was open, and darted inside. Ashley's stare maintained its heat on the back of his neck, but he didn't bother to glance behind. He was not interested in whether she had moved on to her own classroom. He was glad only to be rid of her, although irritable at his own inability to cut her down. To cut anyone down, for that matter. Sometimes he worried that the fast wit of others when compared to his own meant he was stupid, or at least not as smart as other kids his age.

The throb in his temple evolved into a full-blown headache. Something—the "eyeball?"—moved under the skin. Had his attempts to avoid a confrontation with Ashley triggered it somehow?

Tab deposited his backpack in its designated location and took his seat while the other kids yukked it up in the reading corner. What were they so happy about? He wished Lost Hollow School had stayed closed for the rest of the year. Although the news claimed the place had been cleaned, Tab detected a moldy, mildewy odor in the air. It made him think of spoiled milk.

He slapped his sketchbook on his desk and flipped it open. It took some effort, but he managed to page past the image he'd drawn of the pickup truck. He still hadn't decided what to do with the information. Best not to think about it right now.

A fresh blank page confronted him. He plucked his pencil from its holder on his desk, tapped the eraser a few times against his bump, and set about making shapes. His light rocking against the back of his desk drew occasional stares, and at least one giggle, but he didn't care. It was comforting, like the slow beats of an old grandfather clock. The throb in his temple soon synchronized with his metronomic movements. His eyelids felt heavy. He wanted to put his head down, take a rest. Instead, he turned toward the ceiling, his eyes rolling back, the tip of his pencil plummeting to the paper.

First, he drew a vertical rectangle. Inside the rectangle, two identical squares were born, one atop the other. Next, he drew a circle in the center left of the larger rectangle. Together, the elements began to resemble a door.

The point of the pencil again landed inside the vertical rectangle, but also inside its top square. Five strokes later, he had drawn a hand, palm down against the door, holding it closed.

His heart raced, although he was not aware of it. On the right side of the door, as he faced it, he drew a semi-circle that at first appeared to be connected to the door itself. Then he added hair to the semi-circle, and eyes, and part of a nose. A person, feminine, peered from behind the door that was being forced closed. Her eyes became her most prominent feature. They formed from large concentric circles, uncomprehending and afraid.

Below the face, he drew another hand. This one was not pushing. It had wrapped itself around the depth of the door and was shoving against it. From the bottom of the hand, Tab drew a vertical squiggle that then became a series of dots. That string of graphite ended in an oval pool at the bottom of the door. Tab wasn't using color pencils, but if he had he would have stained the pool and every trickle or blob leading to it a dark red.

A moment later, the bell rang, marking the beginning of the school day. Tab started, his eyes rolling forward to their rightful positions. Had he drifted to sleep? He only glanced at what he'd drawn before snapping the sketchbook closed. His fingers wanted to keep going, to find out what he was going to draw next. But he also didn't want any trouble from Ms. Bowman. Or any of his classmates if they saw what he'd been up to. They all thought he was weird already. No sense in confirming it for them.

When the lunch bell rang, Tab forgot all about the new drawing. Three hours after that came the dismissal bell. He snatched up his backpack, crammed the sketchbook among the unorganized books and papers in its unzipped compartment, and legged it out the door while other kids said their goodbyes.

Ms. Bowman busied herself erasing her whiteboard. Tab was supposed to wait until she led the class to the car line, but it was the last day of the school year, and he didn't much care for waiting. What were they going to do? Suspend him? Besides, Jeremy would be looking for him. And his mom was almost always first to arrive for pickup.

Except he didn't make it outside. As soon as he veered into the hallway, a head-splitting wail accosted his ears. The rest of his class, including Ms. Bowman, joined Tab at the mouth of the classroom.

"What is going on out here?" the teacher asked. She wriggled her way through the wall of students and strode down the hall. Her next words were, "Oh, my! Oh, dear! Oh, God!" That was followed by the hurried *slap slap slap* of her flats against the hall's linoleum.

Seconds later, a group of kids from another class—Ashley Reardon's—padded to their classroom from the front of the building. A few, all girls, sported furrowed brows, worried eyes, and turned-down mouths. One, a boy named Teddy, raced back as though he was being chased by a mountain lion. His eyes were alight. A monstrous grin spread across the lower half of his face. Jazz hands waggled on either side of his head.

"Oh, man!" Teddy said. He glanced this way and that, looking for anyone who might be looking at him. "She's all busted up! She's all busted up, y'all! They've called an ambulance!" He locked eyes with Tab, who did not glance away fast enough because Teddy danced straight to him.

"Dude! She's *all* busted up!"

"Who?" Tab asked before he could stop himself.

"Ashley Reardon!" They were nose-to-nose now. Tab could smell Black Cherry Kool-Aid and pretzels on his breath. "She got mashed in the door when she tried to leave. It was like it was possessed or something. Slammed closed on her, even with her pushing on it. I bet she has a broken arm! I bet her lungs collapsed!"

When Tab didn't react, Teddy flailed away in search of someone else to enthrall. A stone sat in Tab's gut, followed by a wave of nausea.

When a clearing opened in the throng of people who had gathered around young Ashley, Tab could make out that she was seated on the floor in front of the doors. Her face was beet red. Her left arm dangled dead at her side as she swiped at her tears with her right.

A tall, foreboding figure he recognized as the principal, Mr. Miller, stepped into view, blocking the clearing.

"Go back to your classroom." He motioned at the hallway in general, but Tab and the others could tell he meant them. Feet shuffled behind him as the other students complied. He backed inside as well, taking long peeks at the front end of the hall, hoping he might see more. The crowd did not part again.

No one in Tab's class returned to their seat, except for Tab. They congregated in the open areas of the classroom, regaling each other with their theories about what happened to poor Ashley and whether she might be deformed or disabled by the experience. A few of the other boys were already trying to make up new jokes based on the accident.

"How much does it cost to get out of this place?"

"If you're Ashley Reardon, an arm and a leg."

They weren't funny, but the other boys laughed. Because to not laugh would have made you seem squeamish. And looking squeamish got you belched at and coughed on during lunch or spit on at recess. Unless you were a girl.

Tab sat his backpack down beside his desk and yanked out his sketchbook. He flipped to the page he'd been working on earlier. In the face of the girl who was being pressed by the door, he could indeed pick out the terrified eyes of Ashley Reardon. The disembodied hand pressing against the door reminded him very much of the calloused hands of a man who works for a living...

A man like Stinkeye Roy.

CHAPTER SIXTEEN

By the time spring rolled into summer, Tab had heard through his mom, who heard through the grapevine, that the broken arm and ribs Ashley Reardon suffered from the school's front doors were almost healed. A local newspaper, the *Hollow River Echo*, latched onto the incident. Its editorial board called out the school and its governing body for their negligence. The building's entrance hadn't been updated since the early 1970s. Until 1995, that wing of the building had been part of the high school.

High school students, the *Echo* argued, were strong enough to open such doors without harming themselves like little Ashley. Middle schoolers and elementary kids were not. Nor were they likely to help themselves by pressing the accessibility button to open the single area of entry it operated. To do so without disability might make them look weak in the eyes of their peers.

The editorial generated outrage, calls for change, and backlash among Lost Hollow citizens, officials, and the county school board. There were the folks who wanted to protect the school children from future harm. Then there were the folks who thought the kids should just suck it up and learn the proper way to open heavy doors. Tab didn't understand this argument. Was there more than one way to pull open a door? The *Echo*'s letters page expanded to two over the issue in one late spring edition. Soon, the story gained enough traction and talk that it was picked up by Channel 6.

Tab paid the controversy little mind after it blew up in the media. The newspaper held no interest for him. He also switched off the television before the syndicated afternoon shows faded into news teasers. His drawings became more frequent, except without the dinosaurs or superheroes he'd fancied in the past. Instead, he drew scenes, people, places, and things he knew or imagined from real life. Often, scary things. He hated being surprised by the news, discovering that scenes he drew in a trancelike state—while his body rocked and his bump burned and stabbed at his temple—had clawed their way into reality.

Once, Tab overheard his mom chatting on the phone about a school bus that had crashed head-on with a semi on a stretch of highway in Hollow River. The bus was ferrying a group of Lost Hollow and Hollow River kids to a summer camp. The driver, who had been drinking, had fallen asleep at the wheel and crossed the center line. The bus plowed into the Mack without braking.

At least no one was killed. The driver's foot had slipped off the gas, slowing the bus. The semi was still in low gear, having just rolled away from a green light. The bus driver lost his job and went to jail. At least one kid got a heinous concussion. Another broke his wrist.

When his mom finished her call, Tab closed himself in his room and paged furiously through his latest sketchbook. Sheet after sheet of the pad was filled with mundane nightmares of modern life: car accidents, shootings. He'd also drawn an overdose, although Tab knew only that he'd depicted a three-quarter portrait of a strange thin man with long hair and an open mouth. Bubbling foam and thick vomit flowed from the corners of his lips like lava rolling out of a volcano.

The final drawing was another of Stinkeye Roy. *Just Roy*, he chided himself. Seated on a short stack of concrete blocks, Roy stared back at him from empty eye sockets, menacing and piteous. A light, paternal smile curled his lips. There was no bus accident to be found among his sketches.

Tab allowed himself to relax. The bus was one disaster for which he would not hold himself responsible. He slapped the sketchbook closed, crossed his arms over it, and laid his forehead on top of them. Tears would not come. He was past tears. Drowsiness and psychological exhaustion held stronger claims. As he drifted, the sensation of a gentle hand on his left shoulder stirred him awake again. He peered over it, but the room behind him sat empty.

There was no bus accident in your sketchbook, his conscience repeated. *You didn't do anything wrong. This time.*

Sleep overtook him. His dreaming mind dropped him into a land he visited often now. It was a world where his dad had died but was also somehow still alive. Dad beckoned to him from behind a wall of milky, semi-opaque haze. He mouthed words. Sometimes, Tab thought he could pick out one or two of them, but most of them were lost. The ones he could pick out in the dream were forgotten by the time he awoke. Except for two. One was *Dad*. The other might have been *Roy*.

Outside his head, Tab snorted and fell into the rhythmic log-sawing of a middle-aged man in the slow-wave stage of sleep. He slapped at a phantom tickle on the end of his nose, shifting so his bump pointed skyward. A tiny dark hole, no larger than an average blackhead, appeared in the center of the bump. It widened in a lateral fashion, ripping apart the layer of temple skin like a sewist cutting a row of stitches.

When the open seam had spread across the entire diameter of the bump, the upper and lower layers folded back on themselves. From within emerged a wet, gray orb full of spidery bottle fly-green and black capillaries. In the center, an angry crimson iris more elliptic than round drowned a pupil about the size of the head of a pin.

The eyeball trembled in its socket, blood vessels pulsing. Hot ichor flowed through them. Tab shifted in his sleep and sat up. His normal, human eyes fluttered open but remained unseeing. Unconstrained by his waking mind, his hands spread open his sketchbook and located a blank page. His right hand plucked a No. 2 from its place in the jar and traced a series of light circles onto the page. The circles later became connected by bolder lines.

Soon, a figure began to take shape: a masculine hand, filthy and spattered with crusting, flayed open flaps of rotting flesh. The hand emerged from solid earth, as though its bearer had been buried too soon, demanding to reside among the living. Wrapped around the fourth finger of the hand was a ring. It bore a striking resemblance to his dad's white gold wedding band, an ivy vine engraved around its diameter.

The image completed, Tab plunked the pencil into the jar, closed the sketchbook, and collapsed atop it again. He would not discover the new drawing until the next day.

CHAPTER SEVENTEEN

His mother's enraged shouts were the first sounds he became aware of the next morning. Tab sat bolt upright in bed, his heart racing. When his brain phased into enough reality to enable him to decipher her words, he realized she was shouting only one: his name. Hot blood galloped through his head, making him flush. What had he done now? His dad screamed at him more often than his mom, which always sent him into panic. Except Dad was dead now. Sometimes, possibly even last night, Tab thought he could still hear him screaming.

He scooted to the foot of the bed, intent on grabbing his sketchbook off the desk before heading downstairs. He'd sit with it in his lap, rocking and tracing the edges of the letters in the Strathmore logo until the tempest passed. It was the only way he'd learned to cope with screaming. Only once had they deprived him of that. It was the time they'd caught him posing for a self-portrait while standing in his underwear in the bathroom mirror. Some of his mom's makeup was spread on the vanity before him: a L'Oréal Paris Colour Riche lipstick named Prosperous Red, some Covergirl rouge, a Maybelline smokey eye shadow palette, and a black liner pencil on which the brand name had worn away. She didn't use these much, so Tab didn't think she'd mind him experimenting a bit.

Mom and Dad had caught him attempting to apply the eyeliner after he'd already smeared the lipstick in a ragged clown-like fashion around his lips. Dad, his eyes aflame and his nostrils flared, had swept the makeup off the vanity with his forearm. After it clattered to the floor around Tab's feet, he'd snatched the boy's wrist and squeezed, forcing him to drop the eyeliner pencil. Then he'd led him away from the bathroom and screamed at him for what felt like hours about the differences between boys and girls, that boys weren't meant to use things like makeup. Dad wrapped his rant by threatening to send him to boarding school "for his own good" and to "make sure he turns into a man."

Tab had meant no harm, thinking only that modeling for a self-portrait as a clown in his underwear would be funny. He also didn't understand why his dad had freaked out so hard about the makeup in particular. Lots of clowns were boys. Most, probably. Heck, lots of his dad's favorite bands wore makeup. Tab had seen the proof in his old rock T-shirts featuring bands like Kiss, Poison, and Twisted Sister. His mom had one from The Cure with "Kiss Me Kiss Me Kiss Me" printed on it. The man behind the type obviously wore lipstick and eyeliner.

On some level, Tab felt anger at himself for not having foreseen this outcome. Both his dad and his brother criticized him on the regular for not being "manly" enough. His classmates, too, for that matter. Ashley Reardon most recently. But if being manly meant not having fun or not looking the way he wanted to look, then Tab would've been happy to have been born a girl. *Or maybe neither*, his mind amended, because his dad also sometimes commented on women no longer being "womanly." He seemed to rein that in whenever Tab's mother was around, though.

What kind of stupid world was it that limited what you could do or enjoy just because you were born one way or another? All Tab knew was that he liked what he liked and didn't like what he didn't like. If girls liked the same things he did, what was so wrong about that? The last thing his dad had screamed that night as he stormed away was: "Kid thinks he's Buffalo Bill or something."

Tab had heard of Buffalo Bill, the Western showman, but didn't know much about him. He'd asked Jeremy to look him up online, wanting to know if Buffalo Bill's Wild West show had involved boys wearing makeup. Jeremy had instead laughed and called him "sheltered" for not knowing about the Buffalo Bill character in some movie called *The Silence of the Lambs* and therefore being unable to make the connection between that and his father's rant.

He shuddered and locked away the memory. Whatever his mom was mad at him about now couldn't involve underwear, makeup, or any alleged differences between boys and girls. That had happened forever ago. It felt like forever, anyway.

His desktop was bare of everything except his jar of pencils. Where was his sketchbook? "TAB! YOU WAKE UP AND COME HERE RIGHT NOW!" His heart leaped into his throat, thudding there as if he'd just tried to swallow a live frog whole.

"I have to pee!"

An exasperated sigh echoed from elsewhere in the house. "Fine! Pee and then come here. We need to talk."

By the time he tiptoed into the kitchen, where his mother and Jeremy were seated, the former glowering and the latter hiding a malicious grin behind his fist, he'd already resigned himself to punishment for whatever crime he'd committed. That soothed his heart a bit. He no longer felt hot, yet he dreaded the reaming to come.

He'd barely had time to pull his chair back from the kitchen table when his mother dropped his Strathmore before him. It was folded open on its spiral to a single page on which had been drawn a cut-up, battered hand in a claw pose. Said hand sported ragged nails and a ring on one finger. It emerged—with force, based on what Tab could see—from a clump of solid grass and dirt.

"Explain this," she said. Her voice was flat but in a practiced way, as if she was aware of Tab's nerves and was trying to dial back her anger so as to keep him honest.

"Is that *my* sketchbook?"

Jeremy scoffed and rolled his eyes. His mother shot him a warning glare.

"Yes, it's your sketchbook," she said to Tab. "No one else here has one. What's the meaning of this?" She pointed to the drawing of the hand with her index finger but did not touch it.

"Someone drew a hand in my sketchbook," he said. "Did you get this out of my room?"

Sandra slapped her hands against her hips and barked a sardonic laugh. "It came out of your room, but it's none of your business where I got it."

Jeremy, he thought.

"You answer to me. I don't answer to you. Now explain this drawing."

"I've never seen it before," he said, although he was already aware his protests would fall on deaf ears. "Whoever took this from my room must have drawn it."

"You know what this looks like?"

"It—" Tab stammered. "It looks like Dad's hand coming out of the ground. Those look like his fingers after he's been working in the field. And that's his ring. But Dad never wore his ring while he was working in the field. Not ever. You were afraid he'd lose it."

A tear crept unbidden from his mother's right eye. She slapped at it as if it was a fly on a picnic day in the park. "That's right. It *does* look like your dad's hand. Now tell me why you would draw something like this, Tab."

"But I didn't," he said again. "Whoever took my sketchbook must have."

Jeremy pounded the fist that had been covering his mouth on the table. "I can't draw!"

"Jeremy, go to your room," Sandra said, not looking at him.

"But—"

"Now. You can come out after we leave." To Tab, "Dr. Clifford had a cancellation today and I was able to make an appointment with him. You can't be drawing stuff like this, Tab. It's scary and it makes me worry about you."

"I didn't!" he said, his eyes welling up. "I didn't draw this!"

Sandra snatched up the sketchbook, holding it by its spiral in one hand as though it was a diaper full of foul-smelling, watery baby dook. She fanned the pages at him, revealing brief flashes of all the black-and-white tragedies and crimes and disasters that had filled it since the end of school. "I suppose you didn't draw the rest of this stuff, either."

"Well, yes I did, but—"

"Go clean yourself up and get ready to go. Our appointment's in two hours."

"But—"

"GO!"

"Can I have my sketchbook back?"

Sandra's nostrils flared. Her eyes narrowed, resembling his dad's when he was about to explode. "TIMOTHY AARON BEARD," she shouted. "Get your butt in gear right now. I'm out of goddamn patience. You'll get your sketchbook back when I say you can have it back and not before. Don't ask again."

More hurt. Not only because his mom refused to return his beloved Strathmore, but also because she'd used a bad word while scolding him. Not that she never used bad words. She did. His dad claimed to have the sailor mouth, though, which he insisted was a sign of higher intellect. Mom was more careful but slipped on occasion. Most of the time, Tab wasn't fazed by them. But when they directed the bad words at him or Jeremy, they stung.

She might as well have punched him in the face.

CHAPTER EIGHTEEN

Both Sandra and Tab cried in whispers, at separate times, on the drive to Dr. Clifford's. There, Tab began to wonder why she'd even brought him along. He passed forty-five minutes in the waiting room beanbag chair without his sketchbook, uninterested in any of the titles on the children's bookshelf. There was much adventure in those volumes, but also a lot of reminders of fear and death. His mother had darted through the door to the treatment rooms with his sketchbook dangling from one hand and her bag clasped in the other.

He considered trying to summon Roy. The ghost apparently made for a terrific spy. He wanted to know what they were saying about him when he was not in the room. More, he wanted to know what they might be *doing* back there. Yet he remained frightened of Roy because there was an undercurrent of conniving and malice slashing at the ghost's truths. Ashley Reardon, the man at the zoo, Tab's dad, all three were events Roy had been truthful about and which he might have caused. Or maybe Tab had caused them. Whether Roy was lying about the nature of what Tab had come to alternately think of as a power and a disability was difficult to pinpoint.

There were also the times that were obviously without malice, though. His cat, Alfie. Roy had been protective of Alfie during the storm. He suspected Alfie, too, could sense Roy's presence. But he had never so much as hissed at or gotten his back up at the ghost. At least, not that Tab ever saw.

He closed his eyes and sank into the beanbag chair. His third eye cracked open as he began to drift, finally enabling him to see inside Dr. Clifford's office. Therein, he lowered his gaze to his feet, orienting himself. What he saw on the floor were a giant's work boots. They connected to thick tree trunk legs hidden by beige coveralls. Above his knees dangled boiling red, cracked hands. Tab wasn't just seeing through Roy. He *was* Roy. The Tab who was not Roy grimaced. His body was too big, his shirt too tight against his belly. Friend or foe, he would never be *comfortable* with Roy.

On the other side of his office, Dr. Clifford held Tab's sketchbook in his lap. The depiction of his late father's hand clawing out of the grave seemed less menacing in the presence of these clinical fluorescent lights. His mother sobbed in heaving gasps, inconsolable. She sat on the couch across from Dr. Clifford, her elbows on her knees and her face in her hands.

"Is there no possible way you could have seen this drawing before?" the doctor asked.

Tab's mom shook her head. "No."

"Tell me about the dream again."

Sandra shivered. "I'm standing in the graveyard," she started. Her voice cracked on the last word. She cleared her throat and continued, "I'm standing in the graveyard, looking at Tim's headstone. I'm wondering if I'll ever see him again, thinking about how much I'd love to feel him wrap his arms around me. I mean, we weren't getting along very well. We'd grown apart, I guess. And his temper got so much worse as he got older. But I remember the days when we couldn't stand to be away from each other. That's the part of me that wants him back. That wants to tell him I love him one more time. I will always love him."

"Mmm-hmm. So what happens next?"

Her eyes widened, images from the dream apparently flooding her head. "All of a sudden, this hand—Tim's left hand—bursts out of the ground at my feet. As I start to back away, his right hand bursts through, too. They claw at the dirt, which in my dream is a lot looser than it was when I was standing on it." Her voice rose, tremulous. "The hands push at the dirt, moving it out of the way. All of a sudden, I catch sight of his face. His eyes are open. They're sad, haunted. He's looking at me, and I think he wants me to help him. But I can't. I can't bring myself to reach out to him because he can't still be alive. I'm afraid he'll be cold. And slimy. I'm afraid if I tried to pull him up that the gray, dead skin would slide off his hands in my grip. I mean, it's been weeks since we buried him."

She sniffled and swallowed. Dr. Clifford wordlessly gifted her the box of Kleenex from the end table beside him. Sandra plucked a tissue from it, dabbing at her eyes and nostrils before continuing.

"I'm trying to decide what to do when he speaks to me. He says Tab's in danger. A man is after him; a man I can't see. All I can think about when I wake up is that ghost Tab thought he saw in his closet before Tim died. All I can think about is what if it's real? What if something is trying to take my baby boy away from me the way it took my husband? How can I protect my kids from something I can't even see?"

That last ended in a sob, which next collapsed into an uncontrolled series of them. She blew her nose into the tissue, trying to recover herself. Dr. Clifford waited, but Sandra had nothing left.

"Okay," he said. His voice was soft, reassuring in an unexpectedly maternal way coming from someone with such an overtly masculine appearance. *Unmanly*, Tab's dad and brother would say. And probably Ashley Reardon, too. "I think I understand. It's not uncommon for anxiety to spread its fingers throughout a household during a time of grief like this. I see why you say your nightmare last night was almost this same scene." He tapped the drawing with the trigger end of his pen. Sandra maintained her gaze on her hands wringing her tissue, not wanting to look at the abomination again. "Indulge me for a minute. Let me give you a different idea of how all of this could have happened in a rational way.

"It's easy to fall into magical thinking when life throws coincidences at you." He closed the sketchbook and set it aside. Sandra's hands fell into her lap. She opened her mouth to protest, but the doctor stopped her with a raised finger. "Listen to me for a moment. Your entire family is grieving an enormous loss right now. Grief within the family unit is one of those rare times when everyone under the same roof is mostly on the same page. You're all noticing the same things, finding reminders of Tim and what happened to him everywhere."

"Oh, you're right about that! I found a wrinkled and water-stained old Marilyn Monroe calendar from 1955 tucked in his sock drawer the other day. I remember it. He found it on the floor of his Aunt Kathy's old store after he'd inherited the land. I wonder if it's worth anything."

Dr. Clifford smiled but transitioned the conversation back to his point. "It's not impossible that you and Tab watched the same TV show or saw the same magazine or book cover somewhere, which triggered this image in both of you."

Sandra chuckled, her eyes wet and sad. "Well, Tim did have a big collection of horror books and movies with some bizarre covers on them. All three of us have been kind of revisiting his things in the house lately, I think. Just remembering who he was." She pointed a finger toward the sketchbook in epiphany. "That drawing is the same as the DVD cover for *Mortuary*! One of Tim's favorite horror movies!"

Dr. Clifford's eyes brightened. "Tab is an artist. A damned superior one, if you don't mind my saying so. It's natural he'd use his sketchbook to process something like this if he's been exposed to a similar image from something that belonged to his father. You've tried to bury your hurt deep down inside because you have to press forward. You're the sole breadwinner now and you have a household and a farm to run. Mostly on your own because of how young your boys are. Because you can't allow yourself to process it consciously, your subconscious—your dream world—is doing it for you."

"But why is Tab saying he didn't draw it?"

"That is a question I'll need to address with Tab," Dr. Clifford said. "Shall we call him in?"

Sandra glanced at the clock. "Oh! I've already used up our whole hour. I wanted you to talk to Tab, too."

"Yes, but I have another one available right now. I think it's important we keep working through this while it's fresh. In fact, I'll give you this next hour for free. That's how important I think it is."

Tab's vision cleared as Dr. Clifford poked his head out from behind the door to the offices and motioned for him to follow. The boy's eyes felt heavy, as if he'd just awakened from a deep sleep. It must have been evident on his face because Dr. Clifford asked him about it.

"Did you fall asleep out there?" the doctor asked, paternal joviality in his voice. It was different from the tone he'd taken with Sandra a few minutes before. Brotherly and mannish. Tab shrugged and seated himself on the couch.

He was careful to leave the middle space open, separating himself from Sandra.

His sketchbook lay closed on the end table by Dr. Clifford's chair. A hot pang of embarrassment, betrayal, and rage stabbed at his chest. Her violation of his privacy infuriated him. Work he took pride in, work he wanted to become his life, had gotten him into trouble with not one, but three people in the space of a day. He retrieved the sketchbook without asking, sat with it, and finger-traced the Strathmore logo on the cover, acknowledging neither of the adults in the room.

"So, what's going on?" Dr. Clifford asked. "Can we talk a little about what happened this morning?"

"My brother stole my sketchbook and showed it to my mom," Tab intoned, his voice flat. He did not look up from the sketchbook cover. "Then Sandra freaked out about a drawing in it I didn't do. That's all."

Sandra looked hurt. "It's *Mom*, Tab," she said. "You always call me *Mom*."

He paid her no mind. "I don't know why she's so freaked out about it. It's just a drawing of a hand."

"It's your *dad's* hand coming out of the *grave*."

"I didn't draw it," he said again. Then, with a hint of mockery, "Sandra."

Dr. Clifford shot Tab's mother a warning glance, stopping her before she could retort. "Let's save this for a bit," he said. "For now, why don't you tell Tab why you were so upset by it?"

"Because of your nightmares," Tab said before she could answer.

Sandra's mouth dropped open. "My—"

"She's told you about her nightmares?" Dr. Clifford asked. "No."

"Then how do you know what Dr. Clifford and I have been talking about in here?" Sandra asked. She transitioned from shock to anger mid-sentence. Her narrowed eyes pierced him. He only shrugged in reply.

"Were you listening at the door, Tab?" the doctor asked.

"No."

"So how do you know?"

"Roy," Tab said, tapping his bump with the end of his pencil. He began to rock, bending forward at the waist and backward into the couch, not looking at anyone. "When we're connected, he can see even though he doesn't have eyes. And he can go places I can't go. Roy was in here with you. He heard you, so I heard you."

"This again," Sandra spat. She folded her arms and turned her back on the boy, glaring out the window at the gleaming tops of cars sitting in the direct sun of the parking lot.

"So through Roy you could hear what your mom and I discussed?"

Tab nodded.

Dr. Clifford leaned back in his chair. "Okay, do you understand that in using Roy to overhear us, you've done the same thing you accuse your brother and your mother of doing? I'm not saying your brother had a right to take your sketchbook. Not at all. I just wonder if you feel any different about listening in on our conversation than you do about your sketchbook."

Hot pins and needles pricked at Tab's cheeks. "Oh," he said.

"Yes," Dr. Clifford said, smiling. "So, do you think both of you can acknowledge the violations of privacy?" He glanced from son to mother and back. "If you can, maybe we can move forward a little and drill to the core of what's going on here."

Sandra and Tab locked eyes. "I'm sorry, Mom," he said.

"I'm sorry, too, hon. Your brother has no business going through your stuff. If you know about my dream now, you know why the drawing scared me so much.

Are you having the same nightmares about your dad I'm having?"

"I didn't draw it," he said again.

Sandra threw up her hands. "Oh, come on, Tab! We were starting to make some progress!"

"Now, now," Dr. Clifford said. "Let's talk about this." He turned his gaze to Tab. "If you didn't draw it, who did?"

"I thought Jeremy did. Maybe Roy did it."

Sandra grunted. "I'm done with Roy. I don't want to hear any more about him."

"But you do," Dr. Clifford said. "I'll get to why. But first, I want to ask Tab a few more questions about Roy. So bear with me for a minute. Tell me something, Tab. When you're in school, do the other kids seem to appreciate your drawings? Do they like them?"

Tab shrugged. "I guess."

"Do any of them ever make fun of you for them?"

"Mom and Dad always said they're jealous."

"Do you show your drawings to other people much?"

He shook his head.

"No? Have any teachers ever made comments to you about your art?"

"They say I have a vivid imagination. But sometimes they yell at me about it, too. They think I'm not paying attention."

Sandra nodded. "We've had a couple of parent-teacher conferences about it," she said. "Ms. Bowman got so frustrated with him for not listening in class."

"What happens then?"

"Well, we talked about taking the sketchbook away, but we were afraid he'd draw on his homework and test papers instead. So we took away television and computer privileges for a couple of days."

Dr. Clifford steepled his fingers, his gaze above their heads. "Have Tab's grades suffered because of his drawing?"

Sandra thought for a moment. "No. As far as I've seen his grades stayed much the same." She smiled, prideful. "Tab's always made excellent grades. He's a sharp kid."

"Uh-huh. And have you considered talking to the teacher about just allowing Tab to draw when he needs to draw if it's not interfering with his schoolwork?"

"But—"

"What I'm hearing is Tab's art is impressive and that he has a vivid imagination," Dr. Clifford said. "What I'm hearing is his drawing during school hours does not interfere with his grades or schoolwork or behavior. Is that right?"

"Yes, but—"

"What I *know*, and this comes from years of experience as well as study, is punishing a child who is exploring a talent can cause the child guilt or shame about indulging in that talent. By choosing to punish Tab, you and his teachers are telling him his creativity is a problem. This is even though you admitted it isn't hurting his school performance.

"When a child does something wrong or inappropriate, it's natural to feel mild shame when corrected. It's even natural for the child to want to deflect blame for it—say, to an imaginary friend named Roy—in order to escape the shame. It only becomes a problem when parents or teachers use punishment instead of reassurance to correct the child."

"But if he's not paying attention?"

Dr. Clifford grinned knowingly. "*Is* he not paying attention? Growing up, you and I learned we had to sit still and sit straight in our chairs, eyes on the teacher. Pay attention or get in trouble. But not everyone is wired the same way. For some kids, forcing them into traditional learning *poses*, for lack of a better term, actually inhibits their learning. I got bored and tuned out as a kid in classrooms like that. I went day-tripping in my own head if I couldn't busy my hands with something while the lectures were going on.

"Tab is an incredibly creative and talented young man. He needs to know it's not something to be ashamed of. Instead of punishing him, try reassuring him. Remind him he's not doing anything wrong. Remind him grownups are nervous people who think he isn't paying attention in class if his eyes are not where they expect them to be. Next, have another chat with his teachers. Tab might need some accommodations from them, for them to understand he *needs* to be able to draw while he's learning. I think if you're able to come to an understanding with the school, you'll find Tab will start to separate criticism and correction from attacks on his character. You might even find he starts to take more responsibility when he *does* make mistakes."

Dr. Clifford returned his attention to Tab. "We all make mistakes. Never believe you should be defined by them. You are not the mistakes you've made. Nor are you the bad thoughts you've had. You're a good person. You're a smart person. You're a talented artist. *That's* who you are."

Sandra sat stone-faced for a moment, pondering the doctor's words. Then it was as if someone flipped a switch behind her eyes. "That makes so much sense."

"Of course it does. Sometimes we have to take a step back from what we—you and I—learned from our parents when we were growing up. My mom and dad thought a slap to the back of the head or a switch on the rear-end was the solution for everything."

Sandra chuckled. "I was so straitlaced. I don't remember ever getting in much trouble. My *brother*, though. Wow. I guess that's why I watched my Ps and Qs so much. It took four years of college before I said my first swear."

Dr. Clifford's face lit. "And what was that swear?"

Sandra cut her eyes at Tab and back to Dr. Clifford, nervous. "Ass," she said.

Dr. Clifford burst into laughter. Sandra followed. And Tab, although he didn't understand what was so funny about "ass," even after he'd laughed with Jeremy and his mom about it in the car. It was another name for donkey. He knew it could also mean butt, and butts were always funny. He couldn't remember having used the term either way. His memory gears ratcheted up anyway, scanning for times he might've embarrassed himself by using "ass" in an incorrect way. Saying swears was one of those things that felt forbidden to him, but also enticing. His brother said them sometimes without consequences. Well, other than his mom shouting his name, which most of the time for Tab felt shaming enough.

Dr. Clifford met Tab's eyes. "Now, let's talk a little about Roy if you're comfortable. Do you remember I suggested you talk back to Roy when he gets in your head? Have you been able to do it?"

Tab squirmed. "A little," he said. It was more lie than truth. He hoped it was not written on his face. Neither Dr. Clifford nor his mother believed Roy was an actual entity. They'd almost had Tab himself not believing it. There had been too many coincidences since then, though. Dr. Clifford eyed him with a puzzled, bemused expression.

He probably knows I'm lying, Tab thought. *I'm going for it.*

"Too many things I've drawn or that Roy has shown me have come true," he said. "He's not my anxiety. He's not OCD. He's real. Sometimes he's in the room with me. Sometimes he's using my eyes to show me things." He turned to his mother. "That's how I knew about your dream. I wasn't listening at the door or anything. I was in the bean bag chair outside, but Roy was in here with you and Dr. Clifford. So I heard a lot. I didn't mean to. I mean, I thought about asking Roy to help and decided not to. Then it kind of happened anyway."

"Really, Tab?" Sandra asked. Her nose was scrunched and her lips puckered as if she smelled something rotten. She leaned back on the couch and folded her arms across her abdomen. "We're going in circles now."

"No, this is good," Dr. Clifford said. He tapped the end of his pen against his lower lip. "Are either of you acquainted with synchronicity?"

"The Police album? Sure. I had a copy of it as a kid."

"No, I mean the idea of synchronicity proposed by Carl Jung and Wolfgang Pauli. It's dismissed by much of the scientific community these days, and with good reason. Unless you're into quantum physics or something. But at its simplest, it's the possibility of meaning or interconnectedness between strings of coincidences. Like after 9/11, when a lot of people were saying they'd seen the numbers nine and eleven everywhere before the attacks. Some people think it's God or the universe or whatever trying to send them messages. Most of us in the sciences tend to agree it's confirmation bias, coincidence combined with some hindsight that fits a few puzzle pieces into place."

"What's confirmation bias?" A kindling of hope sparked in Tab's chest, and he wanted to nurture it. It was hope he might be wrong about Roy, that the doctor might banish all this worry the eyeless phantasm had caused him with a single rational explanation. That Roy might not be real after all.

Dr. Clifford pressed his tongue into his lower lip and glanced toward the ceiling before he answered. "Confirmation bias is when we take something that happens as evidence we're right about a specific idea we have, even if the two things are not related. For example, you thinking the drawing of your friend Ashley getting hurt caused her to get hurt."

"She's not my friend."

"You're right. I'm sorry. Your classmate?"

Tab shrugged.

"I remember the news stories on Channel 6 about your neck of the woods. Parents had been complaining about how heavy those school doors were for years. Some had even predicted a child would be hurt by them one day. It was only a matter of time until one did. It just happened to be on the same day you drew it, a day she picked to harass you in the hallway. Right?"

"Yeah."

"Yeah. It wasn't the first time she picked on you, either. I remember when you were here before, what she said about you in the waiting room. Someone else in your shoes who hadn't drawn the picture you drew would've thought it was karma. She got hurt because she hurt you and the universe answered for you. But because you drew the picture, you think you caused it. It could just be you already knew about the heavy door controversy and drew your picture based on it. By coincidence and no fault of yours, Ashley got stuck in the door. Make sense?"

"I guess. But I don't remember any news about the doors being heavy."

"Well, it *was* brought up in PTO meetings," Sandra said. "We always took you with us to those."

Dr. Clifford nodded, emphatic. "I've said this today already. I don't mean to sound repetitive. But you are an *artist*, Tab. Most artists are astute observers, I'd guess. You're aware of things around you even if you're not *aware* you're aware. So, synchronicity—your sense that your drawings and thoughts are connected to external events beyond your control—isn't anything but your smarts combined with a little bit of our pure human penchant for confirmation bias."

"But *everything* Roy tells me about comes true!"

Dr. Clifford leaned forward, his elbows on his knees. "Does it?"

"Yeah! There was Alfie, the guy at the zoo, Ashley, my dad's accident, you and my mom uh—" He'd almost said *going together*, as in *affair*. He hadn't told either his mother or the doctor about his first bean bag chair vision. They might be angry if they knew he knew. Plus, giving voice to it might make it true.

"Your mom's conversation with me earlier?" Dr. Clifford asked. Tab wanted to affirm but found himself shaking his head instead. "Your, uh, *friendship* with my mother?"

Bewilderment crossed Dr. Clifford's face. His lips parted but issuing no words. Tab examined his mother's expression and found it much the same. He immediately regretted bringing it up.

"What do you mean by *friendship*, Tab?" Sandra asked.

He grimaced. He couldn't talk about the L-word or the S-word with his mother. Instead, he studied Dr. Clifford. "Roy showed me you and my mom doing...stuff people who like each other do. People who *like*-like each other. Grownup stuff. Here. In your office."

"Uh-huh," Dr. Clifford said, cautiously. He thought for a moment. "I think I understand. Look at my eyes, Tab. I can one-hundred percent assure you your mother and I have never been together in that way. Not here or anywhere else. It would be a serious ethical violation on my part, to start. At best, it could damage my work with both of you. At worst, I could lose my license to practice."

"Oh." He screwed up his face. "But you had my mom's makeup on your neck that day."

Dr. Clifford looked surprised, his hand stroking his neck automatically. "I did? Well, I might have had makeup there." He glanced at Sandra. "I imagine your mother and my wife might wear similar shades of stuff like that. And I do make sure I hug my wife before we both leave for work every morning. It wouldn't be the first time we'd accidentally smeared me with her makeup."

"And I'm not that kind of person!" Sandra snapped. Tab winced at the offense in her voice. Or it might have been *defense*. "Your father is just in his grave. What do you take me for?"

Dr. Clifford shot her the warning look again. Tab didn't know what it meant, but it caused his mother to sit back and place her hands in her lap, her eyes wandering the patterns on the gray industrial carpet.

"I'm sorry, Mom," Tab said, a cry creeping into his voice.

Sandra sighed, not looking up. "It's okay. It's okay."

"Here's the thing about anxiety disorders like OCD," Dr. Clifford said. "They trick you into thinking they can predict things, that they *know* things because they seemed to predict things in the past. They also trick you into thinking you can do something to control the outcomes you fear.

"One classic example is repetitive handwashing. People who have OCD and who are afraid of germs are compelled to repeatedly wash their hands in order to prevent themselves from becoming sick. It's called The Doubting Disorder because it tends to make you doubt your own memory and reason. You wash your hands repeatedly even though you think you remember washing them. You become doubtful you remembered to use soap. Or you fear you touched something germ-infested in the bathroom after you finished washing, so you have to go do it again."

"I don't wash my hands that much."

"Well, as I said, that's an example. In your case, your OCD is this eyeless phantom named Roy who has convinced you he can show you things that are happening or will happen. Or make you think you're the cause of them or that you want to cause them. It's called *intrusive thoughts*, and it's a common companion of OCD. The thing is, Roy is playing on doubts and fears already in your head. He's not telling you anything you don't already know or couldn't guess. But he is *lying* to you about the danger those things present and the danger you and your drawings pose to others.

"We've talked about how you might've predicted your classmate's trouble with the school door. Have you considered you could have guessed the fellow at the zoo was going to get hurt? If I remember, you told me he looked unstable."

"I think he was drunk."

"Right. So, isn't it possible you guessed he was going to be hurt and were right? Drunk people get hurt in traffic all the time. OCD—*Roy*, I mean. Let's go ahead and name it. Roy is your OCD and Roy lies to you, too. Tell me. This is sensitive, I know. With your father gone, have you been afraid you will somehow lose your mother, too?"

Tab sat silent for a moment. He glanced at his mother, who took his hand in hers. "It's okay," she said.

"Yeah. I guess I have worried about it."

"Mm-hmm. OCD latches onto our fears. So because Roy could predict what happened to the man at the zoo and the thing with the school doors, he's convinced you he's right about me and your mother as well. He'll probably continue trying to convince you he's right about it. That's another thing OCD and other types of anxiety do. They cause you to constantly seek reassurance. You believe us now, but you might not on the car ride home if Roy decides he's found some other form of 'evidence'." He enclosed the last word in air quotes.

"He'll always be checking for you, searching for hints and pieces to make the puzzle picture into whatever he wants it to be, which is whatever will most likely make you anxious. It might be something you think you saw between your mother and me. It might only be the way we're positioned across from each other. He'll try to latch onto *something* to prove to you he's right."

"The Doubting Disorder," Tab said.

"Exactly. The Doubting Disorder."

"So what can we do to help him?" Sandra asked.

Dr. Clifford removed his glasses and rubbed at the corners of his eyes. "Well, you said talking back to Roy worked a little in the beginning, right? You thought he'd gone away for a while?"

"After Dad's funeral. Yes."

"Okay, I want you to start talking back to him again. Don't only talk back, *fight* back. If he shouts at you, shout back at him. One of the hardest things you have to learn when you have OCD is how to sit with the anxiety and fight the need for reassurance. And by *sit*, I don't mean sit in a chair and try to pretend nothing is happening. I mean allow yourself to feel how you're feeling and what you're worrying about but talk back to it. Remind yourself that you are safe and you are not the cause of the world's problems.

"Tell Roy he's a liar and a trickster. Tell him you're not going to fall for his tricks anymore. I think if you do those things, you're going to see him diminish again."

Tab made eye contact, hopeful. "I'll be cured?"

Dr. Clifford's benevolence shone behind his glasses as he replaced them on the bridge of his nose. "There isn't a cure for something like OCD, I'm afraid. Maybe someday there will be. But if you keep practicing talking back to it, you'll find you can live with it. You'll have some good days and some bad days, but you'll survive.

"Personally, I think you'll thrive. At this point in your life, you can choose any path you want. The trick is to not allow Roy to choose it for you."

CHAPTER NINETEEN

"Well, wasn't that a kick in the butt?" Roy mused after Tab flopped into the back seat of his mom's car and buckled his seatbelt. The boy glared at him, nostrils flaring.

"You're not real," he said. "You're just my anxious thoughts trying to make me afraid. Go away."

He caught his mother watching him in the rearview mirror. When their eyes met, she whispered, "Good job."

Roy bellowed laughter. "I'm as real as you are, buddy. Ask your cat. Better yet, ask your *mom*."

"You're lying."

"No, I'm not. Okay, I fibbed a little when I showed you your mom and the stupid old doctor getting it on. Your mom didn't have an affair with him. She had an affair with me. And *you* are the result."

Tab's mouth fell open. "LIAR!"

In the driver seat, Sandra twitched, startled by the outburst. "Okay, son, talking back to Roy doesn't mean you need to shout out loud. I almost ran off the road!"

"Sorry, Mom, but he's telling me bad things."

"Oh, your mom wasn't *bad*," Roy said, smiling. "She was damned good, in fact. We had a great time together. Made you, didn't we? Your so-called dad? He was a real piece of shit. Murdered me when he found out about us. Gored out my eyes and everything."

Tab scoffed. "Now I *know* you're lying. Dad would *never* do something like that. He just yells sometimes. He couldn't hurt another person even if he wanted to. I can't believe anything you tell me." He eyed his mother's reflection, seeking more approval of how capable he was at talking back to Roy. What he saw wasn't helpful. A vertical line had formed in the middle of her forehead. She stared straight ahead, not acknowledging him or what he'd said.

"Y'see, boy? Your mom knows it's true. You don't believe I'm really real? Watch this."

He passed a hand through the driver's seat headrest and pressed his enormous palm against the back of Sandra's crown. Although the headrest obscured it somewhat, Tab could see Roy's fingers laying against his mother's head. The ghost turned his hand so that the backs of his index and middle fingers pressed there, in a spot where Tab could see. After dipping his middle finger into her hair, he stroked downward, lightly tugging on the long strand. Tab's mother took one hand away from the wheel, reached behind, and swatted and scratched at her scalp as if she had detected a bit of dryness or the nip of an insect there.

Tab glared at Roy, unsure of what to say. His mom's reaction didn't prove anything. If Dr. Clifford was here, he might say that Tab had subconsciously noticed a housefly or a breeze from the Accord's A/C that tickled her scalp and then attributed it to Roy in his imagination. It was as good an explanation as any, he supposed, although something about it didn't feel realistic. Dr. Clifford had a way of explaining how things could happen that felt more *real*. Tab's rational explanation felt less rational and more like rationalization. Although he did not yet know that word, he would have understood the context. He felt like he was lying to himself.

"Still don't believe me, huh?" Roy said. "Get a load of this then." Roy grimaced, straining like he was constipated and trying to force a shit. With the palm of the same hand that had stroked the back of Sandra's head, he shoved her. Tab saw her head snap forward, nearly causing her to strike her forehead against the top of the steering wheel. Sandra gasped and yelped in surprise. She threw her head back against the headrest. Her arms locked straight against the wheel, veins standing out along her forearms and in the crook of her elbows. Tab felt his legs lock against the rear floorboard. The Accord veered over the center line briefly as Sandra tried to regain control. Within one second, she had returned to the car to her lane and straightened it. She'd broken out in a sweat, and her breaths came in heaving gasps.

"Sorry!" she heaved. "Sorry, sorry! I must have nodded off for a second! I'm awake now. We're fine. We're fine." Something in her voice indicated that she didn't quite believe her own story.

Tab snarled at Roy. "Go away!" he said, careful this time to ramp up his volume instead of distracting his mother again with a full-throated outburst. He closed his eyes and cupped a hand over each ear. "I'm not listening to you anymore. You have no place in my head. You have no place in my life. Go away!"

A few seconds passed before Tab realized Roy had not responded. He uncapped his ears and examined the seat beside him. Nothing there. He sighed. A wave of exhaustion overcame him, provoking a jaw-straining yawn.

"He's gone, Mom," Tab said. He closed his eyes and rested his head against the door panel. "I think he's gone now." His mother, eyes wide and knuckles white where she clutched the wheel, did not reply at first. "Did you hear me?"

"I heard you, Tab," she said. There was some amount of ice in her voice. "Listen, we have a long drive home. I want you to do something for me in the meantime. I want you to open your sketchbook and draw a portrait of Roy for me. Can you do that?"

"I already drew him once for Dad when he was watching my closet."

"I know. But I'd like more details about him. Do you know what a portrait is?"

Tab laughed. "Of course I do! It's a close-up of someone's head down to the shoulders."

"Right," Sandra said. "That's what I want you to draw for me. Try to remember as much detail as you can about what Roy looks like and draw him. I think it'll help me figure out exactly what kind of OCD we're dealing with here."

"But what if it brings him back?" Tab asked.

His mother's response was quick and short. "If he comes back we'll figure it out. Right now, I need to see what you see."

Tab took the hint. "Don't expect it to be museum quality," he said. The road home was sometimes a little bumpy, especially after a hard rain. His mother wanted his silence for the rest of the trip. He was able to glean that much from her tone. He opened the sketchbook to a blank page, carefully avoiding the mysterious drawing of his father's hand emerging from the grave.

With a snowy fresh page in his lap, he tapped his pencil eraser three times against his bump before he set the point. Then he was in the zone, although without eye rolling and unconsciousness. It was nice to be aware of what he was creating for once. He neither stopped drawing nor glanced up from the page until his mother announced their arrival home. She did not ask about the drawing's status.

"I have to make dinner. It's getting late. You need any help getting out of the car?"

He shook his head. "No. I've got everything." He piled out with her and vanished to his room. He would not come out until his mother called him for the meal. His sketchbook he left on his desk. The empty eye sockets of the emerging face of Stinkeye Roy stared at the ceiling, unmoved and unblinking.

CHAPTER TWENTY

When the drawing was done, Tab knocked on the door of the family study. Well, what they *called* a study. It was little more than a narrow walk-in pantry in which a desk, chair, landline phone, and power strip had been added to the back wall. The shelves had been removed except for a head-height row containing some volumes of books on machine maintenance, agribusiness, and accounting. His mom's psychology books from Dr. Clifford also occupied the space, their spines crinkled from repeated reads. These days, his mom was in the study more than anywhere.

"Mom? I finished the drawing!"

Behind the door, papers rustled. A drawer opened and closed again. "Bring it in, hon."

He handed the new portrait to her with some trepidation. There had been neither hide nor hair of Roy since he'd appeared on the car ride home. Tab feared drawing him from memory might summon him. Despite what Dr. Clifford had explained, the idea he was causing what he drew remained unshakable. If not the act of drawing him, the act of showing the drawing might prompt a new appearance.

Up to now, neither Tab's mom nor his dead dad believed Roy was real. But seeing is believing. Tab found it puzzling that anyone who saw this new drawing could go on believing Roy was a figment of his imagination. His imagination was powerful. Everyone told him so. But it was not *that* powerful. He hoped.

Sandra scrutinized the page for an excruciating span of time as Tab looked on. Light shining from behind revealed what he'd drawn in reverse. A thick-necked man in a collared work shirt stared at them from scooped eye sockets. His brow was smooth, although thick eyebrows added a sinister element. A round nose flared over smirking thin lips. The red cap sat atop his head, shaded gray, nothing printed on it. From beneath, strands of light-colored hair curled every which way.

Regardless of its subject, Tab basked in the drawing. It was the best picture of a person he'd ever created. But he couldn't stare at it for long without feeling like he'd been punched in the stomach. He allowed his eyes to drift elsewhere. Soon, his mother placed the drawing on the desk and out of his sight.

She sniffled, about to cry, inhaling a ragged breath and letting it out in a long, exasperated sigh. "Tab, I'm going to show you a picture now. It's an *Echo* clipping from a long time ago. Before you were born. I want you to tell me if you recognize the man in the picture. Can you do that?"

Tab's stomach tightened. He needed to go to the bathroom. But he nodded, terrified and curious.

Sandra pulled open the top right drawer of her desk. From it, she produced a thin piece of newsprint about the length and width of a grocery store receipt. An advertisement for a car dealership screamed from the side facing Tab. It had been mangled by the clipping but was no less obnoxious for it. She folded the page to hide the headline from his view. When she turned the article around to show him the picture, she also covered the story's first paragraph with two fingers.

"Do you recognize this man?"

There was no mistaking it. The pictured man was Roy. There was something uncanny about the photo, a creepy lack of clarity to the yellowed half-tone that Tab was old enough to recognize but not yet capable of explaining. From beyond the dots, he saw a man who resembled the drawing he had just handed his mother. The only difference is this man had eyes, half-lidded and staring into the camera. The black-and-white photograph could not reveal their color, but Tab thought they might have been blue or gray. They were narrow, too—not beady, precisely, but more rectangular than he thought eyes should be.

"That's him! That's Roy," Tab said. A tear streamed down his mother's face. She pivoted and swiped at it. "Have you seen him or something?"

His heart thudded with dread. Had Roy told him the truth? Was his mom once in love with a man who was not Tab's dad? Had she been married to his dad at the same time she was in love with this man? If Roy was not lying, the *synchronicity* of the drawing of his dad's hand and his mom's nightmares could also be signs of something very real.

"Have you ever seen this picture before, hon?" No hints in her eyes or her mouth about which way she hoped he'd answer.

Tab shook his head. "No. First time ever."

"You haven't been rummaging around in this desk before? Maybe you were looking for a pencil or something and accidentally saw it at some point?"

He shook his head with more emphasis. "No, Mom. I don't go through your things. Not since the makeup. You and Dad made me promise."

She nodded, running a forefinger under her nose and then under each eye. "Ok. I believe you. Now tell me. Did you touch me or push the back of my head the last time we were in the car? Remember when I said I thought I had nodded off?"

Tab stiffened, inhaled, and held it for a few seconds. "Yes?"

"I wasn't a hundred percent telling the truth when I said that. I don't lie to you, Tab. But right then, I thought that was the best explanation for what happened. It felt like somebody was tickling the back of my head at first. Right here." She ducked and patted her crown with her right hand. "Then, while you were still talking to Roy, it felt like something—I don't know—*pushed* me. The back of my neck is still a little sore from it. We didn't hit a bump or anything that I remember."

"Roy shoved your head through the back of your seat," Tab said. His voice quavered, his lower lip trembling. "I'm not making it up, Mom. I swear. He was trying to prove to me that he was real because I kept telling him he wasn't." He paused. "He could have killed us!"

I ain't no goddamn murderer.

Tab thought, *But you're a liar.*

From her desktop, Sandra produced Tim's DVD copy of *Mortuary!* The cover featured a woman's hand bursting from below earth in front of a gravestone. The hand was open-palm, fingers spread, as if seeking purchase on something. Or someone. The calves of passersby, maybe? To have been buried under the earth, Tab's artist's eye noted that the hand and the arm attached to it appeared remarkably clean.

"Have you ever seen this before?"

He shook his head. "I don't think so. What is it?"

"One of your dad's horror movies from the early eighties. Are you sure you've never seen it before? I'm not asking if you've seen the movie. I'm asking if you've seen the cover art."

"No," Tab said. "I haven't seen either of them before."

Sandra sighed. "I was afraid of that."

"Why? What does it mean?"

She shrugged, her gaze distant, looking at the floor. "Maybe nothing. Does it remind you of anything?"

"The picture of Dad's hand from my sketchbook," Tab said without thinking about it. "And if Roy turns out to be really real—"

Son and mother stared at each other for a moment, each knowing what the other was thinking. "I'll get my keys," Sandra said. "You go get your brother. Tell him we're going to visit your dad at the cemetery."

✳✳✳

The drive to the Lost Hollow gravesite was a short one, but it seemed to Tab as if days passed. He was smart. He left his sketchbook and pencils at home. But because there was nothing to draw and no eraser to tap against his temple, his fingers kept wandering to his bump, worrying at it. It was warm to the touch right now, but no warmer than anywhere else on his face. That meant Roy was not around. Maybe.

The Beard family piled out of the car and located their patriarch's gravestone immediately.

Tab glanced at the lot, unwilling at first to lay eyes on the stone. He dreaded the pangs of loss that might wring from him a fresh round of hot tears. A small shack sat in the corner of the lot. The face of an older man appeared in its dusty window and vanished seconds later. Creepy. But it wasn't Roy.

"Don't look over there," Jeremy said from behind him. "You'll lure old Diggum out here. They say he's crazy."

"Jeremy! We don't use words like 'crazy' anymore."

"Sorry, Mom. They say he's a whack job!"

Sandra rolled her eyes but ignored the slur. She knelt in front of Tim's headstone, placing a hand on it for support as she did. Her knees and the tips of her shoes sank into soft earth. For a moment, Tab had a terrible fear she was going to drown in his dad's grave. It hadn't rained in weeks that Tab could remember, not much at all since the flood. He had imagined that the dirt over his dad would be hard, packed. Unless. Unless, unless, unless. Unless the drawing in his sketchbook, his mother's nightmares, and Roy were all telling the truth.

"Careful," a hoarse baritone said from somewhere behind the family. "I resodded this morning. It ain't took hold yet."

Tab spun his head around. A weathered looking man wearing gray coveralls and an enormous pair of black clod-stomping work boots approached them from the caretaker's cottage. As he neared, Tab smelled the distinct aroma of gasoline. An unopened pack of Winstons peeked over the lip of his breast pocket.

Diggum the cemetery caretaker directly acknowledged neither of the children. Tab didn't like the way his eyes darted to them now and then, as if he was expecting one of them to jump him.

"Flood washed away a lot of the topsoil around here," the man said. "Been working hard every day since to get things looking right again. Sure enough. I try to not bother people while they're mourning their kin, but y'all are standing right on the spot I sodded this morning. Don't want you to fall and hit your head or nothing."

Sandra stood up to greet him. "Thank you. We'll be careful." She considered him for a moment and pushed forward. "Can I ask you something? Have you seen anything weird around here over the past couple of days? Anyone lurking around when they shouldn't be or bothering the graves?"

Diggum's face screwed up in recollection. "Can't say I have. Why? Something wrong with this one?"

"No," Sandra said, shaking her head. "No, I guess not. You wouldn't happen to have any security cameras monitoring the graves or anything, would you? So if someone did disturb something, you'd be able to tell what happened and who did it?"

The man's eyes grew wide, offended. "Hell, naw! That kind of stuff is a privacy invasion. I live here. I don't want no security system keeping tabs on everything I say and do."

"But—"

"Let me ask you something, ma'am. What's with all the questions? You accusing me of something? We got walls here now thanks to the county commission. Had 'em since 2008. We got a gate I lock up at night. You got me living here twenty-four hours a day and seven days a week. You expecting Dr. Frankenstein to come steal some bodies?" Sandra tittered, a blush reddening her cheeks. "No, nothing like that," she said. "I've just—well, with everything going on now I've got it in my head I need to keep watch on it all, I guess. Thank you again for your help." She turned to the kids. "We need to go."

Diggum nodded but did not reply. Tab figured he'd leave them then. He didn't. Instead, he shoved his hands in the pockets of his coveralls and waited, eyes never unlocked from Sandra.

"Come on boys," she said. "Let's go." She reached for both of their hands but only managed to grab Tab's. Jeremy had already stepped out of the way and headed for the car. He was too old for handholding, anyway. Mom just reached for him out of habit.

Tab could sense Diggum's eyes on their backs as they walked. At least he wasn't following them. The cloud of gasoline stink had dissipated.

A warm breeze picked up, stirring the leaves on the few trees dotting the cemetery landscape. The sudden wind stung his bump. That was a new sensation. It made him wish he had bandaged it, or that his mother would allow him to grow his hair longer on that side to cover it up. The breeze whistled in Tab's ears. Somewhere within the sound, he thought he could also detect a voice. A familiar one.

TAAAB, it said. *III'M COOOMING. STOOOP HIIIM*.

"Dad," Tab said. His mother's hand tightened around his own. "Dad's here."

CHAPTER TWENTY-ONE

Guilt wrapped its sinewy constrictors around Sandra's throat and squeezed. Tim had died before she realized she'd left her Facebook message from Seb open on the computer in the study. She never had a chance to discuss it with him. When she'd returned to that computer days after his death, she replayed the private conversation and the sensations it provoked in her. Stuck to the bottom of the monitor was her Post-it note to Tim about Tab's doctor appointments.

He'd seen the message. He must have. She was angry that Tim had discovered it, but at herself more than him. And at Facebook for existing because it made it far too easy for the ancient past to return to the present, like a hand from a grave. "Facebook is shit," she had said. "Seb meant nothing to me and never will." She gazed at the study ceiling, imagining Tim there with her, her hands clasped in his. "I had a weak moment of escapist fantasy. That's all."

It had been at a time when her relationship with her husband had hit the rocks. Sandra still loved Tim despite his angry moments, his get-rich-quick schemes, and all his other flaws. And despite his ham-fisted attempt to avenge her. He'd died thinking she wanted out. Now she'd never get the chance to explain.

Those nasty old feelings—shame and rage—bubbled unbidden to the surface. It didn't matter how much time had passed. It didn't matter how much she had loved and been loved by Tim before he was taken out of this world. It didn't matter how much she loved little Tab. Her mind wandered to the past. The past was pain. Now that her son was struggling—.

Except, he wasn't *struggling*. Not with himself. He was being attacked by a gaslighting ghost that somehow mimicked the symptoms of OCD. He was trying to survive. Did she really believe that now? She wasn't sure she did. On some level, she felt shame for having loaded the kids in the car for that trip to the cemetery based on a gut reaction to what might just be a string of coincidences.

On another, she felt newly scared, ashamed, and alone. Suddenly, she was aware of the tightness of her clothes, pulling at them to stretch them, loosen them so that they no longer clung to her body. She glanced around the study, searching for holes, openings, portals to the exterior of her home through which someone (Roy? Alive?) might be watching her. From the kitchen, she heard the *pop* of their ancient refrigerator indicating that the compressor had stopped. It sounded like a gunshot in her ears, startling her. Outside, some type of muscle car whizzed by, farting fumes at a volume that vibrated the walls. And she was back there again. Back *then*. For the first time in years.

Nothing she could have done would have stopped Roy on that day of horrors, regardless of what conservative pundits and misogynists might say (an opinion she would never express to Tim, even if she thought he might agree with her). Roy outweighed her by a good hundred pounds. He had also disarmed her with the confidence and ease of an experienced predator who had gotten away with rape more than once. Often enough to become a little careless. She'd fought. But she had not defeated him.

Sandra shuddered and forced the memory of that afternoon away. She left the study and switched on the television in the family room, tuning it to a New Wave music station, and began to sing along with as much of Culture Club's "Karma Chameleon" as she could remember. She stood in front of the screen for a while, swaying, singing, and snapping her fingers in time. It helped, but only a little.

All the denial melted away, all the hope that recent events had been a product of Tab's trauma from the flood and the death of his father. Sandra was left only with cold, hard truths. Ice-hard truths immobilizing her will to carry on. If not for Jeremy and Tab, she might go ahead and squeeze the trigger. But she couldn't. Not while they were so young and so dependent on her.

The Hollow County Sheriff's Department had been of little help. Roy was well known to them, of course. They arrested him. Again. It was his second offense according to public records, but Sandra had the impression more than two women had been attacked by the brute over his lifetime. He was out on bail before the sun had set. To add insult, the sheriff's department had allegedly "misplaced" Sandra's rape kit before it could be processed, so the case would eventually boil down to her word against his.

In private, Tim suggested the judge had a bias against anyone who accused Roy of wrongdoing. Was it possible the judge and Roy were acquainted? In his most conspiratorial moments, Tim had stalked Roy, following him to work sites, home, back to work, to the Whitt's store where he had abducted her, and to bars. He was careful to keep his distance. His hope had been to catch the judge and Roy commiserating somewhere. He could take pictures, haul them to the Hollow County District Attorney as evidence the judge was corrupt.

"It's a small town," he'd said. "It's always been a small town and it'll always be a small town. There are things people get away with here that'd they'd never try in places where they don't have a lot of power and status."

It was the smartest thing she'd ever heard her husband say. "Absolute power corrupts absolutely" was all he meant, but she wasn't going to tell him that. He'd think she was patronizing him. He already sensed her resentment over this vendetta on her behalf. She was pregnant with their second child, after all. Something they'd wanted since Jeremy started pulling up on furniture. Rural life could be lonesome for an only child. A little brother or sister might help Jeremy fend off such feelings. She considered reminding Tim that stalking is a crime, but she already knew what he would say. "It's not as big a crime as rape."

Neither of the parents acknowledged, to themselves or each other, the possibility that the new baby could be Roy's. But Sandra thought it gnawed at them both. Tim in particular. More reason for him to insist the child be named Tim Aaron Beard, Jr. if it was a boy. Timmi, Tammi, or Thea if it was a girl. He'd gleaned the last one from a baby names book he'd thumbed through in a Hollow River bookstore. It was short for Timothea, "God's honor." The more Tim imprinted himself on the new baby, the thinking went, the more likely the baby would magically turn out to be his. Not Roy's. *Magical thinking*, Dr. Clifford might say. And it was. Of course it was.

Then came the night Roy discovered Tim following him. The way Tim told it, the man had stumbled drunk from a rarely used backdoor of one of his favorite watering holes. He'd tripped over the curb, smashing face-first into the driver's side window of Tim's Ram. The Ram's tinted windows and Roy's intoxicated eyes prevented him from seeing who sat behind the wheel.

But it didn't matter. Tim's rage boiled over. Adrenaline dilated his airways. Blood thudded through his heart and limbs. Every instinct he had to preserve the secrecy of his war vanished. He shoved open the Ram's door, knocking Roy flat on his ass. "The Last Resort" blasted from the pickup's speakers. It was a ballad about the colonization of the American West, about possession, sad and beautiful but oddly obnoxious when playing through Tim's cranked bass in the night air outside a bar.

"Ow!" the man said. "What the fuck?"

Tim stepped out of the pickup and stood over Roy, legs apart. On the ground, Roy squirmed. He looked like a turtle on its back trying to roll. Tim slid the tire iron he'd taken to carrying with him on these trips—for self-defense, he'd said—from the truck's seat. The straight end tapered into a chisel. Tim considered shoving it into Roy's gaping mouth and through the back of his throat. Instead, he raised the iron high above his head and brought the blunt side down on Roy's face. Again. And again.

Spatters of blood sprayed from the bridge of the man's nose when it broke. A long gash opened across his forehead. Another along his right cheek as he tried to roll away. Each time the iron came down on him, a satisfying crunch of bone harmonized with Roy's yelps of terror and pain.

The heavy bass from the rockabilly throwback songs the house band was playing blared through external speakers mounted along the eaves of the bar, competing with "The Last Resort" in a cacophony of asynchronous drumming. The heavy *boom-chicka-boom* beat covered Roy's screams well, though, Tim thought. The darkness and proximity of the back lot shielded his revenge from the plain view of passersby on the street or bar patrons who had chosen that moment to drive home.

Tim's final two blows landed on the soft areas under Roy's eyes. The orbs bulged outward from their sockets in response. A final swipe of the iron pulled one of them clean out, stalk and all. It rolled a few inches away from Roy's face and lay still, glaring up at Tim with something like shock, even without eyelids and eyebrows to help form the expression. Roy himself had gone silent. He lay still on the gravel, not a finger twitching. The man's bowels let go, the putrid stench of beer-soaked shit that wafted under Tim's nose seconds later confirmed it.

"Fuck," Tim said. He covered his mouth and nose with the palm of one hand. The blood and gore-stained tire iron dangled from the other.

The next few minutes were a blur. Tim tossed the tire iron across the seat of his Ram and leaped inside. He slammed the door, started the engine. The daytime running lights engaged when he shifted into Drive. He couldn't stop that. But he switched off the headlights and anything else that might reveal details about his truck.

The left side of the barroom had no windows. Tim chose to drive that way so no one inside took note of him. He had to fight the urge to stomp on the gas. If he could creep around the front corner, he'd be able to tell whether anyone stood outside. Loiterers might take note of his truck, or his tag, and later put two and two together if he wasn't careful.

Blessedly, no one was there. Still too early for the drunks to go home and sleep it off. Their spouses or children might still be awake if they left now. Most of them, he surmised, had no desire to entertain the kind of judgment they'd get if they arrived home before the tots were asleep. Relieved, he'd driven away from the bar and taken a long, winding back route to Hollow Creek Road and home.

No one discovered Roy's body until closing time, when one of the employees hauled trash to the dumpster out back. Others came running outside when they heard her screams. Roy lay crumpled a few feet away from the garbage, dead and mutilated.

If Roy and the judge had been pals, it hadn't been a particularly strong friendship. The investigation into Roy's death had been quick, dirty, and unproductive. That, or the Hollow County Sheriff's Department and the district attorney's office decided to turn a blind eye to the incident. Given the history of the "victim," Sandra hoped that was the case.

During their investigation, one sheriff's inspector had questioned both Tim and Sandra on their whereabouts the night of the incident at separate times. They were two among a number of Roy's previous "acquaintances" who were questioned, all in a cursory fashion. Sandra had no problem at all convincing the investigators of her truth: she'd been home all night taking care of Jeremy. The child himself had confirmed in his toddler way that the two had watched a few episodes of *Jay Jay the Jet Plane* and *Dora the Explorer* together. The pride beamed on his face when his mother mentioned the former show to the inspector.

"Day Day!" he said. "Day Day!"

Tim's interview was less convincing, but not enough to arrest him. He'd told the inspector he'd been in the barn all night doing maintenance on the John Deere. No one was with him and no one saw him, but he was able to show the man a pan of used oil and an old battery he'd not yet recycled.

"How often do you do this kind of maintenance?" the inspector had asked.

"Not often enough!" Tim had said. "Hard to make time if it's running smooth. There's so much other work to do on the farm."

"Sure, sure," the inspector said. "We'll be in touch if we need anything else."

That had been the last they'd heard from the Hollow County Sheriff's Department. Tim followed the news religiously for months afterward, searching for information about any sign of a break in the case, anything that might lead deputies to his door. None came. Roy had no surviving family, no last will and testament, and no one to claim his body. The state cremated him, then sold off what little property he'd owned. And that was that.

At home, Sandra found herself unable to meet her youngest's eyes after she switched off the television and went to the kitchen for her late day cup of coffee. All this time, she'd thought Roy was her son's imaginary friend or childhood monster in the closet. All this time, she'd thought he'd outgrow it. Or that it was an anxiety condition prompted by the trauma of his father's death. Not once had the name Roy triggered those old feelings in her. She couldn't understand why she hadn't seen it before.

They'd never bothered with a paternity test. Tim didn't want to know the DNA details. Now, with Tab snacking on peanut butter and crackers at the kitchen table, Sandra thought she could see a little of Roy in Tab's features. The eyes: they weren't hers and they weren't exactly Tim's. They, therefore, had to be Roy's.

Sandra poured a fresh cup of joe and sat down at the kitchen table on Tab's left. She blew into the mug, enjoying the warm backflow of steam in her face. As she took her first sip, she cut her eyes to Tab, who was busy spreading a fresh pile of crunchy peanut butter on a Ritz. For a second, only a second, she thought she saw the bump on his left temple split open. Something glistened inside it, moving from left to right. Then—she would swear it—the thing winked at her before sealing itself up again.

Her heart sank into her stomach.

CHAPTER TWENTY-TWO

Tab felt her eyes on him. On his bump, which he imagined sizzling and steaming from the heat of her glare. Something in her expression stopped him from asking her what was wrong. The vibe had changed since she sat down at the table. What had been a simple snack before an afternoon of sketching had become an awkward non-interaction of uncomfortable silence.

Tab's life had been a short one, but until recent days he'd never mistrusted his parents. Without reason, suspicion invaded his mind. She was upset with him. He could tell. Although he did not know what he'd done wrong. No. *Upset* was the wrong word. She looked *afraid* of him.

"Mom?"

"Yes, hon?" She stopped searching her coffee and faced him, her eyes wandering not to his but to the bump on his temple. He massaged the spot, soothing it and obstructing her view.

"Do I have something on my head?"

"No. Just your bump, sweetheart. Is it hurting right now?"

"It burns a little. Kind of a sting. Or it did. I think it's gone away now."

"Mm-hmm. What would you think about us taking you back to the doctor about that? A dermatologist instead of Dr. Patel? She said it was harmless, but you touch it a lot. Sometimes it looks like it's getting worse." Nervousness crept into her voice. Tab found it irritating. "Does it still bother you much?"

"A lot. It bothers me all the time."

"I thought so. I'm going to call Dr. Patel and ask for a referral. We can find someone to take that thing off you. You'll have enough red bumps to deal with when you're a teenager, I imagine. Your brother's already breaking out and he's in middle school."

"Breaking out?"

"Acne, hon. Pimples. Everyone gets them in their teens. Some worse than others. I had them bad in my late teens. Washing my face every night with warm water helped a lot, but it won't stop them."

"You mean Ashley Reardon was right and I'm going to have more of these things?" He indicated the bump on his temple.

Sandra smiled. Tab recognized it as maternal reassurance, but falsity lurked behind it, spuriousness. Although Tab was not yet familiar with that word. "No, not like that one. That's from an injury or something. It's not a pimple. I don't know what it is for sure, but it's not a pimple."

"Will it hurt?"

"Will what hurt?"

"Having my bump removed?"

Sandra inhaled and settled back in her chair. "Not exactly," she said, exhaling the words as if she'd taken a long drag from a phantom cigarette. "If it's a cyst or something like Dr. Patel said, the dermatologist will numb it. They'll use a needle to inject some anesthetic. You'll feel a little pinch or a stick for a second."

She appeared to think for a moment, searching for the words to explain the rest of the process in a way that wouldn't terrify him. "After it's numb, they'll use some tools to open the skin a little bit—"

"They're gonna cut me open?" His voice trembled. Sandra smiled back at him. "It'll be a little cut with a sterilized scalpel. You won't even feel it. They'll squeeze the sides of the bump so the little ball that's living inside pops out."

"Little ball? Like an eyeball?" A thin film of sweat had coated Tab's forehead. He wiped it with his forearm, creating a sheen there as well.

"No, not like that. A cyst is nothing but dead skin cells collected in a little sac under your skin. Most of the time, the sac is ball shaped. They'll take it out and give you a couple of stitches to seal the cut. When the cut heals, you'll have a very small scar instead of a big lump. Scars fade over time. After a while, you won't even remember it's there anymore. I had one removed years ago, before you were born, and now I can't even see where it used to be."

Sandra plopped her iPhone, screen up, on the table in front of Tab. "Say the word and I'll call Dr. Patel and ask for a referral." He detected an urgency in her eyes that she managed to keep out of her voice. She wasn't telling him something. Something that frightened her. In turn, his stomach twisted into a knot.

"Are you sure it's safe?"

"Perfectly safe, hon."

He sighed. "Okay. Let's call."

Sandra unlocked the iPhone. She was about to tap the Contacts app and search for Dr. Patel's office number when Tab's hand slapped hers flat. He snatched the phone away from her and cast it across the room. It hit the floor face-down, bounced, and then landed face up. A crack split the screen's surface in a ragged diagonal line from lower left to upper right.

"What did you do that for?" she asked. "You broke it!"

Tears streamed down his face. His hand remained on hers, which now lay palm-flat on the kitchen table. "I didn't do it, Mom!" he said. "I didn't do it!" Tab struggled to remove his hand from his mother's. Pressure on the back of his hand, mashing it down, prevented him from pulling away, stopping his mother from making the call. Hurting her. "I can't move my hand! Something's holding me down!"

On the last word, Roy materialized. His left hand, gritty and calloused, mashed hard atop Tab's, making the boy's smaller hand the meat of a sandwich. His bizarre eye sockets, thick and swollen along their edges, trained on Tab. His lips spread apart in an effortful grimace, coffee and cigarette-stained teeth behind them.

"Tab, let me go!" Sandra squealed. "I'm trying to help you!"

"I'm not DOING THIS, Mom!"

Sandra wrapped her left hand around her right wrist, using the extra leverage to try to escape. She pulled free just as Jeremy dashed into the room, a puzzled expression etched on his brow, his eyes bleary under drooping lids. He looked as if he'd been startled awake from an afternoon nap. More likely, he'd been staring into the void of the iMac's screen for hours on end.

"What's going on?"

Sandra cradled her left hand in her lap, her mouth twisted downward in a mix of physical and emotional pain. "Your brother tried to crush my hand," she said. "Tab, if you don't want to go get your bump removed, you could have said so."

"It wasn't me," Tab said in a meek whisper. "It was Roy again. Roy."

"Who *is* Roy?" Jeremy asked.

"Jeremy, go back to your room."

"But—"

"Go back to your room now!"

"Fine. Smells like Dad's gross aftershave in here anyway." Tab's older brother sulked away, but not before smacking Tab in the back of the head with an open palm. "Freak."

"And for that, you're grounded. Don't come out of your room until I say it's okay for you to come out."

"What if I need to pee?"

"Jeremy, go!"

"Fine!"

Tab and Sandra sat in silence as the older boy's feet padded into the distance. The sound was followed by the furious slam of his bedroom door. "Ugh," Sandra said. "I don't know where he gets it. Your dad wasn't like that as a kid and neither was I." She recovered herself. Her breathing slowed. Her eyes softened.

"Where is Roy now?"

"Gone, I think," Tab said. The ghost had vanished, popped from existence like a soap bubble, as soon as Jeremy interrupted them. Tab's hand, which still rested on the kitchen table, throbbed. Sandra examined her own hand and then his. "The back of your hand is bright red," she said.

"He was pushing it down. He was holding it so I couldn't move and you couldn't call the doctor."

Sandra nodded, her lips puckered. "You didn't talk back to him this time, though, like how Dr. Clifford said you should do. Like you did in the car."

"No. I didn't remember to do it this time. I was too scared."

"So why did he quit? Why did he leave?"

Tab shrugged.

"Has he ever touched you before? Does he touch you often?"

"No. I knew he could touch other people if he tried hard enough. But I didn't think he could touch me because he never tried." It was the one comfort Tab clung to throughout Roy's presence in his life. The man or ghost or figment or whatever he was had never laid so much as a finger on him, even if he was able to move closet doors.

"What was different about this time? What do you think?"

A fresh tear rolled down Tab's cheek. "I don't know," he said. "Because it was the first time anyone has tried to help me stop him? This thing," he indicated his bump, "is part of him, I think. It only burns and moves when he's there or when he's using it to see. And—"

She waited a moment, but he did not continue. "And what, hon?"

"And once I think he got inside me."

"Like when he was using your hand to stop me from calling Dr. Patel?"

"Kind of," Tab said. "But more like—"

Light dawned behind Sandra's eyes. "More like when he used you to draw the picture of your father's hand coming out of the grave?"

"I think he controlled me. I think he drew the picture of Dad's hand coming out of the grave. I think he used me to do it." Tab sobbed. Sandra slid out of her chair and wrapped her arms around him. "I'm so sorry I didn't believe you," she said.

CHAPTER TWENTY-THREE

There comes a point in every day of every life when even the most logical-minded person can fall prey to the whims of magical thinking. For Tab Beard, the most vulnerable day and hour fell at 10:30 on a Tuesday morning in the examination room of Dr. Elena Morales, dermatologist.

His shoulders slumped when the family entered a formerly sterile waiting room that had obviously been redecorated. Someone had painted over the original brutalism, trying to add some warmth. Textured beige wallpaper was pasted in a haphazard fashion against white-painted walls. Tab knew this because a peeling corner near the door trim revealed it. The orange-yellow glow of incandescent sconces lined the highest area of the walls, replacing the fluorescent overhead lights. Muzak, a grating, amateurish blend of New Age and smooth jazz, whispered from three speakers embedded in circular cutouts in the ceiling.

For Tab, none of it brought much comfort. He searched the waiting room. No sign of Roy. Yet. In the front row of chairs closest to the check-in sat a couple of elderly women. One held the hand of the other. They stared at him, smiling as if he were a cherished Christmas ornament or a cute red panda at the zoo. Tab gazed somewhere over their heads as he continued his scan. His eyes landed on his brother, who sulked in the farthest corner.

Tab's mom forced Jeremy to accompany them to this appointment in spite of the elder brother's furious foot-stomping, hand-wringing protests. For once, Tab was relieved his brother was in tow. Roy almost never appeared when Jeremy was around. Or, in the case of the hand-squashing incident, he disappeared as soon as Jeremy entered the room. It was like his brother was some kind of talisman, an ignorant but protective charm against the wiles of the malevolent ghost. A useful idiot.

Even so, Tab remained vigilant—*hypervigilant*, he remembered. The *crack* of air followed by the soft groan of the waiting room door opening startled him. Each time it happened, Tab's head jerked in the direction of the sound. Once, he imagined Roy peering around the door at him. It turned out to have been an older woman with close-cropped hair and an unfortunate permanent glower.

By the time a smiling, young, dark-haired man in soft pink scrubs called Tab's name, his mom was helping to hold him still in his seat. He'd been rocking and had not realized it. Because the seats in the waiting room were all connected to one long metal tube of a base, his rocking disturbed other patients who were too polite to say so. That's what his mom told him. He suspected it was more likely that the rocking disturbed *her*.

Dr. Morales, who insisted Tab call her Dr. Elena or Dr. El if it was easier, spotted his bump immediately. "I assume this is what you're here for?" she said. "How long have you had this bump? And do you mind if I touch it?"

"Since the whole world flooded a while back," he said.

"He means he's had it since May," Sandra clarified.

Dr. El nodded. "Let's take a look, then."

Tab combed the curls away from his temple, tilting his head so she could better examine it. He hadn't had a haircut in weeks. There hadn't been time. Every member of the

Beard family had grown shaggy as a summer meadow. In secret, Tab hoped his hair would grow long enough to cover the bump. Even after getting it removed, he might ask his mom if he could keep wearing his hair this way. He liked it better thick and wavy. He enjoyed the way it blew backward in the breeze. It made him feel a little like he was wearing Batman's cape.

Dr. El poked and squeezed the bump between two gloved fingers. Her hands were cold, but Tab managed to not shiver. "Yeah, you've got a cyst. It's a little inflamed right now, too. Have you been scratching at it or poking it at all?"

"He has a lot of trouble ignoring it," Sandra said. "That's why we decided to do something about it." Her expression betrayed the lie. "I'm afraid if he keeps picking at it, he's just going to make it worse." She smiled at him when she said it, but it was a rueful smile. The sorrow in her voice was unmistakable. There was a helplessness, too. It grated on Tab.

"Unclench your jaw for me," Dr. El said. "That's better. Yes, I think that's a cyst. We never know for certain until we open them up, but it's very likely. I can try to remove it today if you want. I'll give you a little shot of lidocaine to numb the area. After you're numb, I'll make a small incision in the skin over the bump. Hopefully we'll be able to squeeze the cyst out without too much effort."

She sat and met Tab's gaze. "I do want you to know you might have a small scar where the bump is right now. Once it heals, it won't be very visible. I'll do everything I can to minimize it. Knowing all that, are we sure we want to go ahead and get it removed today?"

Tab looked at his mom, who nodded back. Her eyes had brightened a little. "Yes!" he said. "Let's cut it out!"

Dr. El's nurse—TROY, his name tag read—slid a tray of tools to Tab's left. The doctor plucked a black Sharpie from it and drew a horizontal line across the bump. The ink was cool and wet, producing something of an antiseptic odor. It felt nice against his skin, creating a sensation of tightness over the bump as it dried. Next, Troy draped a blue cloth over Tab's head. A hole had been cut in the cloth, which Troy aligned over the bump so it was the only part of Tab's temple exposed to Dr. El.

"Okay," the doctor said. "You're going to feel a small pinch or stick here as I numb your bump. I'm not cutting into you yet."

He winced at the initial stab of the needle but managed to keep his head steady. That is, until Roy emerged on his right and screamed in his ear. "STOP HER NOW! YOU DON'T KNOW WHAT YOU'RE DOING!"

Tab started, jerking his head away from the offending sound. Dr. El gasped. The needle slid farther into his skin. Too far, before she pulled it out. Something inside the bump popped. Thick warm liquid drooled down his face. The syringe slipped from Dr. El's hand and clattered to the linoleum. Tab clapped a hand against the bump, rubbing at it in an attempt to soothe the pain. The effort sprayed chunky greenish goo with streaks of red into the air. Some of it splashed against the plexiglass visor covering Dr. El's eyes and surgical mask.

In the next second, Roy began to scream. Neither in anger nor in outrage, but in pain. The ghost collapsed to the floor of the exam room and rolled on his back, cupping an empty eye socket in each palm. Tab whipped the blue cloth away from his face in time to see a similar chunky greenish liquid oozing from the places where Roy's eyes should have been. A moment later, he drew breath and seemed to recover himself.

Tab's eyes locked on his mother. "Go get Jeremy! Now!"

"We can't have more family than your mom in here because—" Troy began, but Tab shouted over him.

"NOW!"

Sandra leaped from her chair and dashed through the exam room door, which blessedly opened outward. Troy ran after her while Dr. El attempted to soothe Tab. Her hands were on his shoulders. She was saying something to him, but he couldn't understand her. Her voice was quiet and distant, as if she was speaking to him from across the void separating dream worlds from the waking. He was able to comprehend only two words: "okay" and "down."

Behind her right shoulder, Roy's ruined face rose like a malicious star over the horizon of an unwary town. His lips twisted into a grinning sneer. What remained of his eyebrows arched downward in the middle. He swiped at the chunky tears drying on his cheeks. "You're gonna pay for that, you little asshole," he intoned. "I'm trying to help you. But you gotta help me help you, son."

"I'M NOT YOUR SON!"

Dr. El took an involuntary step back from him, alarmed. For a second, she and Roy were one entity, his ghostly transparency overlapped her corporeal form as if someone had projected an image of him onto her. At the same moment, Sandra jogged into the room, dragging Jeremy along with her. Troy, exaggerating an exasperated eye roll, followed behind. No sooner had the nurse closed the exam room door than Roy vanished from sight. Before he dissipated, Tab thought he'd looked a little startled. Well, as startled as an eyeless man could appear.

Dr. El continued backing up, finally leaning against the block wall opposite Tab. Sandra forced Jeremy down into the side chair she had occupied while Troy, sighing heavily, went about cleaning up the dropped syringe and cyst goo splattering the floor around Tab.

"Is it over?" Sandra asked following an awkward moment of silence among the group. "Is he gone?"

Tab glanced around the room. His eyes lit for a moment on Dr. El's. They were ablaze with shock and disbelief above her mask. Jeremy also glared back at him with something like bewildered amusement. "I don't see him anywhere." In the back of his mind, an ember flared. Hurting himself had hurt Roy. Badly. If he could hurt Roy by creating pain for himself, might he not be able to kill Roy if—.

He snuffed the flare then. That was too scary a last resort to consider.

"Okay. I'm sorry," she said to Dr. El. She was met with silence. "Can we continue now?"

Dr. El slipped the plexiglass visor off her head and pulled down her mask. "Give me a few minutes," she said. "I'll be right back. Troy, when you're done cleaning up, I need to talk to you outside." She left the room. Troy followed her less than a minute later, having wiped up the mess on Tab's face, the chair, and the floor and disposed of the syringe Dr. El had dropped. His gloves made an irritable *snap* sound as he pulled them off and tossed them in the garbage on his way out the door.

"What did you see, Tab?" his mom asked as the door closed behind Troy.

Tab's lower lip quivered. "Roy showed up when she put the needle in my bump. He was screaming at me. Telling me to stop this because I didn't know what I was doing. Then it looked like the needle had hurt *him* somehow when it went in. He was rolling on the floor and holding his eyes."

"Who the hell is *Roy*?" Jeremy asked.

"Shush," Sandra said. "I'll fill you in later."

From outside the room, the sound of raised voices reverberated. Dr. El and Troy were having an argument, or an animated discussion, at least.

"Where is Roy now?" Sandra asked. She did not acknowledge the commotion outside.

"He disappeared when you came back. I think he's scared of Jeremy for some reason."

His brother scoffed. "Scared of *me*? I don't even know the dude! I don't give off any scary vibes."

Sandra smirked. "Well, you are a Ghostbuster, aren't you?"

Tab tittered, nervous. Jeremy peered from one to the other of them, a puzzled expression on his face. "I'm a *fan* of *Ghostbusters*. What does that have to do with anything?"

"Never mind." Sandra patted Jeremy on the knee. "Like I said, I'll explain later."

The door opened. A rushed, dour-looking Troy trod through it pushing a fresh tray of sterilized tools. The lower half of his face was once again covered by a surgical mask. "Okay," he said, attempting to sound cheerful, although his furrowed brow betrayed him. "Let's get this show back on the road."

Dr. El arrived just as Troy placed a fresh blue cloth over the left half of Tab's face. "I didn't push the plunger on the syringe last time, so we still have to numb you up before we start. We punctured the sac wall when you moved. We'll need to squeeze out as much of the gunk as we can before I pull that out. We have to remove the sac if you want to prevent the cyst from returning." She looked at Sandra. "I assume we still want to go through with this today."

Both Tab and Sandra agreed. Jeremy screwed up his face in disgust. "You mean I have to watch this?"

"Look at your iPod," Sandra said, dismissive. "Play a game or something. But we need you to stay in the room."

Jeremy did not reply. He slid the iPod Touch that had seen him through more than one boring family gathering or funeral service from the back pocket of his jeans and disappeared into Angry Birds. For the rest of the procedure, he would go unbothered and unnoticed. Tab suspected that was just how his brother liked it.

"Okay," Dr. El said. "Here we go."

Troy handed her a fresh syringe loaded with a numbing agent, which Dr. El applied without incident. Tab steeled himself for the stick but hardly flinched when it happened. After waiting for numbness to set in, Dr. El sliced a horizontal line across the diameter of the bump, which she then squeezed with care. Sandra grimaced, pinching her nose when the green sludge discharged. It oozed like toothpaste from the slotted end of a tube, or cake icing from a baker's decorating set. But there was nothing appetizing about it.

"Good gracious!" Sandra said. "That's foul-smelling!"

"Weird," Jeremy said. "I only smell good stuff. Old Spice. Like Dad wore."

Sandra eyed him with a smirk. "Doesn't smell like your dad to me. More like moldy cheese or something. Looks like it, too."

Dr. El laughed. "He's smelling Troy's cologne maybe," she said. "These things are full of dead skin cells. There's usually some kind of odor in the stuff around them as well as the stuff inside the sac. Sometimes there's hair or other things, too, but it's more often liquid skin."

"Well, I don't wear Old Spice," Troy said. "I use an unscented aftershave product just in case we have any patients who have strong reactions to perfumes."

"Our policy," Dr. El said. "I don't know what you're smelling. The cyst doesn't smell like Old Spice, though."

It was the second time Jeremy had mentioned smelling Old Spice. Tab never caught the aroma. Was Dad here? If so, why couldn't Tab sense him? It made sense to him that if his dad still existed in a ghostly form, he could attach to Jeremy the same way Roy had attached to Tab. Maybe Roy was afraid of his dad instead of Jeremy.

Troy wiped away the last of the gunk from the edges of the cut and handed Dr. El a pair of tweezers. She inserted the ends of them into the open wound and extracted tissue that looked like a small, deflated balloon: flattened but round and opaque. As Sandra had predicted, the sac would have been spherical had it still been full of grossness.

"There's our cyst," Dr. El announced. Troy handed her a pair of snips. She used them to cut the sac away where it had attached. The whole thing was about the diameter of a dime. The doctor cupped it in one pink-gloved palm and presented it to Tab for examination.

"Weird!" he said. "That's what was in there?" He was not sure what he had expected. The cyst was round and white, like an eyeball. Outside that, it bore little resemblance to the organ. No iris. No pupil for light to enter. No optic nerve through which it could transmit signals. It did not appear to be full of tiny red capillaries shaped like lightning strikes.

"Yep," Dr. El said. "That's what was in there. An ordinary little epidermoid cyst. Nothing unusual about it, except for where it was located. We see them on the face around the eyes. Yours doesn't have anything in it but dead skin cells and oil. Some doctors have seen ones that have hair. Some types of cysts have things develop in them. I have a friend who even removed a rudimentary eyeball from one once."

Both Tab and Sandra swiveled their heads toward the doctor. She did not appear to be joking.

"An eyeball?" Sandra asked. "Like fully developed and able to see?"

Dr. El laughed. "No. Hair or bone or something like that develop more often than something like an eyeball. Even if they do develop, they're not capable of functioning. You won't find cysts with the ability to chew or see or anything." She must have marked Tab's horrified expression because she followed that with, "I shouldn't have mentioned it. I can tell you that in my fifteen years of doing this work I've seen a lot of things, but I've never actually seen a cyst with an eyeball inside it."

She deposited the cyst on a blue sheet that lay near the tools on her tray. Troy replaced it with a needle and some thread. Dr. El pushed the tray away. "We're going to close this up now. I made a very small incision, so I don't think you need stitches for it. I'm going to use Steri-Strips. You'll need to make sure you keep them dry for at least five days, okay?" She looked at Sandra. "Cover the area with a large non-stick bandage when he showers or bathes. That will help. I'd say you'll be healed enough to pull the Steri-Strips off after a week."

"And that's that! Call the office if you have any questions."

She was gone before they had a chance to thank her. Troy began to follow her, but Sandra touched his elbow on his way out the door. "Can I ask you something?"

"Sure," he said. "You need to make a left out of the door here and a right down the hall to get back to the waiting room."

"No. I mean, thank you, but that wasn't what I wanted to ask. We heard you and Dr. El—uh, Dr. Morales—outside earlier. It sounded like you were arguing. Is everything okay?"

Troy nodded, his lips pursed together. "All good!" he said. He started to walk away, then turned back. "No, that's not fair to you. Listen, after Tab reacted badly to the numbing stick, Dr. El didn't want to continue the procedure. She'd already punctured the sac wall, so we didn't want to leave it, either. It could've gotten infected. In the end, I convinced her to go ahead with it."

"Well, why didn't she want to do it?"

Troy paused, thoughtful. "Honestly?" He leaned closer to Sandra's ear and lowered his voice. Tab thought he might be trying to prevent him from hearing, yet he heard. "I shouldn't be telling you this. I'm not a hundred percent sure why I am. We were both a little afraid of the liability after Tab's reaction and *your* reaction to *his* reaction. Not a lot of mothers run out to the waiting room to grab a comfort kid for the kid being operated on, if you know what I mean. Both of you were acting a little...strange, to put it mildly. We weren't sure we could trust your consent."

"You were afraid of being sued for doing a procedure we signed off on?" Dr. Clifford's description of PANDAS from their first appointment bubbled to the front of her mind. "Tab has separation anxiety when it comes to his brother. That's all. It's part of his OCD." When Troy didn't respond, she added, "It's a real condition. He can't help it."

Jeremy glanced up from his Touch and presented first his mother and then his little brother with a skeptical sneer. *Gross*, his expression read.

Troy didn't answer, but he didn't need to. "Talk to Delia at reception," he said, resuming his normal volume. "She'll help you wrap up any paperwork details. Bye, Tab! I hope you feel better!" With that, he left.

CHAPTER TWENTY-FOUR

For the first time in weeks, home felt homey when the family arrived. Alfie awaited them at the door, more dog-like than cat. He curled himself around Tab's calves and ankles, bonking his head against the boy's legs in a friendly "hello." He claimed Tab with the rub of a cheek, then meandered to his water bowl for a drink.

Tab sensed no foreboding about going to his room alone. Nor did he worry about sleeping in his bed at night. He didn't concern himself with watching the news, either. The ride home had passed without incident. He couldn't remember the last time he'd ridden home from a Hollow River doctor's appointment without Roy popping up beside him in the back seat. It was as if the removal of the cyst from his temple had solved every problem he'd had since the May flood. Well, except for one. It didn't bring his dad home.

Or did it?

"What are you smiling about?" Jeremy chided, brushing past his younger sibling. "You're blocking the hall, twerp. The rest of us need to get inside the house, too." He stomped down the hall to the living room, where he collapsed onto the sofa and resumed gaming on his iPod Touch. "Twerp" again. Not "Tabitha." If he must be insulted, Tab thought he preferred the latter. Sure, it meant Jeremy thought he was unmanly. But if being chronically pissed off and an asshole was the definition of manly, "Tabitha" seemed like a welcome alternative.

Tab chose to ignore him, instead addressing his mother. "I can smell Old Spice now," he said, grinning so broad that it hurt his face. "Like Dad's here again!"

Sandra sniffed the air, smiling. "I don't smell it, but I guess I'm glad you do. I got so used to it that I can't smell it anymore." Her smile faded. "You haven't seen *him*, though? The other one? Not since we were in Dr. El's office?"

Tab shook his head. "Nope. Haven't seen him. Haven't felt him at all. Cutting out the bump did the trick!"

"I hope so, hon." She bent at the knees until they were eye to eye. "How's your head? Any pain or anything like that now that the numbing has had time to wear off?"

He thought for a moment, shifting his eyes up and to the right, concentrating so as to detect any odd sensations he might not have noticed after leaving Dr. El's. "Nope," he said. "Not hurting a bit."

"Okay. I want you to tell me if you feel any pain where they cut you." She paused. "And Tab? I also want you to tell me if you start seeing Roy again, got it? Or if you see your dad or anything else that bothers you. No secrets. I can't help you if I don't know what's happening. And whatever *is* happening, I'm going to believe you from now on. Okay?"

Warmth spread from Tab's stomach, along his back and shoulders, and up through his neck and head. It created chill bumps all along its path. "Okay," he said, smiling. "Thank you, Mom."

She returned his smile and stood erect. Her knees popped, prompting a laugh. "Getting old! Let's figure out what we can do about some dinner. I'm starving."

Tab went to his room. The air was lighter, friendly. The room was bright, even with the lights off and the curtains in their half-closed state. He opened his closet doors. No eyeless man in beige coveralls. No malicious face glaring at him from the cut-pile nylon floor. He sat crisscross in front of the closet and stared into its darkness. When was the last time he'd been comfortable reaching inside for his shoes or his blue jeans? When was the last time he'd left the doors open for this long? Not since May, at least.

Dr. Clifford had yet to discuss performing any kind of exposure therapy to help Tab overcome his fear of the well of darkness waiting within his closet. But Tab had managed to reclaim some confidence anyway. As a show of support for himself, he thought he might leave the closet door open for a while. All night long, perhaps. Even while he was in the room sleeping. The house felt safe again. The closet existed inside the house. Therefore, the closet must be safe.

He slid the small garbage can that resided under his desk to the closet, placing it beside the open right fold. If the urge to close the door overpowered him, he would first need to move the trash can or knock it over. Knocking it over might make noises that would wake the rest of the house. He hoped his over-consideration, his desire to not disturb others, would prevent him from acting. He propped the left fold with his desk chair. It rocked backward when he let go, striking the door with a noisome *thunk*.

"What are you doing in there, Tab?" his mom shouted from downstairs.

"Nothing! Moving some stuff around!"

"Well, keep it down! I'm trying to soothe a headache!"

Now he had to deal with two noisemakers in order to close the doors. However, he did not think he would need either of them. He did not think he would be tempted at all to close the closet door. The more he worked against his fears, instead of feeding them by worrying about what *might* happen, the more confident he became that Roy was gone.

In the remaining daylight, Tab sensed nothing sinister about the closet, his room, or anything within. Things felt different at night, when it was quiet and dark. When he was alone on Red Alert. He allowed the *Star Trek* reference to overcome the buzzing in his brain. Jeremy might be the family *Ghostbusters* fan. For Tab, it was always sci-fi in general and *Star Trek* in particular.

His prep for his battle against his anxiety done, Tab grabbed his Strathmore and pencil. He settled in with them after propping some pillows against his headboard. The effort created a seat in which he could comfortably lean, using his upright thighs as a desk. A half-hour after he began sketching, the image of Captain Kirk took shape on the page. Kirk was pointing a phaser at the viewer as he was being transported away.

Someday, he hoped to meet William Shatner and shake his hand. He might even ask him to sign this sketch, assuming he didn't draw another that was a thousand times better before then. It was a good one, indeed. His best so far.

"Tab!" his mom called. He turned his head in that direction and cocked it so he could listen. "Jeremy! Time to eat!"

He smiled and went to close the sketchbook. But before he did, he glanced again at the Captain Kirk drawing. At some point between now and the time he'd completed the sketch and looked away, he had scratched out Kirk's eyes with the tip of his pencil. Puzzled, he set the pencil on the bed beside him. Then he turned the page over and held it up to the window. Two pinpricks of light from the setting sun filtered through the paper. Not only had he scratched out Kirk's eyes, but he'd also poked holes through them.

After closing the sketchbook and flinging it onto his desk, he glanced down at his hands. If he had moved them while he was listening to his mother, he hadn't been aware. There had been no twinge or strain of effort. The graphite marks across Kirk's face had been heavy, as if he'd been stabbing the page with the point instead of sketching on it. The pencil callous on his index finger didn't seem any different. There was no white-to-pink transition like there was after he'd borne down while writing or drawing.

Doubts about leaving the closet door open crept into his mind. He swallowed, trying to maintain the confidence he'd enjoyed all afternoon. The circumference of his pencil was warm to the touch. It wouldn't have had time to cool from his body heat. Of course it wouldn't. It had been a long day with a lot of travel and thinking and work. Surely he had scratched out Kirk's eyes when his mom distracted him with her dinner call.

As if by summons, the call came again. "Tab! Come on, kiddo! Let's eat!"

"Get your butt in here, Tabitha!" Jeremy said. His mother's irritable shushing sound followed the jibe.

"On my way," Tab said. Dinner would help him clear his mind again. Dinner, and then he'd peel back the bandage over his Steri-Strips to make sure nothing bad was happening under there. Dr. El had said to call if there were any problems, after all. It only made sense. He'd need to keep a close watch for them.

Yeah, it was going to be a wonderful night. Everything was going to be alright.

CHAPTER TWENTY-FIVE

Quiet. It was the first time Sandra had experienced it, or at least been aware of experiencing it, since the May flood. Especially so after Tim died. But it was a double-edged sword. She was unable to sleep, having spent most of the night trying to find something to read in bed or to listen to on her iPhone. Morning was fast approaching. She dreaded facing it without rest.

At first there had been peace. The silence of the house meant that Tab's anxieties had finally abated. The removal of his bump had the side effect of removing Roy from the family dynamic. Jeremy and Tab could be their separate selves now if they wanted, and Sandra no longer felt as though she needed to either fear her youngest son or for his well-being.

She'd apologized to Tab for not believing him in the first place. But now that her world had finally started to settle down, Sandra discovered that she still had her doubts. They bubbled to the surface of her mind and over it into her heart, like the foam on top of a glass of soda pop. Yes, there were many coincidences and strange things that had happened around their home and around Tab in particular since the flood. Yet Dr. Clifford had been able to rationally account for ways in which much of that could have happened sans ghost. And if there really had been a ghost, why did it have to be Roy?

Some part of herself that she didn't much like proposed that Tab could have lied to her about never seeing the *Echo* article before. All children lied sometimes, even the notoriously scrupulous ones. Maybe he did it for attention, made himself appear to be haunted by this thing he'd read about, not comprehending just how heinous, inappropriate, even hateful a scheme it would be to force his mother to suddenly relive the worst trauma of her life. Although it if *was* a scheme, it felt a little too devious and sophisticated for a nine-year-old, creative or no.

Seated crisscross alone on the bed she'd shared so long with Tim, Sandra reached for the nightstand and switched on the dusty white noise machine that sat atop it. Ocean waves with the occasional cry of a seagull permeated the air around her. She donned a sleep mask to enhance the effect, stretching out her legs and lying back slowly until the back of her head sank into her pillow. She imagined herself on a tethered raft, anchored but drifting, on the rippling ocean.

She had finally begun to drift when the visage of Seb Tanner, her ocean breeze-ruffled Facebook friend, swam into her mind. He emerged from the ocean beneath her raft, his thick hair, muscular arms, and practically hairless nude torso dripping salt water onto her soft belly as he curled himself over the edge of the float and settled in beside her. His skin had broken out in goose flesh as a gust of wind blew over them. Yet she could feel his warmth beside her. And she longed to entwine her left arm around his right as they lay there together.

Smiling, Sandra tilted her face to his, expecting to find him smiling back at her. Ready to once again invite her to escape, to put Tim, the farm, her trauma, and everything else in the past. To start anew, as if her current life had been someone else's. How many times had she fantasized about that very thing? Innumerable.

But Seb was not there. Suddenly she was no longer on the ocean but standing at Whitt's gas station in another part of Hollow County. On her left, a grime-stained Roy approached, a forced benevolent smile spread over his mug. Just as he drew near enough for her to smell his sweat, the scene changed again. She was at home, having arrived there after dark, disheveled, sobbing, and in pain. She'd had to tell Tim what happened in spite of Roy's warning that she should tell no one. Her husband screamed in her face, although not at her, enraged and bellowing at the top of his lungs. Although he stood right there in front of her, his rage seemed to come from somewhere in the distance, as if she was watching it on a television set.

And there was some other sound there as well. A smaller, pitched higher scream from elsewhere in the house. She recognized the voice but could not immediately place it.

"Mom!"

That's all it took. Sandra whipped the sleep mask off her face, threw back her covers, and spun out of bed. The sleep that had just begun to overtake her bolted away like a family dog during a fireworks display.

Tab. Something was wrong with Tab. The quiet, all too brief, had been broken again. On some level to which she could not entirely admit, Sandra felt relieved.

CHAPTER TWENTY-SIX

Somewhere in the deep of night, Tab sat upright in bed and clapped a hand to his temple. Fiery pain and the distinct throb of his pulse there made him want cry out, but he resisted. Maybe the Steri-Strips had come loose. If the wound had opened and was bleeding, he would need to wake his mom. Until he knew for sure, though, he was not willing to take that step.

He slid from under his bed covers and padded to the bathroom. Peeling back one corner of the bandage, he peeked beneath the covering. What he saw horrified him. A gelatinous orb of sickly yellow pulsed and oozed inside the hollow of the wound, stretching the Steri-Strips. One strip had pulled entirely loose. Thick, sticky pus crept from around the edges. The burnt orange mess pooled at the spot where Tab's bandage remained adhered to his skin.

"Mom?" Tab said. It squeaked out of his mouth. He swallowed, cleared his throat, and shouted, "Mom!"

The response was immediate. Sandra darted toward him, the hem of one of Tim's old hair band T-shirts flapping around her thighs. Tab didn't know who Twisted Sister was, but he'd seen both his dad and his mom wear that shirt before. He admired the singer's tight curls, long hair, and colorful face. A waterfall of blond hair overflowed his shoulders. Toward the viewer he screamed WE'RE NOT GONNA TAKE IT. Once again, Tab wished he could grow his hair out long. Not being able to see his temple might put it out of his mind for a while.

"Mom, something's wrong! It hurts!"

Sandra joined Tab in front of his bathroom mirror. She grabbed the corner of the bandage he had peeled and pulled it the rest of the way off his skin. She examined his wound, then turned on the water and dampened one edge of the gauze, which she used to dab at Tab's temple.

"The doctor said not to get it wet!"

"I know, I know, sweetie, but I need to clean around it so I can make it out better. I'm not touching the cut or the strips." She tossed the bandage onto the sink counter. It was a disgusting mess of wet and slime. Tab gagged when he looked at it, forcing himself to turn away.

"I think it might be infected already," she said. "It's red and inflamed."

"What's that yellow thing?" Tab asked. His voice trembled. "Is it the eye? Is the eye back again?" It was strange acknowledging his third eye aloud to another person. He chided himself for doing so. But if his mother had any concerns about him thinking he was growing a third eyeball, she did not react.

"I think it's just some pus," she said. "Let's clean it up and put a fresh bandage on it. I'll give Dr. El a call when her office opens in the morning. She might have to stitch it up after all if the strips aren't going to hold."

"It's not *him*?"

Sandra smiled, weak. Exhaustion from too little sleep and the slowing of the adrenaline rush created a glaze over her eyes. "No, hon. He's gone. I'm sure of it. A hundred percent sure that Roy is not going to bother us anymore." She unwrapped a fresh square of gauze pulled from a small package of the stuff she'd placed in his bathroom for just such an emergency. "I don't like leaving that strip undone, but I'm not sure there's much we can do about it until Dr. El opens. If it starts to bleed, we'll need to go to the ER and have them stitch you up."

"Do I need to check it?"

Sandra sighed. "No, don't keep checking it. That'll wear out the adhesive on the tape. You'll know if it's bleeding, hon. You'll see some of it soak through the bandage."

There was another horrifying thought in a night full of them. The dry newness of the fresh bandage on his temple along with his mother's careful application provided some comfort. Suddenly Tab felt as sleepy as his mother looked. Through a small textured glass window, the first rays of dawn cast pale blue light. Tab and Sandra noted it simultaneously.

"Morning already," Sandra said, disgust in her voice. It reminded Tab of Winnie Sanderson in Disney's *Hocus Pocus*. He could not suppress a smile. Sandra caught it and knew what he was thinking. "Another glorious morning!" she said in her best imitation of a wicked witch. "Makes me sick!"

Tab laughed.

"Go on back to bed, kiddo," Sandra said. "I think I'm awake now. I'll give Dr. El a call in a few hours when her office is open. We'll fix you up."

Tab stole back to his room, tiptoeing past Jeremy's in spite of the fact that even the sound of Tab calling for his mother hadn't roused his brother. He collapsed onto his bed and shut his eyes, but not before catching a glimpse of—something—amid the darkness on the floor of his closet. He sat up again, squinting, dilating his pupils as much as possible in the wan light of the morning.

There, cross-legged beneath the hanging clothes, sat Stinkeye Roy. Still wearing his beige coveralls. Still with his eyes gouged out. The translucent man seemed to be aware Tab had observed him. He smiled, revealing orange-yellow teeth coated in nasty, wet grime. It looked as if he'd eaten an entire box of Oreo cookies. Or, worse, chewed his way out of the grave.

"MOM! MOM!"

This time, he managed to awaken his brother, too. Jeremy stumbled dully into his room, a mighty yawn and involuntary stretch overpowering him as he did. "What's going on?"

"GET MOM! HE'S BACK!" Tab pointed at the open closet. He and Jeremy followed his finger and looked upon nothing. Roy had vanished. Again.

CHAPTER TWENTY-SEVEN

Sandra opted to not call Dr. El back after all. Instead, she gathered a wailing Tab from his bed and struggled to lead him into their family room. Jeremy followed close behind, still half-asleep enough to not bother with questions, for which Sandra was grateful. She sat Tab down on the sofa and peeled back the dry bandage she'd covered the remains of his bump with not half an hour ago.

The growth was back, as big and boiling red as it had been before their visit to Dr. El's. What's more, the skin the dermatologist had sliced open had healed. The Steri-Strips dangled loose around it, barely attached to Tab now. Sandra peeled them off him, folding them inside the bandage. She pressed an index finger against the bump.

"Ow!" Tab said, squirming. The mound deflated and turned white in the middle only to fill in and return to Rudolph red seconds later. There was no hint of scarring. No sign at all that Dr. El had performed surgery.

"It's back, isn't it?" Tab asked. Immense tears rolled from the corners of his eyes and down his cheeks. "The bump is back."

Sandra nodded, solemn. The bump had, indeed, returned. And Roy along with it, apparently.

She leaned back on the couch. Jeremy, perhaps sensing an imminent family meeting, yawned and plopped onto the floor beside her while Tab sobbed, swiping at the tears and snot with the elastic end of one sleeve of his Spider-Man PJs.

"I think it's time I told you boys some things," she started. "You're really not old enough to know all this yet. I don't think you ever will be. This is not the kind of thing you want to hear from a mom or dad. But considering what's happening around us, I don't think I have a choice anymore." And, she thought, getting it all out might help them find some way to stop it. "Wait here for a minute."

After retrieving the old newspaper article about Roy's arrest from their study, Sandra sat beside Tab. She patted the empty cushion on her other side, beckoning Jeremy to join them on the higher plane.

"A lot has been happening since your dad died."

"Before," Tab said, a hitch of despair in his voice.

"Okay, a lot has been happening since the May flood. I need you both to sit quietly for the next few minutes and let me talk. I have a lot to tell you. Some of it Tab already knows, but some he doesn't. I'm sure you, Jeremy, don't know much of anything about what's been happening. For that, I'm sorry. We're a family, and that means we struggle together and we triumph together even if your dad's not around anymore."

She swallowed. "This is harder than I thought." Turning to Tab, "Let's start by filling Jeremy in on what's been happening with you. After, we can move on to what neither of you know. Make sense?"

Tab nodded. His head indicated certainty, but doubt lurked behind those shiny baby blue eyes she loved so much. Sandra resolved to do her best to make the tale as truthful as possible without creating more trauma for the kid. Or introducing it to Jeremy.

For the next half hour, Sandra and Tab together brought Jeremy up to date on everything the younger boy had experienced since the May flood. Tab went so far as to add information by recounting in full detail the story of the demonic dog he thought he'd seen that night. It was, he explained, how he now believed he got the bump. The coincidences between the dog's attack and Roy's appearance in the cellar were too great to ignore.

Sandra recognized the dog story. Lost Hollow was replete with myths about demon dogs roaming the wooded areas of town. Rumor had it one of them was responsible for the disappearance of Tim's great aunt and her son back in the fifties. No one had ever produced evidence, though. Answers for what happened to Tim's aunt and the other folks who disappeared in the deluge of '55 had never presented themselves. Sandra was surprised no one had written a book about the place. Maybe that would be Jeremy's job someday, given his interest in the supernatural folklore of the town.

For two and a half hours, Sandra confided in the boys about Tim, as well as the man they knew as Roy. She skimmed over some elements, like details about how Roy had raped her. There was no need to provide them. It was enough for the boys to know that what he'd done was terrible and wrong, things that no man should ever do to a woman, or even to another man. She was careful to not reveal to Tab that she suspected Roy was his biological father. That would come later, after she could talk with Dr. Clifford about it, maybe. She didn't want Tab to conflate his entire existence with the evil done to her by Roy.

***

Maintaining her composure was not easy. The man who was not her husband approached, an attempt at an amicable smile smeared over the lower half of his creepy mug. It was not comforting. She'd been taught to not judge a book by its cover, and to extend that courtesy to others who might not look or think exactly like she does. But she'd also been taught to trust her gut. Something about this fellow was... well, *off*. The tingling sensation in her scalp and along the back of her neck, physiological warnings she recognized as the onset of her fight or flight, was evidence enough of that.

"Hey there," the man said. His voice was rough around the edges, as if he was unaccustomed to speaking softly, without anger. "I see you're not pumping the gas at the max flow rate for that pump. I've gotta back my truck in here on account of that's the side where the gas tank is. I also gotta get back to work on account of I'm running late. Can I show you how to make the gas pump faster?"

"I don't see a truck." Sandra maintained eye contact with her own reflection in the slice of triangular window near the back of her car but shook her head. Her upper lip trembled when she spoke. She hoped he didn't notice but was sure he probably did. "And I'm fine," she said. "I have it locked on the maximum. I know how to use a gas pump. You can use the one on the other side."

The man's insincere grin faltered. He gestured broadly toward the right side of Whitt's store, a ramshackle place at which Sandra had never before stopped. She'd only done so today because her tank was on empty and it was nearby. "I have it parked around back right now on account of you're hoggin' the pumps." He swiped an oily hand over the back of his neck and then across the stubble that peppered the front of it. "I don't think you understand what I'm saying. I'm not asking if you need help. I'm asking you to speed it up. That top notch in the lock don't set it to maximum. You gotta hold it and squeeze for that." He inched closer to her then. Sandra shrank back without thinking about it. The shank of the Accord's key protruded from between the second and third fingers of her right hand. She clenched it tighter, readying herself to plunge it into an eyeball if he did not stop.

He cut his eyes toward her fist. "Whoa, there," the man said. "I ain't gonna hurt you. I just wanted to demonstrate."

"I pump my own gas," Sandra replied. This time she eyed him directly, her voice leveled flat, meaning to sound unafraid. A warning. If he backed away now, things might not escalate to a scream for help and call to the police. But it was up to him to make that connection. She could warn him verbally, but in her experience such warnings only added further fuel to an angry man's rage.

"Well, I see you pumping your own gas," the man said. "I'm just trying to show you how to do it faster. That's all. Here, let me help."

Before she could react, the man had crossed the line connecting the gas nozzle to the pump and was behind her, the crook of his left elbow mashing her left arm into her ribs as he gripped the nozzle lever. His right hand landed on her right hip. He moved alarmingly fast for a man of his apparent age and build. He couldn't have been younger than forty-five, and his gut protruded over his belt in an awkward fashion inconsistent with his shoulder breadth and height. Almost as if he was hiding something under his shirt by making himself appear to have a larger belly than he did. His breath reeked of booze. She caught it in whiffs on the breeze, like the scent of some animal that had died and was rotting among the overgrowth along the side of a barren, single lane stretch of road in the middle of August.

His hand disappeared from her hip. She went to grab his left forearm with both hands, use his awkward footing and his own weight against him to wriggle free, but was stopped when he cinched that arm tight around her middle, pinning her own left arm to her side. At the same time, she felt something poke her in middle of her lower back. At first she thought it was his erection, but when he spoke again, she knew it was a handgun.

"Drop the keys. Get into the back seat. Lie down. Scream, and I shoot. Speak, and I shoot. Move, and I shoot. Got it?"

Sandra nodded. She glanced to the left, toward the gas station. There was no attendant in sight behind the large single pane of glass that served as a window into the store. A decal of the Gadsden flag, a coiled rattlesnake against a yellow background and the slogan DON'T TREAD ON ME, decorated its lower left corner. Beside it was pasted a square version of the Confederate flag, a sad familiar sight in Hollow County. There were no other souls in the parking lot now, either. There had been when she'd stopped to fuel up. Otherwise she wouldn't have stopped. Some time between her gassing up and this man's appearance they had all finished their business and driven away.

From her right came the sound of the car door opening. "Drop the keys now." She did. In the next instant, she'd been shoved inside her own car's back seat. She hit her head on the way down, hard enough to make her yelp. The man ducked inside behind her and shoved the barrel of the gun (an intimidatingly militaristic-looking pistol that she would later discover was a .357 Sig Sauer P226) into her rib. "Lie down and shut up. One more peep and I'll blow your head off."

She nodded, holding her breath while he bound her wrists and letting it go after he slammed the door closed. He snatched the keys from the ground, yanked the gas pump nozzle out of the fuel intake, and was in the car and driving before she'd finished her exhale. His movements had a practiced amount of gracefulness and dexterity in their rush contraindicative of the country awkwardness she had thought she perceived in him.

He had done this before.

✳✳✳

She shuddered, tried to dim the memory of what happened next. The boys did not need to know the rest of the details. They did not need to know that Roy drove her to the old rock quarry on the outskirts of Hollow County, a place few but bored teenagers and vagrants ever visited. They did not need to know how he'd forced himself on her, the pistol gripped firmly in his right hand the entire time. They did not need to know about the silent, shameful drive back to Lost Hollow, how Roy had pulled the car over along a barely paved backroad, launched her keys into the dense forested area on one side, and disappeared into a similarly dense section on the other.

"I ain't no goddamn murderer, but if you tell, I kill," he'd shouted as he ran. "You and everyone you love. I know who you are."

The remainder of the details were less important than what happened next, and all of that had been published in a detached, just-the-facts way by the *Hollow River Echo*. Among the things Sandra herself hadn't known until the article hit print was that Roy had stolen ("borrowed," in his words) the Sig Sauer from a radical political extremist group's meeting in a back room of Whitt's where she'd been refueling. Roy was a proud member. In a way, she was relieved she hadn't caught the eye of an employee during the attack. She now thought it was unlikely they'd have helped her.

She swallowed. Her throat was gritty and dry. She showed the boys the mug shot from the newspaper clipping she'd taken from the study, allowing each of them to examine it. The details in the article seemed sanitized when compared to her memory, but even it was too much for the boys, she thought. She summarized it for them in what she felt were age-appropriate terms. Her head swam in what was fast becoming a fugue state of unreality for her, the sensation that it was all happening again. That there was nothing she could to do stop it.

She was careful to ensure that her sons understood that sex itself is not evil. She explained, as best as she could, that Roy was a bad man who abused sexuality, although she wasn't sure how much Tab could comprehend of what she was saying. Tim had already had "the birds and the bees" discussion with Jeremy but had not had the chance with Tab. Sandra dreaded having to have that chat with the younger son herself, especially after having to tell him about Roy. At what age does a boy need to understand that sex and sexual desire are natural but should never be forced? Tab had not yet shown any interest in girls, or boys either for that matter. How could she know when the time was right?

Soon, the time came to tell them about what Tim had done. She glossed over the graphic details about what had occurred in the rear parking lot of the bar that night, but she did reveal Tim's role in it. That was a risk. They might talk, implicating their mother as part of a murder cover-up. She pushed the thought away. Who would they live with if she went to prison? Their grandparents were too old and sickly to take them. No, trust was not easy, even with her own offspring. But for now, it was a survival issue.

"I need you both to know that wronged people often feel like they need justice in order to move on with their lives," she said after telling them about Tim's deed. "Only a few ever get it. Sometimes, when you can't find justice under the law because of the Old Boys network or whatever you want to call it, you think you have to take justice into your own hands. Even if doing so can cause you serious trouble with the law. And society.

"Now, your father acted out of rage as well as the injustice the county and state inflicted on me. He shouldn't have killed that man. It's true what they say: two wrongs don't make a right. But all in all, your dad was a good man who made a terrible mistake in the heat of the moment. He suffered the consequences for it, too. He was almost never an angry man before that night. I wish you both could remember him before all of his yelling and nerves. I could not say the same for Roy."

"Is that why we're being haunted now?" Tab asked. His voice was small and weak. "Because Dad killed him?"

"I think so."

"Why is he just haunting me? Why does he go away whenever Jeremy's around?"

Here comes the hardest part, Sandra thought. She caressed Tab's cheek and brushed a lengthy strand of curls away from his forehead. "I wasn't looking forward to this part of the conversation," she started. "But I guess it's only right you learn about this sometime. By telling you now I hope I can save you some therapy later in life."

Jeremy scoffed. "We already know Santa Claus isn't real." Sandra eyed him. His tone was peak Jeremy, but it appeared to be an act. His face was drained of color, his brow furrowed. The older boy put on a good show, but deep down in there somewhere lurked some humanity.

"That's not it," Sandra said. "Now listen to me, because this concerns you, too. I have a feeling Tab and I are going to need to rely on you more than we have if we're going to be rid of Roy forever."

Tab's breaths came more rapidly now. He'd seen the doubt and worry in her eyes, and it was scaring him. "What is it?" he asked. "Just go ahead and tell me."

She laid her hands on his shoulders, forcing back tears and disregarding a sudden need to blow her nose. "It is possible your dad was not your biological father," she said, relying on more formal language to describe the latter role.

She hoped it might lessen the sting. She also never liked the words "real dad" when it came to defining whoever injected the sperm that fertilized her egg.

"When—" she gulped down a thick wad of snot. "When this ghost, Roy, attacked me, he was still a man. I was not yet pregnant with you. I got pregnant with you not long after, though. Your dad, beautiful soul that he was, decided he did not want to take a paternity test to find out for sure whether he or Roy fathered you. As far as he was concerned, you're his and you'll always be his no matter what the DNA says."

Moisture glistened at the rims of Tab's eyes. Sandra's heart raced. "I don't want you to think or believe your dad was not your 'real dad,'" she said, employing air quotes around the last two words. "Tim Beard, the man you were named after, is your real dad. He put food in your tummy. He put sketchbooks and pencils in your hands. He taught you how to use a toothbrush and how to tie your shoes. He loved you and your brother the same, and both of you more than anything else on this planet. Always remember that.

"As you grow up, you'll remember things from this time in your life that make you wonder whether he loved you. It'll be a time he shouted at you for something you did or something else he didn't like. The man could shout! Or it'll be a time when he was too distant, unwilling, or unable to help you when you thought you needed his help. But I want you to know none of those things dim the light of how much he loved you."

She cleared her throat. "We all—men and women alike—think of the male half of the species as simple creatures, but that's far from the truth. They don't show their depths. American men in particular have been taught it's what men are supposed to do: shove their fears, their emotions, and their hurt down as far as they can. Pretend they're not bothered or that it doesn't exist. What they don't understand is all that pressure has to release sometime, like stretching a rubber band to its limit. Eventually, it's going to snap.

"But you should know that when your dad was angry or distant, it wasn't because of you. It was because other things haunted him he couldn't express, or couldn't deal with in an external way."

Tab sobbed. Two giant tears spilled down his face, one from the corner of each eye. On Sandra's other side, she heard Jeremy clear his throat, as if he, too, was fighting back tears. *I broke the ice with him*, she thought. Jeremy had always been a smart-ass. Sandra told Tim more than once she feared he'd grow up to be the guy everyone called a dick behind his back. At this moment, though, his humanity surfaced. It was a small umbrella of relief in a downpour of despair.

"Am I going to turn into a bad guy?" Tab asked. His voice was hoarse, quiet. "I don't want to turn into a bad guy like Roy."

Sandra shined a sweet, loving smile at him. "No, sweetheart. You will turn out to be whoever you want to turn out to be. I promise. Our traumas and our mistakes and our life experiences do *influence* who we become, but they don't decide who we are for us. Nor do other people and their opinions."

"Why do some people turn bad, then?"

Sandra cleared her throat. It was a wry sound. "That's a question people have been trying to answer since humans evolved," she said. "My point is you don't have to be a clone of Roy. Yes, you *might* have Roy's DNA. And that's still a *might*. Unless we do a DNA test and compare it to your dad, we won't know for sure. You're also half me, though. That's a *fact*. So even if Roy fathered you and your biological roots have any determination over who you're going to be, you'll never be Roy. Your blood might be your heritage, but it's not your destiny."

Tab breathed a sigh of relief. Sandra felt her oldest son's hand on her shoulder. She turned to him and, to her surprise, discovered tears streaming down his face, too. "Am I Dad's son?" he asked with a tremor.

"You're definitely the son of Tim Beard," Sandra said, laughing. "I think I'd know even if I wasn't two hundred percent sure about your DNA. You have your dad's swagger." She smirked. "If not quite his temperament."

Jeremy swiped at his tears and running nose with his bare forearm. "So why am I here?"

Sandra's response was immediate. "You're here to stick up for your little brother. Roy disappears whenever you come into the room. I have a theory about that. If Roy is Tab's biological father, he's somehow using that to attach himself to Tab. That's why none of the rest of us can see him." She paused for a second, reflecting. "That's why your bump grew back almost as soon as we got rid of it. The bump isn't what connects you to Roy. It's just something he accesses to manipulate you. There's an old saying, 'blood calls to blood.' Some truth to it, I think. If Roy's blood is in you, that's how he's able to reach you."

"And because Dad's blood is in Jeremy—"Tab said. Sandra nodded, encouraging him to continue. "Because Dad's blood is in Jeremy, then Dad is connected to Jeremy!"

"Right!"

Jeremy scowled. "But I haven't seen anything like what y'all said Tab's been going through. No ghosts. No weird stuff happening I don't remember."

"You weren't attacked by the dog or whatever it was the night of the flood, either," Sandra said. "That seems to have been the catalyst for the whole thing with Tab. And you *have* been smelling your father's aftershave."

"What's a catalyst?" Tab asked.

"Accelerant," Jeremy said. "Like when you pour lighter fluid on charcoal and light it."

"More or less." Sandra leaned back against the couch and wrapped an arm around each boy. "Now, what we have to figure out is how to use the tools we know we have now to stop Roy for good."

Jeremy wrinkled his nose, puzzlement in his eyes. Then he gasped. "Mom! I can't spend every second of my life babysitting Tab. I want to go to college someday. Or start a paranormal investigation service or something, like those guys on Travel Channel. I can't have *him* hanging around all the time so his invisible friend doesn't show up."

Sandra smirked and patted her eldest son twice on his left hand. "I'm not asking you to do that. Chill out. Tab, can you remember any specific things you were doing or thinking any of the other times Roy wasn't around?"

Tab shook his head. "I don't know. He's shown up in the back seat of the car a lot, even when Jeremy is around. He showed up at Dad's funeral, too, when—when—"

Sandra waited, nodding encouragement.

"When Dad's hand grabbed me from inside his casket!" The words ended in another gigantic sob. Sandra snatched a tissue from a Kleenex box sitting on the coffee table in front of them and dabbed at his eyes. "It's okay," she said. "You never told me about that."

"He said he was going to help me. He reached out of his casket and grabbed my arm and said he was trying to warn me. But I think I'd already started to wonder about Dad being a good man. I started to think Roy was the good man and Dad was the bad man. I didn't know what to believe." He stopped short of telling her that his dad had called her a whore. It didn't feel right to disclose that after she'd spoken so glowingly of him. Something clicked in

Tab's head at that moment. If his dad had murdered Roy for raping his mom, why had he contradicted that story from the grave?

Sandra pulled Tab close to her, pressing his damp face against her shoulder. "I'm sorry, sweetie. I'm so sorry. But listen, I can confirm for you that your dad is the good man, okay? Roy? He's just mad he didn't completely get away with what he did."

"Are you sad you had me?" Tab asked, glancing up from her shoulder to meet her gaze. His eyes were wide and sorrowful.

Sandra smiled, warmth in her expression, and shook her head. "Not at all. I'm grateful I have you, Tab. I'm grateful I have both of my boys. I can't imagine what life would be like without you both and I don't want to."

"But if it wasn't for Roy—"

"Shh." She pressed a finger to his lips. "I know. I know. Dr. Clifford always says in his books that even our trauma can sometimes create positive things. When we work on fixing the trauma. It might be a higher sense of self-esteem, or a better understanding of all the things that make you who you are. In my case, the best thing to come out of the trauma I've been through was you, Tab." Her eyes stung, misting over. "If you're asking whether I would trade you for not having to live with the nightmares and the trauma of what Roy did to me, or not having to live with your dad's act of revenge, the answer is 'no.' I wouldn't trade you for the whole world on a silver platter."

"Dr. Clifford," Tab said. He sat up and pulled himself free of his mother's arms. "Dr. Clifford!"

"What about him?"

Excitement washed over Tab's face. His small blue eyes glowed with it. "The tools! When y'all thought Roy was just my imagination, Dr. Clifford kept talking about 'tools' we could use to keep Roy from taking over my head. After he told me to try talking back to Roy, I did and it sort of worked for a while."

"Hurrr durrr, then why'd ya stop?" Jeremy asked.

"Jeremy!"

"Sorry."

"I already told you. I believed him when he told me he was here to help me. He was supposed to help me, protect me." He stuck out his tongue at his brother, squinting his eyes as he did.

"Alright, now. Let's stay focused." Sandra fought the urge to send Jeremy to his room. It had become her go-to correction for him. Too easy. That, and it was not working. Separating them would only allow Roy to return. Even if Roy didn't, it would solve nothing to shove the older boy out of the loop again. Besides, the boys might finally get along better if they spent a little more time around each other.

She motioned for them to stay put while she went to the study bookshelf and pulled a Dr. Clifford paperback, *Soothing the Obsessive-Compulsive Beast*, from its space there. The spines of the other Clifford books were so cracked from rereads that the titles were illegible. This one she'd not read as much, but it sounded right for the situation.

She opened the book to its Table of Contents, using two fingers to skim down the list of bold chapter titles. There was the obligatory foreword by an esteemed colleague, chapters describing what it's like to live with OCD. Information on OCD as disorder and as a symptom of childhood trauma followed. The book was a complete self-help recipe, like a wizard's spell book from a fantasy movie. The first chapter in the third section was titled TALKING BACK TO THE BEAST. Five chapters followed, each beginning with a gerund and ending with the term "beast."

Sandra shut the book, tucking it at her side. She started back to the family room but broke into a run when a reverberating *thud* preceded the sound of shattering glass. Dashing back to the family room, she discovered Jeremy sprawled on the floor there. He lay unconscious, bleeding from a wound on his crown. Tab sat at his feet, rocking to-and-fro on his bottom and clasping a knee in each hand. Sandra ran to Jeremy first, allowing the book to fall from her hands. She rolled him onto his back and patted his face, trying to rouse him.

"Tab! Call an ambulance!" was all she could think to say.

CHAPTER TWENTY-EIGHT

His brother was breathing, but that was all. Tab grabbed his mother's iPhone, unlocked it, and dialed 911. He put the call on speaker and laid it on the floor beside his mother and brother. As the remote end of the call rang, Sandra said, "Go get the ice pack out of the freezer. Get some towels, too. Dampen one of them. Hurry."

By the time Tab returned, the 911 operator was assuring Sandra an ambulance was on the way. He handed his mother the towels and ice pack. With the damp towel, she dabbed at blood around the cross-shaped puncture wound in Jeremy's scalp. The dry towels she rolled and placed under his neck. This allowed the back of his head to rest on the floor and his mouth to hang open. After clearing away enough blood to reveal the wound, she used a clean corner of the damp towel to apply direct pressure.

In the distance, the warble of one of Hollow County's ambulance sirens swelled. "I can hear the ambulance coming," Sandra shouted to the iPhone. Then she turned on Tab. "What in the blue blazes happened in here?"

A lump rose from somewhere in his chest and plugged his throat. "I—" he started. "I think I tripped him on accident. He hit his head on the coffee table. He's going to be okay, isn't he? He's just knocked out, right?"

Before Sandra could answer, the ambulance arrived. Blessings of a small town with a satellite EMT station.

"Go meet them," she said. "Bring them right here." She stroked Jeremy's forehead with two fingers and kissed him.

Tab dashed outside to meet two EMTs. A tall man, taller than he had ever seen, with smiling green eyes, curly blond hair, and enormous hands carried some rectangular equipment in one hand. A smaller woman, brunette with broad shoulders and muscular forearms, strode beside him. Tab motioned them inside. "He's in there." He indicated the family room, leading the way and creating a Tab-sized breeze behind him as he ran.

The two EMTs kept pace. In the family room, they knelt by the supine boy. The man hooked up his machine, which transmitted heart rhythm and breathing information to a small monitor. The woman took over attempting to rouse Jeremy as Sandra looked on. His mom's ashen face was lined with worry. For the first time, Tab saw what his mother might look like when she became an old lady. Her crying beside his unconscious brother broke his heart.

He sat in the rocker-recliner by the couch and trained his eyes on the black television screen on the other side of the room. It was the one on which he watched his syndicated game shows and, sometimes, the news. He wanted to snag the remote and pop it on, but instinct warned him it would be bad form. His brother was not well. Might die because of him, in fact. Turning on the TV would make it seem like he didn't care.

He rocked, as muted as he could, his ghostly reflection swaying to-and-fro in the blank screen. In the lower left corner, his mother crouched over the other figures on the floor. The lack of light on her face distorted it, obscuring her distress in the reflection. He preferred to focus on himself. Blocking the scene allowed him to dissociate from it, to pretend he was somewhere else. Soon, he saw another figure materialize behind him.

Roy's malicious grin swam into focus first. Then his torso and hands appeared. His emergence seemed slower in the screen than it was when he appeared in Tab's closet. Was he weaker? Because Jeremy's here? The man's enormous fingers clasped the back of Tab's rocker, one on the left side of the boy's head and one on the right. The arms attached to those hands swung back and forth in the same rhythm as Tab himself.

"Well, now," said the mocking voice from behind. The Roy reflected in the television lip-synched the words. "I wondered how I was going to take care of the little chore that was your asshole of a brother. You done went and did it for me!"

"It was an accident!" The EMTs ignored Tab's outburst, but Sandra twisted toward him. "I didn't hurt him on purpose. He stood up to go find Mom. I was going to go with him. Our legs got tangled as we were standing up and he fell!"

"I told you both to stay put," Sandra said. Her voice was flat, emotionless.

"I told you both to stay put!" Roy mocked, his imitation unrealistically shrill. "Well I, for one, am glad you didn't stay put, little man." He bounded around the rocker. His work boots glided through the calves of the woman who was trying to wake Jeremy. She shivered but seemed otherwise unbothered. He rounded in front of Tab and knelt so they were eye-to-mangled eye sockets. Tab did not turn away but tried to focus *through* Roy, like drivers in a blinding fog who stare at the painted lines to find their way.

"I didn't mean to hurt him!"

The male EMT spoke up. "Of course you didn't," he said, his voice soothing in spite of the burly man he was. "We need to try to wake him right now." To the other EMT, "No airway obstruction. BP is 118/79. No obvious signs of cardiac arrest. Heart rate is bit fast, but not alarming. Pupils dilate. Blood sugar is 100 milligrams. I assume he's eaten recently?" He glanced at Sandra, who nodded. "He's got trauma to the top of the head."

"Trauma drama!" Roy said. "Could of told 'em! In fact, y'all *did* tell them, didn't ya? They're just running up the bill with all these other tests, I bet."

Tab squeezed his eyes shut and plugged his fingers in his ears. "I don't see you. I can't hear you."

Roy answered inside his head. "Oh, you can see and hear me alright. Your brother's dying and look what you're doing. You're sitting there like a lump on a temple with your fingers in your ears and your eyes shut, trying to pretend like it ain't happening. Is this the kind of man you want to be? Is this what Tim Beard raised?" He scoffed. "I coulda made you a man, son!"

"He's not dying!" Tab said. "And I don't want to be a man. Not like you!" Fingers wrapped themselves around his wrists and guided his hands from his ears. He opened his eyes to the blurred visage of his mother leaning over him.

"Tab, please calm down," she said. "I can't deal with both you and your brother right now. No, he's not dying. He'll be fine. They've got him awake now. See?"

Tab followed her nod and saw Jeremy's eyes were open. He tried to prop himself up on his elbows, but the EMTs made him stay flat while they continued their work. One of them began the "follow my finger" concussion test. Based on their reaction, Jeremy seemed to pass it with flying colors.

"See? He got his bell rung a little bit, but he's going to be fine."

As if to confirm, the burly man spoke up then. "Since he was unconscious for a bit, I do think a doctor should have a look. Just in case. I don't think he's going to need stitches.

It's a nasty looking little puncture wound, but it's not as bad as it appears."

"But all the blood—"

"Head wounds bleed more than cuts on your arms or hands," the man said. "Trust me, this is a minor one. We'll ready him for transport, though. Better safe than sorry. Do you want to follow us?"

Tab's rage boiled over. He spun around on the cushion of the rocker, his knees sinking deep into the nap, and screamed at Roy. "YOU LIED TO ME AGAIN!"

Except Roy wasn't there anymore. Only empty air and the hallway filled the space behind the rocker. On the floor was the copy of Dr. Clifford's book that his mother had dropped. Tab returned to his seat, cutting his eyes to the left to see if the EMTs were staring at him. The man and the woman both averted their gaze and went back to doting on Jeremy.

"He was here, wasn't he?" Sandra asked. "Roy."

Tab nodded solemnly. "I guess he left when Jeremy woke up. He's going to come back as soon as Jeremy is away or asleep. I know he will. I'm never going to be rid of him, am I?"

Sandra pursed her lips, eyes focused somewhere above him for a few seconds. "Does he have to be transported?" she asked the EMTs. "Can we take him to the ER ourselves or something? If not, can Tab ride in the ambulance with him while I follow behind in the car? The little one doesn't like being separated from his brother in weird situations like this."

That was a lie, of course. Current situation aside, the brothers had an unspoken understanding. Neither of them wanted to be bothered by the other. Their disparate interests and at-odds personalities meant they interacted only when they had to. Or when there was a Batman movie on. Even then, they seldom spoke unless Jeremy wanted to lob insults. Tab's trust in his mother's honesty had faded some since Roy's appearance. For reasons not the least of which were the questions over Tab's own lineage. He could forgive this white lie to the EMTs, though, if it meant he could keep Roy at bay until they figured out how to do so without his brother.

The male EMT sighed. "As a rule, we allow one family member to ride along, and only if they ride up front so they can be buckled in. It's an older family member most of the time, though." He nodded at Tab. "He isn't five feet tall yet. State law says a kid under five feet has to ride in a rear seat."

"Okay, so what if we take him to the ER ourselves?"

The man's tone changed, his expression betraying the offense in his head. "Are you refusing transport?"

"Yeah," Sandra said. She combed her hair out of her face and met the man's eyes. "Yeah, I guess I am. If it's safe for us to load him in the car, we'll take him ourselves. Can you walk, hon?"

"I think so," Jeremy said, his voice strong as ever. Tab took it as a sign that he was fine after all.

"Let's see if you can even stand up first, huh?" the EMT said. "Try standing up. I'll help you." The EMT sat Jeremy up and wrapped one thick arm around the boy's waist. He draped Jeremy's left arm over his own shoulder. Together, the two pushed upward on their legs until Jeremy was on his feet. The EMT released him, but without much distance in case he started to collapse again. He didn't.

"Are you dizzy or anything? Everything look steady?"

Jeremy nodded. "Yep. Seems normal to me."

"Okay. I'm right beside you. I want you to take a few steps. Can you walk to that TV and back?" Jeremy did, and did so at a normal pace. The EMT shook his head, smacked his lips, a sardonic grin spread across the lower half of his face. "Well, I guess you're good to go." He turned to Sandra. "If y'all don't need anything else, we'll mark you down as having refused transport and be on our way."

Sandra thanked them, and they were gone. Tab wondered what they might be saying to each other as they drove away, discussing his strange outbursts from the rocker. What might they say about his odd mom, too, insisting her injured son not ride in the ambulance because her younger and apparently healthy son might miss him.

"Mom," Jeremy said as she monitored the ambulance turning left out of their driveway. "I feel like I'm going to throw up."

"Everybody in the car," she said, snatching the Dr. Clifford book off the floor. She shoved it into a purse she grabbed from a table near the front door.

CHAPTER TWENTY-NINE

Despite being haunted and harangued by Stinkeye Roy, the sheer terror of his mother's fraught drive to the ER overshadowed Tab's previous anxieties. An hour's trip on a normal day, Sandra and the boys managed it in forty-five minutes. Tab gaped at the sedan's speedometer as it climbed past the 55 mph mark. At one point it landed on 90 but backed off when the ass-end of a trundling semi hauling two layers of brand new Subarus loomed large in the distance. The truck's hazards flashed an ominous beat in the candy-like colors of Subaru paint jobs.

"Mom, slow down!"

"Not now, hon," she said. "This is an emergency."

He tucked his hands under his thighs, choosing silence for the remainder of the trip. Now and then, his brother's head wobbled on his neck, as if he was about to pass out again. He never did puke. That was a good thing. But he was not well. Tab feared Jeremy would fall unconscious again, that he would be left to deal with Roy alone. Dealing with Roy at all was bad enough, but dealing with him by himself was the worst. His mom was too distracted to care. And Jeremy? Jeremy never cared at all.

The lights of Hollow River's downtown—most specifically the red glowing EMERGENCY ROOM sign—were a welcome sight when Sandra made the turn into the facility. Here she was forced to slow down because families and outpatients had to cross her path to get to the parking lot. She ground the Accord to a halt in front of the ER doors. In a flash, she was helping Jeremy out of the passenger side before Tab even unbuckled.

"Hurry, Tab," she said. Was she irritated with him now? Blaming him for Jeremy's condition because he couldn't handle Roy on his own? A part of him began to doubt whether Roy was the big deal he'd made him out to be. Jeremy's predicament seemed so much larger, more serious. At least at that moment. Was he just being dramatic, as Jeremy liked to say girls were? Jeremy did sometimes called him "Tabitha," after all, trying to insult his masculinity. Although Tab would not say so, he thought the name was beautiful. So what if Jeremy thought it was a *girl's* name? What was so wrong with being a girl? Unless that girl was Ashley Reardon, of course. She was all kinds of wrong. And not very girly, at least according to his brother's understanding. Tab had begun to suspect that people did not always fit into such firm molds as his brother's definitions of boy and girl.

"Tab! Come on!" Sandra was already halfway to the door, struggling to keep Jeremy upright as his lanky, nearly a teen frame trembled and his knees threatened to buckle.

Tab leaped from the car, slamming the door behind him. Ten skips later, he stood at his brother's side. His mom shot him a grateful glance when Tab also put his arms around Jeremy. Or was she chiding him? Was it "thank you very much" or "it's about time?" He found them difficult to distinguish but tried to swallow the hypervigilance so it didn't prompt him to bother her for reassurances. She had a lot on her plate. Like she often said his dad did. One son is tortured by a ghost. Another has a medical emergency.

Add to that a dead husband and it was no wonder she was hard to read.

"Thank you," Jeremy murmured. Tab wasn't sure whether it was directed at him or his mother, but his brother's head had lolled in his direction when he said it. Therefore, Tab decided to accept the acknowledgment for himself.

"Help!" Sandra shouted when they pushed through the door together. This grabbed the attention of two techs, who rushed to their aid. At reception, Tab recognized the EMT who had wanted to transport Jeremy. Leaning against the wall, his thick arms folded, his lips twisted into a smirk. "Told you so," the look said.

Tab summoned the courage to glare back at him. Instantly, the mocking green eyes collapsed. Tendrils of goo melted from their sockets, the droplets playing Plinko through his five o'clock shadow.

Tab blinked, and the EMT was Roy, his expression unchanged even without his eyes. A second blink, and the space at which Tab had been staring was empty save for a small group of people wandering the hall in the distance, searching for the restaurant, gift shop, or bathrooms. "It's this way!" Tab heard one of them announce. Then they, too, were memories.

He glanced at his brother. Jeremy had been provided a wheelchair at the reception desk while their mother dug her insurance card from her purse and handed it to a scowling older woman with an auburn beehive atop her head. Jeremy looked awake, although barely. His half-lidded eyes stared straight ahead, seeing nothing. His jaw hung open slightly, as if his nostrils were plugged and he had to breathe through his mouth.

Roy had managed to manifest even when Jeremy was conscious and nearby. "He's getting stronger," Tab whispered. "Not weaker like I thought. He can look like other people. And he's getting stronger." He shuddered and sidled close to his mother. His left hand closed around her purse strap where it connected to the bag. He didn't want to distract her, but he needed the comfort of the touch at the moment. His fingers brushed against her copy of *Soothing the Obsessive-Compulsive Beast*. Dr. Clifford's shining bald head and smiling eyes beamed at him from just beyond the title, peeking at him over nut brown artificial leather.

Tab plucked the book from his mother's bag. She did not appear to notice. He felt momentary guilt about taking it from her, but then considered she had meant it for him anyway. He carried the book to a seat in the front row of the waiting area and paged to the Table of Contents.

"That ain't gonna help you," Roy's voice said from somewhere to the right of him. Tab gasped and spun his head to locate the source. Roy sat beside him, now in his beige coveralls, grinning his rotted, mocking grin. Tab had never seen his eye sockets so close. Pulsing red and blackened meat surrounded the perimeter of the holes. There was familiarity there. It was not dissimilar to the mess of gore he thought he'd seen in his bump that day back in May.

While Tab stared, a maggot fell from the ceiling of Roy's left eye and landed in his lap. The man pinched it between his thumb and forefinger and popped it into his mouth. He swallowed without chewing and resumed his grin.

"Man's gotta eat! You're scrawny and you look like a little girl. It's because you don't eat enough." He jerked a thumb at the book. "That quack don't care about you. He only wants to diddle your momma. Now you've killed your brother, your momma's gonna put you up for adoption. She's gonna run straight into that dude's arms. Mark my words. She don't care about you any more than he does because you're *my* boy."

Tab fingered the bold chapter title that read TALKING BACK TO THE BEAST. It was the only topic he'd covered in any depth with Dr. Clifford so far, and the only thing that seemed to work besides Jeremy's proximity. "I'm not *your* boy," he said. "My mom does love me, and I won't believe you. I don't care what you say about it."

Roy nodded toward Sandra and Jeremy. She had knelt in front of the older boy and appeared to be testing his eyes the same way the EMT did when they were at home. Jeremy scrunched up his nose and swatted her index finger away.

"Come on, Mom. I'm fine. Just tired."

"Look how she dotes on him," Roy said. "She don't even remember you're here right now. She don't even care that you got your own problems. She's only worried about Tim's boy."

"Tim Beard was my dad, too," Tab said. "Not you. Even if you are my biological father, you're not my dad." He pronounced "biological" syllable-by-syllable, as if saying the word for the first time, staring into Roy's eye sockets as he did. Even without his eyes, the ghost's hurt expression seemed genuine. He sniffled and wiped his vaporous nostrils with one transparent sleeve of his coveralls.

"I woulda been. I woulda been your dad if Tim Beard hadn't murdered me. Your momma didn't tell me about you. If I'da known I'da fought for you."

Tab narrowed his eyes, his fists resting atop the pages of the open book. "She didn't tell you because you attacked her. You *hurt* her. And *I'm not your son*."

"She showed you the story they wrote about me in the paper, huh? Ain't true, boy. Ain't a word of it true. *Echo* has a vendetta against me on account of some of my, uhm, political associations. Your momma won't say so, but she thinks the same way I do. She wouldn't have met me at Whitt's that day if she didn't. She just feels guilty about being married to Beard while she was fucking me. So I got the blame for it all."

"That. Is. Not. True," Tab said. "Mom stopped for gas. She didn't know it was a racist hangout."

Roy grinned and leaned over him, pretending to examine the book's contents. "It's *all* true," he said. "Every word I said. He pointed at the TALKING BACK line with his middle finger. "How's that working out for you right now? Huh? Clifford is a fucking quack. I told you. You're talking back to me right now and I'm still here. You ain't getting rid of me, boy. Not easy, anyway."

Tab inhaled, resolve bubbling to the surface. If it was time to behave more "manly," then so be it. He'd try one of his brother's tactics: "Oh yeah? Well F—FUCK YOU!" Blood rushed to his face as the words escaped. It was his first swear. Out loud, anyway. A tingle ran up his spine when he uttered it. It sounded unnatural, coming from his mouth that way. But there was something about finally allowing himself to say it that also felt...*good*? Roy vanished, allowing Tab to see the elderly woman who had been napping two seats away from him. She was awake now, looking at him with the most horrified, offended gray eyes he'd ever seen. Shame immediately replaced his momentary lapse of good feelings.

"Sorry!" he said, diverting his gaze to the floor. "I'm sorry! I wasn't talking to you!"

Sandra and Jeremy were suddenly there with him. Jeremy remained in the wheelchair, groggy, both there and not there. Sandra squeezed herself between the older woman and Tab, the space Roy had occupied only a moment before.

"We *never* spoke to our elders like that when I was a young'un!" the older woman huffed. She addressed Sandra, not Tab. "You need to control your boy. Teach him some manners. Why, my dad would've hauled me to the back of the woodshed and whipped my bare behind with a switch if I'd done what he did."

Sandra gritted her teeth audibly. "Well, your dad's not here, is he? My son apologized. We don't hit at our house."

"Well, you should!" the woman said.

"Yeah?" Sandra shot back. "Well, if your dad had been less abusive maybe you'd be able to loosen your grip on them pearls a little, eh?" She spun away from the scene. "Sorry for calling you out on your swearing, boys. Let's go take care of some shit."

"I—" the woman started but was halted mid-sentence by the *thud* of the door to the examination rooms. A pleasantly smiling nurse in pink scrubs with her blonde hair tied back in a ponytail called Jeremy's name. Sandra grabbed Tab by the hand and stood up with him. She guided him to her side, opposite the older woman.

"That's not appropriate language in public, Tab," she whispered through gritted teeth. Together, they pushed Jeremy's wheelchair through the examination room and away from Tab's humiliation. Blessed relief, although it did not last long.

As they strode the length of the hall behind the nurse, Roy peered from around the corner of an open door to a darkened room. He sneered as the trio passed and hissed, "I told you talking back wasn't gonna work. You're gonna be mine yet, boy!"

Tab ignored him.

"All we gotta do is get rid of your brother first!" the ghost said from behind him. It was impossible to tell from how far behind. He resisted the urge to turn and check. Instead, he glanced at the next chapter title in *Soothing the Obsessive-Compulsive Beast*. The words SITTING WITH THE BEAST: MINDFULNESS AND OCD floated in his vision. That was something Dr. Clifford had not yet discussed with Tab, or with his mother. Tab had no idea what "mindfulness" was or how to use it. He would need to read the chapter, or at least skim it. He hoped he had time.

CHAPTER THIRTY

Roy whooped and hooted every single time Tab turned a page. It was loud, annoying, and more than once caused the boy to lose his place and have to backtrack. The ghost sat in a chair opposite Tab, who had planted himself on the floor beside his mother with *Soothing the Obsessive-Compulsive Beast* open to the mindfulness chapter in his lap. When he shot the ghost dirty looks for interrupting, Roy simply grinned back at him.

"What? You think it bothers me that I'm bothering you? Ain't nothing you're gonna learn in that book to help you. I'm just trying to save you some damn time. You searching that book for freedom? You ain't gonna find freedom there. You won't be free until you kill your brother. All those times he picked on you, called you names. Just like his bad old daddy, that one. You ain't like that, though. You're like me."

Jeremy was not asleep, but that was okay. He also wasn't in his "right mind." He muttered things, most of them at too low a volume to comprehend, as if speaking from inside a dream. On occasion, a single word bubbled loud and clear from the back of his throat. "No!" he said once. Later, "Dad." A nurse collected his vitals, surprisingly normal for him, and hooked him up to monitors for reasons she didn't explain. A doctor had yet to appear at their door.

Tuning out the sounds of the monitors came easy. The beeps and boops occurred at regular intervals, which could have been maddening in a water torture kind of way, he supposed. Yet somehow, they were not obnoxious.

Roy operated on an altogether different annoying frequency. The *oo* sounds in the middle of each *whoop* and *hoot* hit harder than the consonants, coarser in his ears. Something tickled the inside of his ear canal every time he hit those notes. Tab clenched his teeth so hard he thought they might break. Once, he bit the inside of his cheek and had to force himself to not scream. He tongued the little flap of damaged flesh inside his mouth, trying to shove back the fold so he wouldn't bite it again. No luck.

He closed his paperback and allowed a few minutes to pass without looking at anything in particular. Eventually, Roy vanished again. It could have been coincidence, but at the same moment Jeremy sat up in his hospital bed and shouted the first complete sentence he'd uttered since they'd arrived at his room. "Alright, I'll help!" He then settled back onto his pillow and spiraled into incoherent babbling, most of which arrived in whispers.

Rather than trying to read again, which would surely prompt Roy to hoot and holler in his ear more, Tab set the book aside and looked at his mother. "Mom, what's mindfulness?"

"A trend," she said. Her eyes remained trained on her oldest. The corners of them were turned down with worry, mirroring the shape of her mouth. There was a distance in her gaze that Tab didn't like, as if she was worried about her boys yet distracted by something else. Something that only she could understand.

Tab pressed on. "But what does it mean? How do you do mindfulness?"

Sandra met his gaze, irritability in her expression. "Why?"

"I think it might help with…*you know*." He whispered the last part.

"Tab, you have the book. I'm sure Dr. Clifford covers it in there. I'm not an expert and I've never used it."

"But every time I try to read, *he* stops me. He keeps making these hooting and hollering noises. They hurt my ears. I don't get it, either. How do you do it?"

"Oh, for god's sake. Is Roy here right now?"

Tab shook his head. "But he will be if I try to start reading again."

"Okay, the best I remember, mindfulness means that instead of trying to ignore or shut out your bad thoughts or feelings, you allow yourself to feel them. Acknowledge them, and then let them go. Like, if you're remembering something you did in the past you think was bad and that you're ashamed of, you should acknowledge what happened in the past and allow yourself to be totally aware of every feeling you feel because of it. The trick is you have to do it with *calm*."

"Calm," Tab repeated.

"Right. So if the bad thing you did in the past makes you feel shame, let yourself feel it without trying to control it. Don't try to do anything to fix the feelings."

"But—"

"I know, I know," Sandra said. "When you feel bad feelings you want to get rid of them. Some people use medication. Others pass the hot potato to someone else, vent, or find fault." She grinned. There was no mirth in it. "That's what causes a lot of the road rage these days, I think. People who are raging about uncontrollable things in their own lives decide to take it out on someone else. And who is a better target than the guy who cut you off in traffic?"

Jeremy moaned. Before he lost her to the son who ailed in a visible way, Tab spilled his last question. "So if I read this book and let Roy do whatever he does, that's mindfulness? Just ignore him?"

"Pretty much," she said. "Sit with his interruptions, but calmly. Don't talk to him. Don't stare at him. It's the same advice your gramma always gave me when I was growing up and other kids were pulling my pigtails. 'Don't let it bother you.'"

With that, her gaze shifted to the agonized expression on his brother's face. Her lips hung partly open, as if she was about to say something else to him but forgot what it was. She closed her mouth seconds later, not uttering another word. Lost in her thoughts.

Sounds easy enough, I guess, Tab thought. He cracked his neck, an act that would have normally attracted derision from his brother but was now met with silence, and spread the book open again. Roy's return was immediate.

"What'd I tell you about book sense, boy?" he asked. "Book sense ain't worth a damn if you ain't got the common sense to go with it. Right now, you ain't got the life experience to have no common sense. Put that thing down and let's kill your brother like you almost did back at the house."

Tab shut his eyes and breathed deep. He allowed the air to fill his lungs, almost to a point of pain, and blew it out slowly through parted lips. He did not allow the exhale to explode from him, nor fill his cheeks. It followed the path of his tongue and through his teeth. Natural. Relaxed. The book remained open on his lap. His palms lay flat atop the spread, one on the left page and one on the right.

"You listening to me, girlie?" Roy asked. "I'm talking to you. You're too old to think the world goes away on account of your eyes being closed. Unless you do think that. Maybe you *are* Tim Beard's kid after all!" He followed that with a guffaw so obnoxious Tab thought even those unaware of Roy's presence might react to it.

He did not open his eyes to check that theory, though. Tab's stomach cramped at the sound of Roy's voice. That made him bear down, trying to squeeze through the pain. How can you *not* react to something like that? His body was his body, after all. It was going to do what it was going to do. *Just ignore him.* Gramma's old advice sounded better to him than "mindfulness." Maybe he could let his body be his body and just drown out Roy with his own thoughts.

Tab has a powerful imagination. The voice in his head was not his, nor anyone specific. It was the voice of every teacher, every relative, and even Dr. Clifford all rolled together in a chorus of epiphany. *He has a powerful imagination, and he can make magic happen with the stroke of his pencil.* Maybe, Tab thought, he could imagine the sound of the ocean in his head or something else to drown out Roy's obnoxiousness. Some kind of magic words or phrase he could think on repeatedly.

Roy is here, he thought. *Abracadabra and Presto. Now he's gone.* He opened his eyes. Roy now sat on the floor in front of Tab, a mirror image of his posture if not his expression. Roy beamed a shit-eating, grimy toothed grin. His eye sockets pulled themselves into a narrow, mocking shape.

"Bada bing!" he screeched in Tab's face. "Bada bing, bada boom! I'm still in the room! Gotta help me send your brother back to the womb!" The playful menace on his face transitioned to something more sinister. Suddenly, Alfie was there with him, curled in his lap and purring contentedly as Roy stroked him with the tips of two grave-pickled fingers. "You're gonna help me, boy. Whether you want to or not. If you don't, I'm gonna hurt everything you love. Don't think I won't. I'll find a way. I ain't no goddamn murderer, but I will defend myself."

Before Tab could react, Roy twisted the cat's head off its neck, the same way his dad might twist the top off a beer bottle. Hot salt water filled Tab's eyes, his mouth dangling open in shock.

"Al—" he stammered. "Alfie! Oh my God, no!"

Roy grinned, and the vision was gone. "Fuck off, your cat's still at home and doing fine," he said. "Fucking baby. Like I said, I ain't no goddamn murderer. Well, except for wanting to kill your brother. But that's out of necessity. Self-defense, you know? And I can't do it myself. You gotta do it for me."

"My brother can't hurt you," Tab replied, choking on the word "can't."

Roy waved him away. "You don't know. You don't know shit about shit."

A waft of sulfur assaulted the boy's sinuses. It caused his left nostril to clog and then run with clear mucous. Tab allowed it to happen, swiping at it with neither palm nor sleeve. *Abracadabra and presto. Go away, Roy.*

He shut his eyes again. After three long inhales and exhales, he became aware of hot breath tickling his left earlobe. Or was it the scruff of a whisker? He wrinkled his nose, then smoothed it out again. *Abracadabra and presto. Abracadabra and presto. Abracadabra and presto, dammit! Abracadabra and presto!* The unwelcome hot breath filled his ear canal. It felt as if it might burrow beyond his ear, puncture his eardrum, and penetrate his brain. Is that what Roy had wanted all along? To enter Tab's mind? Become him?

When he could not discern whether seconds or minutes had passed, Tab opened his eyes and examined the room. The hot breath was gone. He hadn't even noticed when it vanished. There was no sign of Roy, either. Only his mother, his brother, and the beeps and boops of the monitors.

"It worked!" Tab said. He tugged on his mom's sleeve, intent on telling her how all he'd needed was some magic words to get rid of the boogeyman. She turned to him, a strange broad grin on her face. Too broad. Sandra had a pouty, petite smile that just cleared the width of her chin, even when she was at her most amused. The corners of her mouth now curled Grinch-like toward her cheekbones, almost the distance of the opposing corners of her eyes.

"What worked, honey bunny?" she asked. Her eyes were too wide: crazy, wet, red-rimmed, and unblinking. Her head wobbled crazily on her neck, looking as if it might roll off her body and into his lap at any moment.

"The, uh—" he said, searching now for what he'd meant to say to her. It was gone. "Nothing," he said. "Never mind. I can't remember what I was going to say."

"Well," the thing he thought was his mother screeched with insane glee. "I'll shake it out of you." She reached for him with both hands, bending at the waist to snatch him from the floor. As she did, the enlarged phantom hands of Stinkeye Roy came undone from her and protruded outward. Within seconds, he emerged from her body and grabbed at Tab's armpits. Tab screamed and pivoted away, using the leverage of his back against the wall to roll himself panda bear-like toward the door of the room.

"I told you it wouldn't work," Roy snarled. He followed it with a choked laugh, sounding as if he'd chain smoked an entire pack of cigarettes and chased it with a hot mug of beach sand and broken glass.

Sandra snorted herself awake. She had dozed off in the chair while Tab was meditating. "What's going on?" she asked, smacking her lips. "Tab? What's happening?" Even having just roused from sleep, there was sorrow on her face and in the sound of her voice.

"Nothing's working!" Tab said. "He's back. He tried to grab me. He was inside you and looked like you and I thought he was you until he tried to grab me!"

Roy burst into belly shaking gales of mocking laughter. At the same time, Jeremy gasped into full consciousness and sat up, pulling taut the cables connecting him to the monitoring devices. He looked around the room, bleary eyed at first. His gaze lit on Roy.

"Back off," Jeremy said, but it didn't sound like Jeremy. It sounded like his dad's voice spilling from his older brother's mouth. Both Sandra and Roy seemed to also detect the difference. Sandra, fully awake now, leaped to her feet and ran to Jeremy's side. She summoned Tab to join her. He scrambled to her without question, wrapping his arms around her waist. She one-arm hugged him around his shoulders, pulling him to her while she held Jeremy's uncabled left hand in her right.

"Who are you talking to, son?" she asked Jeremy. There was a pause before the last word. It came out slow, as if she had at first considered using a different noun to address him. Tab saw Jeremy's hand gently squeeze his mother's. It was the only sign he had heard her.

"Get out," Tim's voice said from Jeremy's mouth. "Get out of this room and get out of my son's life. You don't belong here. Your fight is not with them."

"He's not your son." Roy's voice had changed, too. Low and growling like a wolf who had learned to speak English. His eyebrows knitted, creating an almost perfect vertical line down the center of his forehead. Although his hands were open, his forearms and legs were locked in a boxer's stance, as if he was about to throw punches.

Jeremy released his mother's hand and began to disconnect the monitor cables from his body without looking at them. He maintained full eye contact (well, as much eye contact as one might have with an eyeless ghost) as each cable pulled loose with a fleshy *snap* sound.

"He *is* my son," Tim's voice said. "He will always be my son. What his DNA does or does not say does not matter to me." Tab's eyes misted over. He swiped at them and squeezed his mother tighter. "You've done enough harm to this family. It's long past time for you to leave us alone."

Roy's lips twisted into a sneer. He bared his grotesque, broken teeth. "He has my blood. Not yours. I ain't ever gonna leave him. Not ever!"

Jeremy's face contorted into rage unlike anything Tab had seen before. His brother was mean, irritable, but rarely appeared angry. His nostrils flared. His upper lip curled outward. His ears pricked upward into the mop of his hair. Before anyone could react to stop him, the boy leaped from his hospital bed. He landed on all fours, sprung frog-like from his calves, and lunged at Roy.

Jeremy's arc through the air lasted an eternity. Tab anticipated a connection, heard the slap and crack of flesh against flesh and bone against bone. But it wasn't real. Jeremy ducked mid-air as if to head-butt Roy. Instead, he passed through the ghost, emerging from the back. His expression transitioned from anger to fear to shock as he rammed head-first into the bathroom door. There was the definitive *crack* of snapping bone, and Jeremy went down. He landed chin-first on the floor behind Roy. A second, louder *crack* echoed on impact.

Sandra and Tab screamed in harmony. "*NO!*" Tab released his mother as she attempted to push him away. Together, they made an end-run around Jeremy's hospital bed, Sandra destined for her oldest who now lay broken on the floor like some child's forgotten Raggedy Andy. Tab, tears streaming from the corners of eyes engorged with blood rage, ran at Roy. His hands balled tight into fists, his jaws locked together and braced for combat. His arms and legs thrummed; the cords of muscles he never knew he had wound so tight he thought they might erupt through his skin.

Like his brother before him, Tab ran with his head down, a bull fueled by hate charging a matador at full steam. He leaped into the air as he closed the distance, aiming for the same spot his brother (*dad?*) had. He expected to fly through the body and smash into the wall as well. He was on some level prepared to try to stop himself, prevent himself from suffering the same fate as Jeremy. To his surprise as well as apparently to Roy's, the entities connected.

Tab's head smashed into the middle of Roy's bulk. The ghost stumbled backwards, pinwheeling his arms against gravity that should not have been capable of pulling him down. He fell on his transparent bottom near the head of Jeremy's sprawled and broken body. Tab's forward momentum carried him just a couple of steps shy of tripping over Jeremy and slamming into the same door that had taken out his brother. His sneakers squeaked against the linoleum as he brought himself to a full stop. He blinked twice, at first unable to decide what had happened.

Roy seemed equally flummoxed. He looked at the boy from his fallen position: knees up and arms behind his back, propping him up. He closed his open mouth, wrinkling his nose into a canine-like snarl. He lunged at Tab and disappeared before his path hit its apex. Just as he vanished, Tab thought he saw Roy's expression switch from fury to surprise.

Tab next became aware of rapid footfalls echoing in the hallway outside. These were accompanied by the sound of hard rubber wheels or casters rolling and tumbling along the floor. Someone had gotten wind of the commotion or realized Jeremy had become disconnected from his cables. People were coming.

CHAPTER THIRTY-ONE

Something wet trickled down the left side of his face. He dabbed at it and came away with a shiny crimson stain coating the pads of two fingers. Blood. While his mother and the nurses saw a groggy and incoherent Jeremy back to bed, Tab crawled to his feet and went to examine his reflection in the bathroom mirror. It was blood alright, drooling from the center of his bump.

He snatched two brown paper towels from the dispenser and ran them under cold water. Balling them in his left fist, he squeezed out the excess and squished the gooey mess against the bump. Direct pressure stopped bleeding. It was one thing he remembered from the fire and first aid lecture the chief of the Hollow County Volunteer Fire Department delivered at his school earlier that year.

While he waited on the bleeding to stop, he explored the floor outside the bathroom, seeking what he might have hit. A couple of small dark droplets of his blood dotted the linoleum tiles outside the bathroom, but nothing shown in the area he'd landed before Roy disappeared. No hospital equipment or furniture with hard edges stood close by, either. He didn't remember striking his noggin on anything at all.

Noggin? he thought. It was not a normal word he used to describe his own head. It sounded like an old-fashioned word, something Gramma or Grandpa might have used when they were trying to be funny or folksy. Or by an adult using euphemisms to smooth over a painful experience suffered by a child. It was a Roy word.

Tab left the bathroom, piling himself on the floor by his mother's chair. The nurses continued their attempts to comfort his brother. Jeremy fought them, probably unaware he was doing so. When one of the women tried to reattach a cable he'd ripped loose, he batted her hand like a kitten playing with a shoestring. Otherwise, his face was frustratingly blank. The second nurse produced a pair of arm restraints from her cart. She attached them to the bed and had one around each of Jeremy's wrists before anyone could protest.

"It's only until he can relax and be himself again," she said to Sandra. His mother watched the procedure with haunted eyes brimming with unshed tears. "With the state he's in right now, he might end up hurting himself or you or one of us."

"It's all happening at once," his mother whispered. "Everything's happening at once."

Anger boiled up from Tab's gut. Jeremy not only being hurt but looking stupid while doing it annoyed him. His mother's tears annoyed him. Her tremulous voice even more. Once annoyed, it was an easy transition to frustration and, from there, anger and hate. Tab was the one with the big problems. Tab was the one being haunted by a nasty man he'd never met but who claimed to be his real dad. The only reason Jeremy got involved at all was because his own dad had connected to him somehow and that scared Roy away. Well, it used to.

I ain't scared of him, Tab thought. Then: *Of course I ain't scared of him. Tim Beard is my dad. Why would I even think I would be scared of him?*

Jeremy might have been scared of him. Jeremy seemed to be scared of a lot of things. That's why he was such a jerk. If he hadn't been stupid enough to trip over Tab's ankle when he stood up to go after their mother at home—. Hell, if he hadn't been stupid enough to get up and go after her in the first place, he might not be in the hospital now.

Or you should've kept your feet to yourself, his brain replied. *Or you should've kept Roy from getting inside your head like he is right now.*

"Oh," Tab said aloud. "Oh no."

***

The next thing he became aware of was a stiff breeze in his face and a repetitive slapping sound in back of him. He opened his eyes to a set of bright yellow double doors at the end of a long corridor. The hall was painted in a duo-tone with white on top and gray on the bottom. He sped toward those doors faster than he could walk. It dawned on him then that he was strapped in a wheelchair. Whoever was pushing it seemed in one hell of a hurry. The slapping sounds were the soles of shoes against the floor.

The wheelchair slowed to a stop when they reached the door. A meaty, hairy masculine hand and forearm stretched out from behind him and slapped a giant square button, opening the door. Beyond the opening stood a nurse's station enclosed by thick glass above the countertops. Behind the glass stood a series of long black vertical bars, presumably made from some kind of metal. It made the enclosure look a lot like a prison cell. A small sign at the window read CHILDREN'S PSYCHIATRIC.

"Mom?" Tab's voice was weak and tremulous. He drew breath and then shouted, "Mom?"

"I'm right behind you, sweetheart," she said. A wave of relief washed over him at the sound of her voice.

"What's happening?" His stomach turned over. He gagged once, but nothing came up. The hairy nurse's arm finished pushing Tab's wheelchair up to the station window, then slapped a sheet of paper on the counter and shoved it through. A series of slapping sounds faded into the distance. "Where are we?"

Tab's mother appeared at his side. She knelt while the silver-haired severe-looking nurse behind the glass gave the paper a once-over. She had not yet acknowledged either Tab or his mother. "We're still at the hospital, hon. You had a, uh—you had an *incident* back in your brother's room. I'll tell you about it when we're settled."

"Where?"

She didn't answer him.

Moments later, the severe nurse wheeled him into a cube-shaped room of sparse furnishings. Two walls gleamed a Tweety Bird yellow. The others loomed institutional gray. One window populated with reinforced panes allowed a sliver of light to permeate the area above the bed, which was clothed in Batman-themed sheets. The bed, the nightstand, and a short bookshelf were all of the oak-stained particle board stuff one might find at a Target or Wal-Mart. If not for the hospital whiteboard and the beeps and boops of equipment in other rooms, it might've been a hotel designed for a child.

"What are we doing here?" Tab pleaded as the nurse assisted him out of his wheelchair and onto the bed. He sat with his legs dangling over the side, unwilling to lie down in this strange place. "Mom?"

"You're going to be okay," the nurse answered for her. She didn't seem as angry to him now as she had behind the glass. "Your mom's here with you and your brother is fine."

Tab glanced at Sandra, urgency in his eyes. "What does she mean? What happened to Jeremy?" His stomach twisted into a knot when the nurse cut her eyes to Sandra, who nodded at her in response. Whatever had been exchanged between them felt ominous. The nurse collected the empty wheelchair and rolled it out of the room, closing the door behind her.

"Son," Sandra intoned. Another ominous sign. She sat beside him on the bed and placed a soothing hand on his right knee. "First, Jeremy is fine. You didn't hurt him."

"I—?" Tab started, but she cut him off.

"What do you remember?"

He thought for a few seconds. Soon it came back. "Roy! I jumped at him. I was able to hit him and knock him over, Mom! I didn't think I would be able to do it, but I did. Then…then he got inside my head, I think. The last thing I remember is thinking he was inside my head."

Sandra scoffed. "That explains a lot."

"What do you mean?"

"You might want to take a few breaths," she said. "This isn't going to be easy to hear. You attacked your brother."

"I *attacked* him?" Tab's eyes went wide. The first two fingers of his left hand went to his bump. He massaged it, but only became aware of it because it felt different now. There was a small hard crust in the center of the outer layer of skin. Like a scab. He resisted the urge to pick it off.

"You did." She cut her eyes to the ceiling. "How can I best describe it? It was weird. Almost like you had gone into a trance or were having a seizure or something. Your mouth was open. Your eyes were rolled back in your head. All I could see of you was—" Her voice hitched. She swallowed and recovered herself. "All I could see of your eyes was the whites. And you were making some kind of weird sound, like you were trying to scream in your sleep. It was this long *ahhhhhhhhhhmm* sound. The closest thing I can compare it to would be a white noise machine, a long constant humming but through your open mouth.

"It was *disturbing*, I guess would be the best way to put it."

"It was *him*," Tab said. "He took me over." A revelatory thought occurred. "Oh my gosh! I'll bet that's how the drawing happened. The one of dad's hand coming out of the ground! I bet Roy drew that! He was using me to try to make it come true the way the other stuff I drew did! To make dad come back! But why would he want that? He's afraid of Dad. That's what I thought, at least."

Sandra shrugged. "I don't know, hon. But that's not as bad as what happened next between you two."

"Between Roy and Jeremy," Tab said. Sandra waved it away. "One of the nurses who came running to help Jeremy had a pencil tucked behind her ear," Sandra said, punctuating it with a short chuff of air that approximated laughter. "That's something you don't see often anymore. When I was your age, all our older women teachers in elementary school used to have at least one pencil tucked into their hair and behind an ear. Some of them had one on each side of their head."

Tab giggled, prompting Sandra to do the same. The room felt little lighter as a result.

"While they were getting Jeremy back into bed, I guess you saw the pencil. You jumped up and grabbed it. Nearly took the poor lady's ear off with it, I think. She was still cradling the side of her head with one hand when they carted you out of the room."

"Roy," Tab corrected. "Roy did those things."

"Right. Roy." But it didn't seem to register with her. "After you grabbed the pencil, you ran toward Jeremy with it. You were holding it weird, not like you were going to use it to draw or write something, but more like a weapon. You had it balled in your fist with the point facing outward like it was a knife. I don't know what you were planning to do for sure, but you ran straight at Jeremy. It took me and both nurses to hold you back and knock that pencil out of your hand. We had to hold you up by your arms and let you dangle in between us. Your legs kept trying to run at your brother in mid-air."

She closed her eyes, remembering. "If we hadn't stopped you, I think you might have killed him."

Tab gulped. A hiccup arose from deep down in his gut, blowing out his airways. A hot stream of tears spilled from his eyes. "I didn't know what I was doing!" he said. "I'm sorry, Mom! I didn't mean to hurt him. I don't remember anything. It was Roy!"

Sandra pulled him closer to her, nestling his face in the hollow of her neck. "I know, hon. I know. It was Roy. It's all been Roy. Ever since he attacked me, in one way or another, it's been Roy." Tab relaxed against her, and that seemed to open her heart more. "I guess deep down I've always known nothing had been *fixed*, you know? Yeah, Roy died, and you and your brother have been the absolute lights of my life. But there's been something dark in me ever since that day. Something I can't put in the past. Believe me, I've tried!

"You know how when you have some homework you don't want to do as soon as you get home, you kind of set the books to the side until you're ready to deal with them?" Tab nodded, rubbing the top of his head against her jawline as he did. "Well, that's how I dealt with what Roy did to me. I put it *over there*, you know? In some locked closet inside my head where I hoped it would never escape. But you can't do that with my kind of trauma. You can't.

"I have dozens of books on psychology and trauma and recovery, but none of them have done me any good. Know why? It's because I've never been ready to deal with it." She sniffled. "Now, because I've waited so long, he's back. He took my self away from me. He took my husband away from me. And now he's trying to take you. And Jeremy, too." The last few words of the sentence wavered in the air as Sandra choked back her own tears. She cleared her throat and righted Tab, looking him in the eyes.

"Now I *can't* do anything about him," she said. "I mean, I can work on how the whole thing has affected me. I can make some appointments with Dr. Clifford for myself, let him guide me through all the crap and hope I come out better for it. But I can't stop something I can't see or hear or touch. I can't fight *him*."

"Only I can," Tab said.

"I think so. You and Jeremy, maybe. Except Jeremy is hurt right now. The doctors thought you were having a nervous breakdown because of what you saw happening in his room. They thought that's why you *acted up*, as they put it."

"I think," Tab started, unsure at first how much worse he was about to make things for his mother, "Dad took over Jeremy. Dad can see Roy just like I can, and Roy can see Dad. But they can't hurt each other unless they're real. Unless they become us. I think that's what Roy wants." He tapped at his bump. "When he went inside my head, I got mad all of a sudden. I got mad at Jeremy because of how he looked in bed, but I was mad at Dad, too.

"Jeremy can't see Roy and I don't see Dad, at least not since the funeral. But I think Dad is here. I think he's trying to help." He swallowed a thick glob of mucous that had pooled at the back of his throat. "Roy wants me to hurt Jeremy. Kill him. Because he thinks it will stop Dad or at least hurt him the way Dad hurt Roy."

Sandra sat granite-faced, eyes locked on the closed door in front of them, jaw set. She sat there long enough that Tab became uncomfortable. He mashed his hands into the bed mattress to scoot himself away from her. Then she turned back to him, expressionless.

"He doesn't want revenge on me," she said, her voice flat. Then, as if realizing it for the first time: "He wants revenge on Tim. None of this has been about what he did to me at all, has it? It's not even about *you*. As far as Roy is concerned, *he's* the one who was wronged. By your dad. At the bar that night when he lost both his eyes and his life."

"I guess so."

Sandra sprang from the bed and pressed her forehead to the door. Her upper back and shoulders heaved. Her breaths came in huge, gasping sobs. She spun, eyes aflame. Her nose and lips pulled into a snarl similar to the enormous black dog Tab had seen the night of the storm. Her cheeks and the center of her forehead had gone pink.

"Roy is not the victim here!" she shouted, causing Tab to wince. "He did what he did *to me*. *He* hurt *me*. And because he hurt me, he also hurt your dad, and Jeremy, and you. That, that, that *motherfucker* has no right thinking your dad or any of us owe his miserable ass anything."

Fear gurgled in Tab's belly. Not fear of Roy this time, but of his own mother. He could not remember having seen her this angry before. Especially over something he had said. It reminded him of seeing his dad angry. He scooted backwards on the bed, pulling his knees up to his chest. His mother must have noticed because her eyes softened.

"I'm not mad at you, honey," she said. "Not in the slightest. I just—" She was interrupted by a knock at the door and stepped out of the way in time for it to open. Behind it stood a broad-smiling older man in a lab coat with mostly white hair and a smattering of salt-and-pepper around his ears.

Tab sighed. Another doctor.

CHAPTER THIRTY-TWO

Fifteen minutes elapsed from the time the new doctor entered the room and his diagnosis that the boy was not a danger to himself or others. He could rejoin society. However, the children's psych ward was almost empty. The doctor said Tab could rest in this room while Sandra returned to Jeremy. Policy might state otherwise, but the ward's director happened to be on vacation. Her fill-in was a buddy of the doc's.

"There's probably some paper and crayons in the drawer of the nightstand," he'd said. "If you want something to occupy your time while you wait for your mom. I'm sorry there's no TV in this room."

Tab had to admit to some comfort in knowing he had access to drawing tools, even if they were the instruments of a—well, a *normal* child. The word vibrated in his head. *Normal*. It was not something he was, but it was something he longed to be. Right now, anyway. Not always. Thoughts of worrying about nothing but homework and online games and when their next trip to the swimming pool might be appealed to him more now than he could remember. If the word *nostalgic* had been in his vocabulary, that's how he might have described those feelings. He was a nine year old nostalgic for the innocent days of seven or eight, when there was no anxiety or OCD. In the hustle and bustle of leaving the house for the hospital, he had neglected to grab his sketch pad and pencils. *Bet that's why Roy went for the one behind that nurse's ear*, he thought.

"Are you okay with staying here while I go sit with Jeremy?" Sandra asked him after the doctor left. She choked on the older boy's name. Her brow was wrinkled, the edges of her eyes and lips bordered by deeper lines. "I'll double-check with the nurse's station to make sure they know you're still back here. They can look in on you while I'm gone."

Tab pulled open the nightstand drawer. Inside lay a small composition notebook. It was college ruled, intended for writing. No matter. His brain could ignore those thin blue guides as his images took shape. An eight-color box of crayons branded with the hospital's logo sat atop the pad. Tab tossed both items onto the bed. He started to shut the drawer and heard a rolling sound along its bottom. Double-checking, he located half a No. 2 pencil with a worn eraser and rounded point. He grinned, holding it up so his mom could see.

"I'll be fine," he said.

"Good. Oh, and I picked this up as we were leaving Jeremy's room." She retrieved the paperback copy of *Soothing the Obsessive-Compulsive Beast* from her bag and pitched it on the bed beside him. "I don't know if it'll help anymore. I'm starting to doubt everything we were going to try since it all ends in such a—."

She wanted to say *disaster*, Tab thought. It was a favorite word for when things went wrong. Most times, it was too strong for the situation. She might describe burning biscuits in the toaster oven as a *disaster*, when it was only a charred side item and a bad odor. Given all the events of this day, *disaster* wasn't strong enough. Sandra allowed the thought to hang unfinished. She kissed him on the forehead, telling him she'd return soon. Then she hurried out the door without a look back.

Tab grabbed the notebook and opened it to the first page. It was blank except for an illegible word scrawled in the top margin. It was as if someone had started a page of homework and been interrupted. Tab flipped to the next page, which was clean, poised to draw...what? For the first time in months, his mind blanked. There was no urge to replicate something cool he'd seen elsewhere. No desire to draw a superhero in an exciting pose. No visions of *disaster* that he might have seen on the news. He drew a single arc in a thin stroke across the middle of the page, then erased it.

Frustrated, he tossed the notebook and pencil onto the bed and looked around the room, seeking inspiration from an environment that was half-heartedly kid-friendly and sterile. Dr. Clifford's book caught his eye. He picked it up and thumbed past the mindfulness chapter. "Well, that didn't work," he said. "Let's see what other weapons we have."

A section page separated the mindfulness chapter from the next. On it was printed a simple warning: ADVANCED TOOLS. Dr. Clifford must have intended for beginners to baby-step into recovery, graduating to the advanced level only after completing the others. But this was no time for baby steps. Tab flipped to the next page. On it, in bold print, was EXPOSING THE BEAST: THE ROLE OF ERP IN OCD.

He read the chapter in twenty minutes. At first, it sounded again like the old advice his mom said his gramma gave her as a kid: "just ignore them." Further reading revealed more complexity. ERP, Dr. Clifford wrote, stands for "exposure and response prevention." It is gradual exposure to distressing environments. By exposing the beast in a gradual way, say a finger or toe at a time, the OCD sufferer can learn to control their compulsions. If you can sit with the beast's toe but not react to it, you graduate to a foot. Or a full leg. Then you move on to expose more beast.

Tab's heart sank. It sounded like a long process, not helpful in an emergency like right now. Where had Roy gone? The last time Tab remembered seeing him was before hearing the man's voice in his own head. Was he still in there? How long until Tab lost control of his own body again? Or had Roy departed after the nurses stopped him from stabbing Jeremy with a pencil?

Control, he thought. *I don't want to be controlled. I want control.* Kids were powerless in a world built for grownups doing grownup things in their selfish grownup ways. Except when Tab sketched. He seemed able to exert some power in this world when what he drew came to pass. The problem was allowing himself to draw those things intentionally, without falling into trances or forgetting what he had done and why.

The drawing of his dad's hand? He didn't remember it at all. Yet when they got to the cemetery, he'd heard the voice of Tim Beard on the wind. Now even his mom believed his dad worked through Jeremy to stop Roy. Before, there had been the drawing of Ashley Reardon getting slammed in the school door. And the quick sketch he'd done of the man from the zoo. Not to mention all the other stuff he'd confirmed on the news.

At first, he'd blamed Roy for reading his mind and making those things happen. Roy had been involved somehow. But what if the power was all Tab's? What if he *deliberately* drew something he wanted to happen in order to make it come true? He snatched up the notepad and pencil again, tapping the eraser against his bump as he tried to think of some way to test his idea. His stomach growled. When was the last time he ate?

He began to draw. The first image to take shape among the blue rules was the rectangle of the door to his room in the psych ward. Touching pencil to paper again was sublime. He smiled as he worked, intent on his process. He hardly noticed the warm pulsing in the bump on his temple. The sensation rose toward the center and spread outward over the surface of his skin. It turned his cheeks a pink hue, dampened his forehead with a thin sheen of sweat.

He next worked on the figure of a woman standing in the emptiness of the door frame. Her face round. Mouth smiling. Eyes kind. Her hair framed her face like a halo. Tab drew it so a viewer might interpret it as bound in a ponytail. She wore scrubs. Tab was tempted to color them in with the blue crayon from the small pack he'd found in the drawer but decided against it. He'd not previously added color to his drawings. Safer to replicate his earlier successes as much as possible.

A small badge bearing a name, which Tab drew as a squiggle, was pinned above the woman's left breast. As a final touch, he drew a paper bag in her right hand. It was turned outward to display the McDonald's M logo on the front.

After completing the image, Tab set the notepad and pencil aside. He folded his hands in his lap, dangled his legs over the edge of the bed, and waited. Ten minutes passed. Fifteen. The ticking of the clock hanging over the door to his room was the only sound. Maddening. He retrieved his tools and drew the clock above the door, setting it three minutes ahead of the current time, which was about 7 p.m. The second hand slowed, ticking and tocking once for every two or three seconds that passed, dragging into eternity.

Then it was time. The clock's minute hand landed on the exact time he'd drawn and stopped. The second hand went dead. The ticking fell silent. Tab felt his bump burning, as if the drunk man at the zoo had snuffed another cigarette on it. He stared at the clock, unbelieving, wondering whether it had actually stopped or if his trauma-addled brain might have imagined it. Maybe it had been stopped all along and his mind had tricked him into thinking it worked. After all, he hadn't detected the ticking sound when his mom was in the room.

A knock startled him. The door swung open before he had a chance to call out to whoever lurked outside. A round feminine face appeared from behind it. "Mr. Beard?" said a sweet lilting voice. "Tab? You awake in here?" She saw he was and pushed open the door the rest of the way.

Tab's heart fluttered. She was a nurse, like he'd drawn in the notebook. She wore blue scrubs. Her gold-streaked hair was tied back in a neat ponytail. A black badge with white lettering was pinned above her left breast, although she was too far away for Tab to read the name. She grinned, stretching a brown paper bag toward him as if it was a gift. The McDonald's logo was emblazoned on the front. The unique aroma of the restaurant's fries permeated the room as the nurse walked it over.

"Your mother thought you might be getting hungry since it's past your dinner time," the nurse said. "She didn't think you'd want anything from our cafe, so we sent a volunteer to Mickey D's for you. They forgot the drink, though. Want me to get you a Coke?"

Tab grinned. He'd forgotten to draw the Coke.

CHAPTER THIRTY-THREE

His cheeseburger came with a side of small fries. It wasn't a Happy Meal, but that was fine with him. He never cared much for the puzzles and games on those thin cardboard boxes. The toys this summer were from *The Last Airbender*, a movie that held no interest for him. He'd missed the Marvel Heroes toys by a month or more. The *Shrek Forever After* watches by a couple of weeks. No matter. His imagination was a much more potent toy for playtime. But for now, playtime would have to wait.

His belly full after a warm and reverberant belch tasting of salty fries, Tab set about his new drawing. He drew the head first. Always. He sketched a series of light circles over the same space of blank page. The center he filled with a curved cross to obtain perspective. A number of other ovals and rounded rectangles formed a torso, arms, legs, hands, and feet. Before working on the face, he added a plaid flannel shirt tucked inside a pair of denim overalls. The final touch was the John Deere cap on the figure's head.

The face was the hard part. As days turned into weeks and weeks into a month, conjuring his dad's face had grown harder. There were glimpses, faded snapshots. His dad beaming over his new Batman drawing. His dad screaming at the television in outrage whenever the angry guy with the tall hair on Fox News told him about some new thing "the liberals" were doing to destroy America.

Tab didn't know for sure who "the liberals" were, but he didn't like people shouting over each other like they did on the show. He feared the hate he saw in his dad's eyes and seized-up jaw when he watched. It made him look insane. Demonic. Liable to throw punches at anyone who ventured too close. He shuddered at the memories of his angry dad.

Choosing to focus on the smiling Dad instead, he drew something of a caricature of Tim Beard. His more prominent features—colossal round eyes with delicate brows, tall forehead, roundish cheeks and chin—became cartoonishly emphasized. When he was done, he sat the notebook on the bed and eyed the completed work with some skepticism. It was one thing to put ideas in the head of his mom or a nurse, both of whom were living beings. It was quite another to use the same technique to communicate with a ghost.

Tab sketched a rough speech balloon above the figure. Inside, he printed the words HEY, TAB, LET'S TALK ABOUT ROY in all capital letters with a period at the end. On second thought, he converted the period to ellipses, something he'd seen in a library book once. When he'd asked Ms. Bowman about it, she'd explained that three dots indicate a pause or the trailing of a thought. "Don't overuse them, though," she'd said. To his credit, this was Tab's first time. That done, he pushed the notebook away and lay back on his bed.

His eyes never rolled back in his head. He discerned no sensations in the bump on his temple. No heat, no pulsing, no insect-like movement or rotation under the skin. He tapped the bump with the eraser, hoping to prompt some kind of activity. Nothing. At first.

The hospital pillow was more comfortable than he'd thought. The silence of the room and the fact that this was the first time he'd lain down in—well, who could remember how long it had been? Since he'd awakened that morning, at least. Tab drifted in and out of consciousness, becoming aware of his surroundings and not aware at regular intervals. It was like peeking at the room through the slats of his closet. *Must be what Roy sees when he hides in there*, Tab thought. Or he said it aloud, because the response was almost immediate.

"Hey, Tab," came the soft but gruff whisper of Tim Beard, a voice he used only when communicating with his young sons or when smoothing over an argument with Tab's mom. The boy smiled when he heard it. Something about it recalled warmth and security. Dad was home. He was safe. Everything would be okay now. "Tab? Son, we need to talk about Roy."

His smile transformed into a grimace. He opened his eyes, half-expecting Stinkeye Roy to be standing over him instead of his dad. Or nothing at all if the voice had been little but a waking dream, a hint of sleep paralysis like on that one episode of his mom's *Unexplained Phenomena* show. Sleep paralysis informed by his desire to talk to his dad again. However, he was not disappointed.

At the foot of his bed stood the figure of Tim Beard. The real deal. To Tab's relief, his father's face, only half-visible and out of phase, resembled how he looked in life. It was not a nightmarishly realistic version of the caricature he'd drawn. He doubted he would've lasted long enough to chat with the man if he'd had to look at a three-dimensional version of that. The bump on his left temple throbbed. This was real. Really, really real.

As if to confirm, the figure stretched out a hand to him. Tab reached back, not thinking it could be Roy in disguise again. Not thinking that it could be some other malevolent spirit he'd conjured out the graphite point of a No. 2 pencil. Their hands met. Tab felt a chill in the phantom as his fingers passed through its palm. Goosebumps raced up his arm, down his back. There was *some* solidity to his dad's ghost. Tab sensed the resistance of pressing against another person.

"It's me, son," Tim said. His voice reverberated throughout the room, the sound of a lone actor speechifying to an empty auditorium.

"Where have you been? Why haven't I seen you until now?" An indignant tone permeated his words. He didn't intend it, but very much meant it. "It's been *forever*, Dad. People have been hurt. One man died. And now I'm able to touch Roy the way I was able to touch you. He's turning *real*, Dad, and he wants to kill Jeremy! Maybe me and Mom, too!"

Tim stretched one translucent arm around Tab's shoulders, sorrow in his eyes. "I'm sorry, but it's not because I didn't want to be here for you. I couldn't get through. I tried. I tried so hard, son." A crackling cry broke up those last words. He appeared to swallow it down and continued. "You weren't able to see or hear me, not even at the funeral."

Tab's squinted his eyes, puzzled. "You *did* talk to me at the funeral, though! You grabbed my arm from inside your casket. Scared me to dea—uh, scared me bad!"

Tim shook his head, somber. "That wasn't me, son. It was Roy pretending to be me, like he's pretended to be your mom and the EMT you saw in the ER. It was all Roy trying to manipulate you, to groom you away from your mother and me. Son, even when that man tells you the truth, there's lie in it somewhere. He wants to own you, and he needs us out of the way to do it."

Tab opened his mouth to speak but found nothing to say. His eyes glistened. The inkling of having been set up, lied to, and treated as if he had no intellect sat on his stomach like a lead ball. His mom was innocent after all, not a whore. He'd already believed her. But to have it confirmed by his dad—his *real* dad—the same dad who he'd thought told him his mom was a cheater, kindled fresh rage inside Tab. At Roy. The liar. The predator. The monster.

"I didn't know why you couldn't see me at first," Tim said. "All I knew was I could see Roy hanging around you. Roy was able to see me, too. The closer he got to you and the more you seemed to grow to trust him, the further you drifted from me. I tried reaching out to you from this weird half-world. It was like walking in a dense fog with occasional bright spots, places where reality would come into focus again and I was able to see and hear you and those around you."

"Jeremy?" Tab asked, although it wasn't really a question.

Tim nodded. "Jeremy. Whenever you two were together, I was able to see and hear again. Once, I thought he was able to hear me trying to talk to you both." He chuckled. "Your brother doesn't have quite the imagination you do, son. That could be why he was never able to see or hear like you. He's too, I don't know, *immersed* in the fantasy worlds fed to him by TV and movies and the internet to bother exploring his own mind. Or, I don't know, maybe he's afraid of what he'll find in there. He seems to have developed some of my anger problem."

"But he's your blood," Tab said. He stared at the floor. "He's your blood and I'm not, so that's why you were able to join with him and not me. Right? I'm—" he gulped. "I'm *his* kid, ain't I?"

"I wondered," Tim said. "It was always in the back of my mind. But, listen, even if you *are* his by biology, it was *me* who loved you and took care of you. That's what makes a dad. Not his DNA." He sighed, steeling himself. "There's no reason to lie to you because most times you're more of a grownup than most grownups. Including me. I did worry about how you were going to turn out. We're all products of our genetics and our environment. But as far as I'm concerned, it's up in the air how much each makes up somebody's character.

"You've got a good heart, kid, and a good head on your shoulders. You're a good person, no matter what Roy tries to tell you or what dark thoughts you have sometimes. I didn't get a chance to tell you this in life, so I'm telling you now. The world is going to try to stomp that heart and imagination right out of you as you grow up. They'll tell you it has no place in the real world. They'll tell you what I told you: to man up. But don't you dare listen to it. I've been watching you, son. I think you're going to change the world.

"Also, I want to tell you that I'm sorry. It took dying for me to see how all my angry outbursts, all my rage and screaming were affecting you. And your brother. And your mom. I got inside my own head in the last part of my life, and I didn't like what I found there. That's why I lashed out. I was never mad at you or anyone else. I was mad at myself. None of it was your fault."

Tab began to cry. "But you're here because I drew you," he said. "So the man at the zoo *did* die because of me. And Ashley Reardon *was* hurt because of me! They weren't just coinc...coinc..."

"Coincidences," Tim finished for him.

"Yeah."

Tim patted him on the knee, although Tab could not feel it. "Son, we all have bad thoughts sometimes. God, I wish I'd shown you some old episodes of *Mister Rogers' Neighborhood*. That man knew how to talk to kids." He tossed a hand in the air, swatting away the regret. "Through every part of our lives, we're going to give into anger and wish hurt on other people sometimes. You didn't know you had this power. You couldn't have known. You were just doing what any artist does: drawing what you saw and infusing it with how it made you feel."

"But I thought my drawings might be coming true and I kept doing it!" Tab said. His cheeks felt hot. The ends of his mop of hair grew damp with his sweat. They stuck to his forehead.

Tim nodded. "Because you were trying to convince yourself it wasn't real. You were testing, drawing things you thought couldn't possibly happen. If they didn't happen, you weren't responsible."

"Except they did happen."

"Yeah. They did." Tim smiled. "But you figured it out and turned it around, didn't you? You got hungry and you drew the nurse bringing you food. You needed help figuring out what to do about Roy, and you drew me. I'm here now, ain't I? You have power you can choose to use for whatever you want. You could use it for good. You could use it for evil. You could be selfish with it or you could change the world for the better. Heck, you could be all of those things with it at the same time! There are no pure good or pure evil people in the world, son. It doesn't matter what's on the news or what daggers people sling at each other online. Human beings are complex creatures. We live way more in the moment than we like to think. Mostly, we're all just damaged goods trying to figure out how to fix ourselves."

He laughed. "Hey, remember the time we were at your cousin Mike's wedding? You got mad at your brother and pushed him into a car."

Tab frowned and ducked his head, as if he'd like to disappear into the neck of his shirt. "It was the car they'd decorated with TP and shaving cream," he muttered.

Tim roared, wiping a finger across his right eyelid to clear away nonexistent tears. "Yeah, there was shaving cream and soap and toilet paper and beer cans all over it. When your brother hit that car, all those things were smeared all over him and his new suit. Remember?"

"Yeah," Tab said, following it with a sigh.

"You felt so horrible! You gave Jeremy your dessert for a week afterwards and told your mom you'd donate your allowance for the dry cleaning."

"I didn't mean to do it!" Tab wailed.

"I know! That's the point. You got angry. Your anger got the best of you. It happens, son. It'll happen again. It happened to me all the time. But it doesn't make you a bad person. It just makes you a person. We handle things the best we know how. Sometimes we succeed. Sometimes we fail. The trick is to learn from both."

Tab pulled his legs onto the bed and began to rock, not looking at the ghost of his dad. "So how do I fix this?" he asked. "How do I get rid of Roy? Make him gone?"

"I don't know that you can, son. If Roy is part of you, part of him will always be part of you. I mean, he isn't *who you are*, you know? You decide that. All you can do is make him a smaller part of it. Unfortunately, life doesn't have an eraser." He thought for a moment and tapped the half a pencil Tab had used to draw him into reality. "But this does."

"You mean I can erase him?" Tab brightened, the tears on his cheeks had begun to dry and evaporate.

Tim laughed. "Well, I don't know about that. Like I said, I think Roy is always going to be an ingredient in the stew that is you. But think about how you use an eraser when you're working on a drawing. Do you ever use it to erase the entire thing and start over?"

"No. If I don't like what I'm doing at all, I throw the page I'm working on away and start a fresh one."

"Exactly. So what do you use the eraser for?"

"Mistakes, like when I make a mark where I didn't mean to." His eyes lit up. "Or when I want to make a tiny change! It doesn't even have to be a mistake. If I decide there's a detail I don't want anymore, I'll erase!"

"That's right! Whatever power this is you have, and however you got it, it's been growing inside you. You're getting stronger. Hell, you didn't even have to go into a trance to get me here. If you use that power for good, great! But you also have to learn how to *control* it or exert some influence over it. Not like when you drew my hand coming out of the grave, but more like when you drew me just now. Or that nurse who brought you the cheeseburger."

"But I didn't do the hand drawing!" His voice sounded whiny in his own ears. He'd grown weary of having to explain that he wasn't responsible for the drawing his brother had stolen and that had so upset his mother.

Tim smiled, empathy in his eyes. "Yes you did, although I know it hurts you to think so. Like I said, I've been watching you. You made the drawing, though I don't know that you were aware of doing it. Your eyes! Man, that was scary. They'd rolled back in your head. I don't think you even looked down at the paper the entire time you were drawing it. You summoned me with that drawing, Tab. You were using every bit of the power you had, and it was draining you as you were drawing me. It drained you so bad you don't even remember doing it."

Tab picked up the notebook on which he'd drawn the full figure of his dad. "But it didn't happen this time," he said. "Not with this one."

"No, not with this one. Or the nurse with the McDonald's. That's why I think it means you're getting a handle on this ability as it's getting stronger." He scratched his chin. It made a sandpapery sound despite his lack of scruff.

"Let's try an experiment. Just a little one. Something that won't hurt anybody, okay?"

Tab nodded, but his heart constricted in his chest. Dad's ideas? Oof. Some of the failures were spectacular. Like the time he'd run over his own foot with a lawn tractor—which was not running, thank God—while he was working on it. Instead of chocking the tires with wedges made for the job, Tim had used a couple of rocks. Neither was the correct weight or shape. The man had walked with a limp for two weeks afterward.

Tim jerked a thumb at the remains of Tab's discarded dinner, which he had yet to toss into the garbage can by his nightstand. "Let's turn to a new page of your notebook. I want you to draw the McDonald's bag. Do a quick sketch of it, but make sure it's as accurate as possible. That'll be important in a minute."

Tab examined his father's face. He was serious. The boy began to draw. An initial simple rectangle with a serrated top became a cube with more vertical length than horizontal and more horizontal length than depth. On the front face of the cube, Tab drew a McDonald's "golden arches" logo in its stylized fashion. The art was complete when he added the company trademark notification and a rectangular background.

"A marketing agency couldn't have done any better," Tim said. The ghost had switched locations without Tab noticing. He now sat behind the boy on the bed, peering over his shoulder at the work in progress.

"Thanks."

"Hey, you've got talent, kiddo. Now, that's enough. Take your eraser and change something about the bag. Doesn't matter to me what it is. I want you to use that imagination of yours. Change the design, or the shape or size of the bag. Whatever you want. Make sure you concentrate on it. Take control of it. Like you want to make it happen. The same way you concentrate when you're drawing? Do that when you're erasing."

Tab looked at the bag on his nightstand, then back at his drawing of it. The resemblance was remarkable. He had even drawn the little recycle logo on the left side of the bag. Tab flipped the pencil between his fingers with the dexterity of a magician and erased it from the drawing. When he peered at the genuine article, the recycle logo was still there.

"It didn't disappear," he said. "Nothing changed."

Tim groaned. "You didn't concentrate on it, son. You need to start thinking of the eraser end of your pencil the same way you think of the lead. The eraser isn't for getting rid of something. It's for changing it, extracting it. I know shit about art, okay?" Tab giggled at the expletive. Tim smirked, pretending to look ashamed. "Sorry. I don't know much about art, but one thing I did learn in my short time in community college was you can create art by addition or by subtraction. You know who Michelangelo was, right?"

Tab acknowledged he did.

"Well, Michelangelo painted, but he also sculpted. When he was painting, he was using paint to add shapes and colors to an existing canvas or whatever. But when he was sculpting? What was he doing?"

"He was taking away!" Tab exclaimed.

"That's right! He was removing stone from a big old block of it in order to create something new from it. That's how you need to think about that eraser. In fact, let's don't even call it an eraser anymore. That's your chisel. Got it?"

Tab brightened. "Got it!"

"Alright, let's try this again."

The boy closed his eyes, eraser (*chisel!*) poised over his illustration of the bag. Thoughts about Roy, his dad, his mother, his brother, and everything else buzzed through his head. He hummed atonally, unaware of his own attempt to match the frequency of his brainwave. Tab had never had occasion to hear the term *mantra*, but that's what he was doing.

His eyelids fluttered open, revealing blank orbs. But he was not unconscious this time. Not zoned out. The bump on his left temple itched. He diverted his focus, acknowledging it, allowing it to expand and grow. Soon it throbbed with each beat of his heart. An image of his room surfaced in his mind. His father's spirit stood left of him, smiling down at him. Tab's terrible third eye had opened, ready to serve.

Tim Beard either whispered or mouthed the words "Do it now." Had Tab heard it in his ears or inside his head? In his trance, he nodded. He turned his face to the lights inset among his hospital room's ceiling tiles. His hand dropped to the notebook. The pencil eraser, his chisel, hit first. It landed dead center in the golden arches. Tab rubbed at the drawing in small circles, not watching what he was doing. Still aware of the space in which his erasures occurred.

"Good," his dad said. "You're doing great."

Tab tried not to smile, nor allow himself any pride. Doing so could break his concentration, pull him out of the trance. His grip on the pencil loosened. Wood *clack*ed against the notebook and rolled away. He shut his eyes again. When he opened them, they had righted themselves. The pulsing of the bump on the side of his head ceased. An after-warmth embraced his body but faded, creating chill bumps. The room was blurry at first, as if he'd just awakened from a nap. When it cleared, he noticed his dad looking at him.

Tim's patient smile broadened into a satisfied grin. He raised his eyebrows and nodded towards the notebook. "Look what you did, son."

He did. The McDonald's bag on the notebook page now displayed only the two longest sides of the M logo. In the middle, where they would have met, nothing shown but the blue rules of the paper. The two remaining elements of the M almost looked like two McDonald's French fries bowing to each other. He giggled at the thought, wondering whether he should add bowties or belts around them to enhance the effect.

"Now, take a gander at the real bag."

He'd almost forgotten about the real bag, which was the point of the whole exercise. Tab spun around, expecting to be disappointed, and did a double take. The M logo on the real McDonald's bag matched the drawing in his notebook to the smallest detail. There was no evidence the middle part of the logo had ever been printed. No smears, no fades to indicate a printer's error. The area of the bag where the logo's middle would have been was clean brown, like the other unprinted spaces.

"It worked!" He turned back to his father. "Holy shit! It worked!" He clapped a hand over his mouth, embarrassed that he had said the S-word in front of his dad. Tim belted genuine laughter, as he sometimes had in life. "It sure as shit did!" he said, and that made Tab blush.

He wished he could throw his arms around his dad's neck and hug him tight. He almost leaped up on the bed and tried, but he could see the yellow wall of the hospital room and the furniture shoved against it through his father's body. That dissuaded him. He didn't want a repeat of his brother's lunge at the phantom Roy.

"Dad?"

Tim's eyes drooped at the corners, his smile dissipating. "Yes, son. I think I'm going now."

"But I still have the drawing!"

"I know. Power fades over time, I guess. It can't be sustained. Or you can only spread it so thin. Drawing the bag and chiseling away the logo might've drained whatever strength you were using to keep me cohesive here."

Tab began to cry. "Don't go!" he said. "Please! Roy doesn't show his face whenever you're around. I miss you. And Mom and Jeremy miss you, too!"

"I know, son. I know." Tim's voice was more distant. It had rung crystal clear for the few minutes before Tab began to work on the McDonald's bag. Now it sounded like it had at first, far away and tinny, a voice in a memory or a dream. "I'm still here. You won't be able to see me now, but I'm still here. Even if I can only connect through Jeremy."

"I need you!" Tab said. His face grew bright red with strain, both from focusing on his father and making himself heard. "You have to help me get rid of Roy!"

"Fight him, son!" Tim said as the last particles of the apparition flickered out of view. "You have the power. You have the tools. Fight him!"

Tab flipped back to the notebook page on which he'd drawn his father. The figure there had also vanished, leaving behind only a crisp, clean, blue-ruled page. None of his other drawings had disappeared, not even the ones he wished like hell he could undo. Why had his dad vanished? He'd drawn a ghost into a reality. Ghosts, like memories, faded with time. It was all he could reason.

He collapsed face down on the bed. His notebook and pencil rolled away and clattered to the floor, forgotten.

CHAPTER THIRTY-FOUR

Tab's hospital room was not a prison. Nor was Tab a prisoner. That didn't mean he didn't feel a twinge of misgiving about not staying put. The nurses in the children's psych ward had been sweet enough to him, even if one nameless doctor had been somewhat dismissive. Tab pressed his ear to the door, listening for footsteps or carts rolling the hallway outside. Nothing.

He had stopped the clock on the wall in his room with a drawing. It was functional again, but he had no idea how much time had passed. He'd had no word from his mother since the nurse brought him dinner. His dad had returned to oblivion, or wherever ghosts went.

He opened the door a crack, enough to peer into the brutalist, fluorescent-lit hallway beyond. The starkness of the places adults trod was not lost on the boy. It filled him with new dread of growing up. Why did grownups, men especially, insist on bland lives of furor and stress?

In the distance lay the nurse's station. The stern woman who had greeted him sat behind the glass, her back to him. Outside the station, also with his back to him, a janitor clad in short-sleeve gray coveralls swept a mop across linoleum. A wheeled bucket of cloudy, nasty looking water dragged behind. The man slung his mop past the nurse's station and whirled out of sight. Tab had a minute tops before the janitor completed his circuit. He had to move now.

He pressed a hand against his back pocket. The half a pencil and composition notebook were secure there. He'd had to fold the notebook in half to fit it but fit it he did. He feared the resultant crease might affect the magic he and his dad had discovered, but it was necessary. He'd have to lope on all fours past the nurse's station to prevent her from spotting him. If he walked upright, they'd lead him right back to his room on account of his mom and brother couldn't be bothered right now.

Tab considered fighting Roy from the solitude of his hospital room, but something there didn't feel right. Roy was stronger without Jeremy (and, by proxy, Tab's dad) around. If he waited, fought Roy on his terms in the presence of his mother, his brother, and his dad's ghost, he would be fighting a weakened, more nervous Roy. Advantage: Tab.

The nurse hadn't budged from her position at her station. She must be working on her computer, or surfing the web, or playing Solitaire. Whatever. It held her attention.

Tab collapsed into a crouch, then pulled the door open enough to slip through. A couple of quick glances left and right revealed he was alone on this part of the floor. He allowed the door to close behind him but kept a hand on it to ensure it didn't slam.

A sense of vulnerability crept in now that he was outside the shell of his room. It was cooler out here. Every shadow cast on the floor he perceived as a threat. After two leaps forward, making minimal sound and with no reaction from the nurse or the shadows, his confidence began to grow. He grinned. He was James Bond now, one of his dad's action movie heroes. The thrill of secrecy and remaining undetected intoxicated him. He wondered if ghosts like his dad and Roy must feel this way around people who can't see them.

"Maybe we do and maybe we don't," a gravelly voice on his left said.

Tab hung his head, exasperated. Roy. Fucking Roy. Goddamn fucking Roy was here and honing in on his thoughts again.

"If you gonna fight me, boy, do it here. You chicken?"

He didn't look at the ghost. Except for the quiet sigh that escaped before he could catch it, Tab didn't acknowledge him at all. He closed his eyes, clearing his mind. *Abracadabra and presto!* The hospital air created chilling sensations on his forearms. He felt the pressure of the smooth floor tiles against his fingertips. He curled his toes at the ends of his shoes.

Lurching forward, he pressed himself as close to the wall as possible. He dodged adjacent door facings, his fingertips supporting his upper body. Most of his "walking" was on crouched legs. In school, they called it a duck walk, but Tab always felt more like a frog. Whatever they called it, it seemed to be working.

"What d'you think that's gonna do, boy?" Roy said, more behind him than beside him now. "What d'you think you're gonna do when you're out of here?" His voice grew louder, more enraged as Tab departed. "What do you think you're gonna do? I *hope* you're going to your mom! I *hope* you're gonna go to your brother! You know why, you little shit? Because if you're there, I can kill him! I can get rid of your dumbass fake dad forever! All I gotta do is kill the last remaining drop of blood he has on this Earth and he's gone, Tab! He's *gone!*"

The stretch of hallway he traversed ended in a T. To the left was the nurse's station and the hallway in front of it. To the right was a shorter hallway ending in the double doors through which he'd been shoved in the wheelchair. Tab allowed himself one glance behind. Roy was gone, if he had ever been there. In her station, the stern-looking nurse remained glued to her computer. She coughed once, turning her head when she did, but without enough periphery to catch sight of him.

Tab dashed around the corner. He imagined a mouse skittering through a kitchen at midnight. A few more frog-leaps, and he stood upright. He slapped the rectangle to open the doors, ran through them in a flash and was suddenly power-walking a new section of the floor to—where? He didn't know.

He skirted a corner and was greeted by a series of signs, one of which pointed to the elevators. A glance at the number on the closest room revealed he was on the first floor. Jeremy was on the third. Room 314.

Another janitor, his back to Tab, stood between him and the elevator niche. Tab tried to bypass him on the left, but the silver-haired, coverall-clad old man swept his mop that way as soon as he did. Tab veered right, but the janitor performed the same maneuver. He waited for the man to sweep left again, but he didn't. Instead, he paused in his work to pluck an iPod from his back pocket. He leveled the device in front of his eyes and began to poke at it with one damp, smudgy finger.

"Excuse me," Tab said. "Excuse me. I need to get by."

No answer. Tab again ran left. Just then, the man swung the mop handle around, connecting with Tab's shins. The boy lost his balance and sprawled on the floor slicked with mop water, his hands and legs outstretched. He rolled onto his back to find the janitor glowering down at him, menace in the hazel eyes behind his rectangular wire-rimmed grandpa glasses. In a moment, those eyes collapsed into the man's head, and Tab was again face-to-face with Roy.

"I can't stop you from going up," he said. "Even if I wanted to, I can't. I don't know why. Something won't let me. But I *can* force you to do what I want when you get there. I almost did it before they sent you to the looney bin." He sighed through his nostrils, leaning forward on his mop handle. "I'm sick of these games. All I want is some justice, son. You'd think my own blood would let me have that."

"Don't call me 'son,'" Tab said. He scrambled to his feet and dashed to the elevator. After punching the Up button harder than was necessary, he glanced back from where he'd come. The janitor was gone, and so was Roy. The old man had been another disguise. Not real. Most likely a visage adopted by Roy from someone he'd seen that night.

The location lights above the elevator announced the box was stopped on the eighth floor. Tab snatched the notebook and pencil from his back pocket, grateful they weren't lost in his tumble, and turned to a blank page. He drew a quick and dirty sketch of Stinkeye Roy in the form in which they'd first met: the coveralls, the missing eyes, the scruffy round face, the baseball cap. The Roy figure stood in a symmetrical pose, his hands at his sides and his feet together as if at attention.

When the figure was finished, Tab sketched outlines of other figures surrounding him, near but not touching. He fashioned empty silhouettes that could be interpreted as masculine or feminine, young or old. He even outlined a small dog and cat, anything he could imagine that Roy might imitate. In the spaces between the figures and Roy, Tab drew small squiggly arrows, a shorthand that these were other identities Roy might assume.

The elevator chime sounded. Its doors opened. Tab stepped inside without looking up from his drawing. He glanced at the control panel to ensure he was pressing the correct floor number and then swapped the pencil's point for its eraser. His chisel. He closed his eyes, ready to concentrate. Suddenly, a new voice spoke to him. Young. Feminine.

"Well, look who it is."

He swiveled his head to the left. There stood Ashley Reardon with her right arm in a sling. She snuggled a crutch in her left armpit. A malicious sneer spread across the lower half of her face, teeth clamped behind pulled lips. Her eyes glistened with hate.

"What are you doing here, homie?" she asked. "Or should I say 'homo?' You never did answer me when I asked you which way your thing swings." She caught him looking at her busted arm and leg. Had she broken her leg, too? Tab's mother hadn't told him that. "*You* did this to me, didn't you, you little shit? You and your drawings. I always knew you were a freak."

"I—" Tab said, but snapped his mouth shut. As far as he knew, no one but his mother, his brother, and Dr. Clifford knew about his drawing of Ashley. Unless Dr. Clifford had betrayed him to the girl and her mother, but he doubted that. The elevator doors opened on the third floor and Tab stepped out with Ashley right beside him, glaring at him, inching her face closer to his. Closer to his bump.

She wasn't real. Tab shut his eyes and leaned his head back. The calm state came more easily than it had the first time. He concentrated on the sensation of the pencil between the fingers of his right hand and the texture of the notebook in his left. The buzzing of the lights overhead drowned the doubts and other voices in his mind. *Abracadabra and presto!*

"You aren't gonna get away with this," the "Ashley" entity whispered in his left ear. On that, he stabbed the drawing he'd been working on and rubbed the eraser in small circles until he'd formed a larger void around the figure of

Roy. The eraser chiseled away the middles of the arrows he'd drawn between Roy and the other figures, leaving gaps of blank page between their starts and ends. When he was done, he opened his eyes. Ashley Reardon was gone, replaced by a furious Roy. Tab had severed his ability to don disguises. Temporarily, at least.

"That's CHEATING!" Roy roared. "You're a LITTLE CHEAT! Come here, you little cheat! I'm going in. From here on out, you're mine."

Tab ran, although he knew full well running from a ghost was useless. Roy could disappear and reappear anywhere he wanted. It didn't matter how much distance Tab put between himself and the apparition. But when fight or flight takes over, as Dr. Clifford had written in his book, the rational mind checks out. His legs wanted to run. His arms wanted to pump. So he let them.

A sign at the next T pointed him to the right for rooms 300 through 315. Tab took the turn at full speed. The tips of his sneakers squeaked to a halt at the change in direction, nearly costing him his balance. He righted himself and kept going, but there was a new twinge in his left ankle. The last few feet to Room 314 became a fast limp. He was still looking at his feet when he butted head-first into the belly of a nurse in pink scrubs who blocked the door of his brother's room.

Tab steeled himself and stared directly at her face. "Are you *him*?" he asked, his voice flat, less James Bond and more Harry Callahan. Another of his dad's heroes, although Tab had only ever seen one or two famous clips from the *Dirty Harry* movies. His mom had always refused to allow his dad to show those movies to him and Jeremy. Tab asked often but was always disappointed. He'd heard about the little dog named Meathead ripping a fart. That would be a hilarious thing to see.

"Am I who?" the nurse asked. She bent at the knees, resting her palms on them so her face drew near to his.

Tab checked his notebook. The image he'd drawn of Roy surrounded by other figures was still there. The gaps in the middle of the arrows looked narrower now but were not healed. His power couldn't hold off Roy's ability to assume other shapes forever. Roy was a ghost, like his dad, but the fact that there remained gaps on the page was a clue that his shapeshifting abilities hadn't returned yet.

"My brother is in there," Tab said. "So is my mom."

The nurse's green eyes brightened, contrasting brilliantly with her reddish orange mane and pale skin. "Are you Tab?"

He nodded.

"Oh, sweetie, you're not supposed to be down here right now. Your brother's sleeping and your mom's trying to sleep. Let's take you back down to your room on One, huh? We can give you anything you need down there. You don't need to bother your brother or your mom for it."

Tab snarled. "I don't *need* anything. Except I need to be in there with them."

The nurse straightened up. Confusion, offense, and then resolve replaced the patronizing helpfulness in her eyes. "I'm sorry," she said, "but it's past visiting hours. Only one family member is allowed inside at a time until nine o'clock tomorrow."

"But I'm allowed in any time!" Roy said. The voice came from behind Tab. He was not startled by it. Somehow, he'd already sensed the ghost's presence. A chill gripped him but was gone in a second. The same chill must have hit the nurse. Bumps rose all over her freckled forearms. Then Roy's head and neck poked through the door of his brother's room. He looked like Porky Pig bursting through the drum at the end of those old cartoons on Boomerang. Roy said in a mock stutter, "Ah-bedee, ah-bedee, ah-bedee, I'm inside, folks!"

Tab reached for the door handle, but the nurse was too quick. She stepped in front of it. "I told you, 'No,'" she said. She pursed her lips together, the patience gone from her face. Grabbing Tab's shoulders, she spun him around. "Back to One with you. I'm going to call security for escort. You can just sit on the floor until they get here." She pointed at the wall opposite 314 and motioned to another nurse who happened to be passing by, whispering something to him. He nodded and walked back the way he came. Tab supposed he went to round up a security guard.

Rage swelled in his chest. He felt it press against the walls, bubbling until it boiled into his head. He wanted to explode at the nurse, to call her all kinds of names, to kick her in the shins, to do something to move her out of his way. He was tempted to shove her, but they would haul him away sooner for something like that. It might get him locked inside the little room they'd reserved for him in the psych ward.

He plopped down against the opposite wall and opened the notebook to the now blank page on which he had drawn his father. He scanned the nurse from top to toe, then sketched her standing in front of the door. The room number of 314 was visible to the right of her head. The name tag on her scrubs read MOLLY, so he sketched that as well. When he was done, he flipped the pencil and allowed the eraser to hover over the illustrated Molly's head.

"I need to see my brother," he said to the real Molly blocking the door.

She sighed. "I'm sorry, son. But no."

"I'm not your son." She rolled her eyes but did not reply. Tab shut his own. He drew in a deep breath and tried to swallow the rage. *Abracadabra and presto!* He was angry, yes, and anger is an emotion normal people feel. He didn't want to hurt the nurse, but he did want her to leave. She was making it difficult.

His anger contained, Tab redirected it into his bump. The blemish filled with hot blood, pulsing against the thin membrane of skin on his temple. The third eye opened. "This is only temporary!" he shouted, then dropped his eraser onto the page and rubbed at the drawing of Molly the nurse. He rubbed until he heard the paper crinkle under the pressure of his touch. When he opened his eyes, Nurse Molly on the page was gone and so was the nurse at the door.

Tab flipped his pencil. Guilt stabbed him in the back of the neck. Where had she gone? He couldn't answer, even if he was responsible for sending her there. He considered redrawing her, tracing the impressions of the lines he'd erased. Could it make things worse? His drawings effects on ghosts were temporary. His effects on humans so far had been unfortunately permanent. Nurse Molly had not been a ghost. Had he killed her? Or would the fact that he only wanted her to go away for a little while eventually bring her back? His mom and dad would call that *intent*. He didn't have intent to kill Nurse Molly. If his intent mattered, and the erasure was only temporary, he might create *two* Nurse Mollys on accident if he tried to redraw her. Was intent enough? Maybe wait, find out if her erasure—what? *Expires*? It was the best word he could think of.

He buried the feelings. Wherever Nurse Molly had gone, he hoped she wouldn't remember it when she came back again. *If* she came back again, his brain amended.

Tab braced against the wall and pushed himself to his feet. He folded the notebook in half and stowed it along with the pencil in the back pocket of his jeans.

"Murderer," a voice said beside him. "You're a goddamned murderer, Tab. You little shit. I saw what you did to the lady what didn't do nothing to you. She was doing her job, Tab. Wasn't no reason to send her into the beyond like that."

Roy had appeared on his left again. Tab allowed himself a glance in his direction. The ghost of the man stood facing him, his shoulders slumped and his chin hung low on his neck. He shook his head, crestfallen.

"What do you know about the beyond?" Tab asked. He shouldn't acknowledge the ghost. He knew that. But he couldn't help himself. The accusations fused with his own doubts and pangs of guilt were too much. "All you ever do is hang around me."

"I know enough," Roy countered. "It wasn't until your little third eye there opened up that I was able to break free of it, to see the world clear again, to move around in it like a goddamn normal person. Ain't nothing in the beyond but fog, boy. Just empty, dank fog and the echoes of your own footsteps and sobs."

Tab sneered. "For people like you, maybe. Bad people. Or you're stuck. I've seen enough of my brother's ghost hunting shows to know things like that can happen. Ghosts can get stuck here. Between here and there. Especially if they think they died too early to do whatever they were put here to do."

"You think *I'm* the bad guy?" Roy scoffed. "You murdered an innocent person, you stupid little shit."

"You hurt my mom. And you *want* to kill my brother!"

The ghost leaned in close to Tab's face then, his nostrils flared and his lips pulled back in a demonic grimace. "I ain't hurt nobody!" he snarled. "Your momma gave herself to me, and it don't matter whether you believe it. Innocent until proven guilty. That's what the law says. And there wasn't no evidence, least there wasn't after the sheriff's department lost it." He bellowed laughter at that. "And killing your brother is in self-defense."

Tab balled his hands into fists. His forearms and biceps tensed, the muscles thrumming underneath his skin. "Just because they can't prove it doesn't mean you didn't do it," he seethed. "I'll believe my mom over you any day of the week and twice on Sunday. She wouldn't lie to me."

"Oh, yeah?" Roy's grimace transformed into a smirk. "She lied to you about who your dad was."

Tab laughed out loud at him. "Tim Beard *is* my dad," he said. "That's all they told me. He raised me. He sent me to school. He taught me things. *You* were never my dad."

"You got *my* blood!"

"*If* I do, I hate I do," Tab belted. Had he had the presence of mind and words to say so, he would've added, "If blood is all that matters for a legacy, it's a crying shame you have one when there are good men who don't."

"I'm a good man," Roy said, although it was unclear whether he had somehow "heard" the more complex message Tab was trying to convey. "I'm a *good man*! Fuck you, kid. I'm a *great man*! It's the rest of y'all who are broke. Ladies love me, boy. They just don't know it when they first meet me."

"Shut up," Tab said. He leveled a finger at Roy. It was an impressive, intimidating command to issue from the mouth of a child. Perhaps to the astonishment of them both, Roy did indeed shut up. Maybe he saw the grownup resolve behind Tab's glare. Maybe he'd run out of things to say.

Either way, Tab sensed a shift in the power dynamic as he locked eyeball-to-socket with the ghost who had tormented him for these many weeks. For the first time, Tab's confidence did not wane. For the first time, he refused to be the one to turn away.

Roy, also for the first time, flinched. He took one step backwards, his brow and mouth downturned and his head tilted to the right. It was as if he was a dog trying to make sense of a high-pitched trill. Tab grinned.

"You know, Roy, I erased that nurse." He held up the notebook page on which he'd depicted her. "The drawing hasn't come back yet. Maybe that means you're right about me. I *am* a murderer!"

Roy was agog. "So you admit what you did to her? There you go! Murderer! Like your dad!"

Tab's grin widened. "You called Tim Beard my dad."

Roy howled. Whatever brief power Tab wielded over him exploded in a flash of rage and hate. He took two more steps backwards, but they lacked the trepidation of the one before them. He was preparing to launch. "I'm gonna kill you, boy. First I'm gonna use you to kill your brother. And when your skin is covered in his blood? And your nostrils are full of his stink? And you're deaf from his screams? Then I'm gonna kill you, too."

He leaped.

CHAPTER THIRTY-FIVE

Tab crashed into Room 314. The door bounced against the wall behind it and rebounded, almost bopping him in his nose. He escaped with a video game soldier-like strafe to his left. Jeremy sat upright on the bed, clothed and bright-eyed. He and their mom started at the sound of the door. Together they glared at Tab with a mixture of confusion, fear, and...was that hate? It looked like hate.

"Oh my God, Tab," his mom gasped. "You scared us to death! What are you doing here?"

Tab grinned. His mouth felt strange. More, his teeth felt broken and gritty, as if he'd been eating dirt. His breath came in gasps, his chest heaving as if he'd barely escaped a tiger.

"Just came to check on my big brother," he said. "It was boring sitting in the looney bin."

"Tab!"

He sneered. "Well, that's what it is, ain't it? That's where they put all the crazy kids. All the ones all you grownups is always scared of?"

"'Crazy' is not a nice word either, son," Sandra chided. She looked him up and down, suspicion mounting in her expression. "What, uh—what's wrong with your eyes, Tab? They look black, like your pupils are too big. Did they give you something downstairs?"

Jeremy hitched, hiccuping and gasping at the same time. "Mom?" he said. "That's not Tab."

"What do you mean? Of course it's Tab. That's your little brother. Don't you recognize him?"

"No, Mom," Jeremy said. He addressed her but maintained eye contact with his brother, who only grinned back at him. "That's the look he had when—" His eyes widened with sudden recollection. He leveled a finger at Tab. "When he tripped me at home. On purpose! He did it on purpose, Mom. That's not Tab. That's Roy!"

Roy laughed. "Way to go," he said. "You're able to put two and two together. Reckon they do still teach kids something in them public schools now and then, don't they? Betcha don't know cursive, though."

Sandra stood, positioning herself between Roy and the bed her oldest son occupied. She set her jaw, eyes narrowing. Her hands balled into fists. "Get away from my sons," she said. "Go back to whatever shit-infested dimension you came from. You're dead. You don't belong here."

Roy stamped his right foot. "YOU don't belong here! *I* should still be here. Your dead-ass husband is the only reason I ain't!" He tossed Tab's folded composition notebook away. It landed beside Sandra's chair, open to the image Tab had drawn of Roy surrounded by other figures. The arrows he'd cut in half with the eraser had healed. Roy snatched up the pencil, holding it with the sharpened end up. He wielded it at Sandra and Jeremy like a knife. "Now I'm gonna be rid of him for good."

"Uh uh," Sandra said. "Nope. I've seen this movie before." She grabbed the corded remote control attached to the side of Jeremy's bed and jammed her thumb on the button labeled with the nurse icon that somehow everyone always recognizes as a nurse even though nurses don't wear those strange little hats anymore. At least not in Hollow River Medical Center.

Roy lunged at her. He was stopped mid-step by the voice of Tim Beard coming from behind Sandra. "Leave them alone!" She likewise recoiled at the sound.

Jeremy crouched on his hands and knees on top of the bedsheets, resembling an Amazonian panther ready to pounce. A shock of his bedhead formed a single fang-shaped bang, a faux widow's peak over his brow, enhancing the effect. "Your fight is not with my sons or my wife. Your fight is with me. So let's stop hiding behind the kids and handle this like the men we used to be, huh?"

"Murderer!" Roy said. He lowered Tab's body into its own strangely squirrel-like Spider-Man crouch. To anyone watching, it might have looked like two toddler gunslingers dueling doodies at dawn. From somewhere inside Tab's head, Roy heard the boy screaming laughter at this notion. "Shut up," he said.

Jeremy/Tim arched his left eyebrow. "I didn't say anything," he fired back. "And so what if I'm a murderer? My 'victim' was a fucking rapist pile of shit."

"Not you, asshole," Roy said. "Your brat." The kid's laughter was contagious, it seemed. In spite of himself, Roy struggled to suppress a smile. Jeremy/Tim, seeing this, fought back a grin as well. It was Sandra who spoke then, snapping the tension.

"Can we all calm down for a minute?" she asked, sincerity in her voice despite the unreality of the circumstances. "I don't want either of you—Roy? Tim?—hurting my boys. They're innocent in all of this. This is ridiculous. You both look like you have to take a massive shit."

Grins surfaced on both boy's mouths, but it was Jeremy/Tim who broke. He snorted, tried to contain it, and had to wipe a long trail of snot away from his nose and upper lip with his forearm. Roy swallowed, but was unable to prevent Tab's diaphragm from joining in. He barked a laugh, cleared his throat, and swallowed. The kinetic tension he'd been holding in all of Tab's muscles dissipated like scant morning dew evaporating from shriveling grass in the dryness of a late summer drought.

"You're losing, Roy," the invader heard Tab's mouth say. Sandra, Tim, and Jeremy heard it, too. They all stared at him as the words left Tab's mouth without Roy's consent. Their internal dialogue had been severed. He could not hear Tab inside Tab's head.

Roy glanced down at the boy's hands, which were planted firmly on the floor in front of him. A hazy aura of blackish red surrounded the fingers. It was as if he was watching an old-school 3-D movie without the special red and blue glasses. "You're losing, and do you know why?"

Roy tried to sneer, but Tab's face would not cooperate. "Why?" he asked. He couldn't determine whether he'd said it aloud.

"That's the *second* time you've called me *his* son," Tab said.

Jeremy and Tim laughed together. "He called you dad's 'brat,'" Jeremy said from behind possessed lips. "But your reason is sound."

Tab squinted and stuck out his tongue in a playful act of derision. His brother responded in kind, but without anything resembling malice for once. Finally, they were on the same side.

"No," Roy said. Then, stronger, "No, I am not losing. I get payback. I will have justice for my life. I want back what I had. I want my life back. And *I WILL HAVE IT!*"

He sprang. With or without Tab's body, Roy had grown weary of waiting. The recoil sent Tab reeling backwards. He landed on his hands and butt. The point of the pencil in his right hand snapped on impact.

"Shit!"

He scooped up the pieces and scrambled backward, slamming his back against the door. The composition notebook lay where Roy had tossed it. It was open to the page on which he'd drawn the man. Tab snagged it as the ghost's hands locked in Jeremy/Tim's. Roy shoved Jeremy's hands backward on his wrists. The strain made cords stand out on his brother's neck. Tab's mom joined the fray. She stood behind Jeremy, pressing the backs of his hands, struggling in vain to shove them forward again. "Let. Him. Go!" she said between halting breaths. "You're dead! You're both dead! Let him go!"

She fought for Jeremy, but Tab sensed his mother was referring to both of her sons: the one gripped by his protective father and the one battling his own inner demons that allowed Roy to wreak havoc on the living members of his family. Yes, they were both dead. Both dad and both dead. Tab was reminded of a Jimmy Buffett song Tim had played endlessly after Hurricane Katrina ravaged Louisiana and Mississippi. "Breathe In, Breathe Out, Move On," a song about dealing with what life throws at you and allowing the past to stay in the past.

"There's nothing to see here," Tab said, quoting a statement Dr. Clifford had offered in *Soothing the Obsessive-Compulsive Beast*'s section on rumination. "There's nothing to see here because the past is in the past. It's dead and it's gone. And so are you."

He closed his eyes, relaxing against the door. The eraser end of his pencil dangled over the image of Roy. The grunts, groans, and protests of struggle from Jeremy's hospital bed loomed large in his consciousness. With some effort, they faded into a hum of white noise.

Tab focused on the buzzing of the fluorescent lights and the roar of the hospital HVAC. His mind blank, his eyes rolled back in his head. He positioned the eraser on the page and began to rub.

CHAPTER THIRTY-SIX

A guttural moan followed by the most blood curdling, coyote-like howl of pain he'd ever heard broke his reverie. The pencil fell from Tab's hands. His eyelids fluttered open and, when his vision cleared, he was met with the image of Roy lying flat on his back on the floor in front of Jeremy's bed. The ghost brayed in pain while Jeremy/Tim leaned over the bed railing, agog. Sandra had backed away from the scene, unable to see what was happening but understanding, for now, Roy was no longer a threat.

His hands were missing.

No blood flowed from the stubs at the end of his arms. There was no gore. No blood vessels, muscles, or bones. Both of Roy's arms ended in nothing. He continued to yawp and groan as if someone had kicked him in the balls, but Tab doubted the ghost could experience pain, or anything at all. If there were no joints or muscles or blood, how likely was it Roy had the inner workings necessary to send pain signals to his brain? It wasn't.

Tab stepped forward, staring at the writhing figure on the floor with fascination and revulsion. Jeremy, too, remained locked on Roy, apparently able to perceive him as long as he was connected to their dad.

"What's happening?" their mom asked. She sidestepped Jeremy's bed and stood beside Tab, clasping her hands together beneath her chin and staring at—well, at nothing as far as she was concerned. "What's going on?"

Jeremy answered her in his own voice, not his dad's. "Tab did something to him," he said, a hint of admiration in his voice. "He doesn't have hands anymore." He burst into a gale of uncontrolled laughter. "He doesn't have *hands* anymore because Tab erased them! That's *hilarious*! Way to go, bro!"

"Stand up," Tab said, ignoring both his mother and his brother. "And stop crying. You're not hurt. You're not even bleeding."

"My hands!" Roy screamed. "You took my hands!"

"Yep. I'm gonna take the rest of you, too, but I want you to hear this first. Stand up. Or sit up. I don't care. But if you don't stop squalling I'll take your mouth, too. I'm tired of listening to it."

"Fuck you."

Tab smirked. "Alright." He closed his eyes and positioned the eraser over the drawing of Roy. He was about to fall backwards, into the blank pillow-like realm of his concentration, when Roy spoke up again.

"Okay, okay. You win. I'm sitting up."

Tab opened his eyes and confirmed it. Roy sat on the floor beside Jeremy's hospital bed, his elbows resting on his knees. His incomplete limbs dangled there, empty wrists pointing down at his work boots. His eye sockets formed teardrop shapes, narrow at their outside corners and arched near the bridge of his nose, as if he'd been crying. The frown on the lower half of his face stretched from jowl to jowl, creating deep folds on either side of his chin that made him resemble a ventriloquist's dummy.

Tab squatted and plopped down on the floor across from him, assuming a posture similar to Roy. Although Roy would've been a foot and a half taller than him in real life, Tab was able to stare him in his eye sockets. He was hurt, losing power. By all accounts, he was now a small man. Tab opened his mouth to speak but was interrupted by two firm knocks at the door. A second later, the door opened, and Nurse Molly appeared.

"Mrs. Beard, I—" She spied Tab seated on the floor. To his great relief, she looked the same as she had before he'd erased her. Except for a haze or gloss over her eyes. She looked as if she'd recently freed herself from an anchor that had dragged her into a fathomless afternoon nap. "There you are! I'm so sorry, Mrs. Beard, I have no idea how he got by me. I was standing right outside. He was there one minute and gone the next. Do you want me to take him back to One?"

Sandra shook her head and smiled in a forced way. "No, no thank you. We're fine. We need a bit of alone time, please."

Nurse Molly bowed her head to indicate she understood and backed out. The door clicked into place behind her.

"You're a part of me," Tab said as if he'd never been interrupted. "Don't know if it's because of blood or that thing that attacked me in the storm, but you're a part of me. I don't think I can do anything about it unless someone re-wires my brain. I guess you saw Nurse Molly is back from wherever she went. I didn't *murder* her, like you said. I made her go away for a little while. She never even knew. Look, your hands are already starting to come back." He nodded at Roy's stumps. Faint outlines were appended to them now, hints of fingers and knuckles there and yet not quite there.

"You can't kill me," Roy said. His voice was low, quiet, as if speaking more to himself than Tab.

"No, I can't kill you. But I *can* make you go away. I can make you go away every time you pop up. I don't care what shape you take and it doesn't matter where we are. I don't think I even need to use my pencils or erasers to do it now. They're just...things."

"Ceremonial objects," Jeremy said. "Like the stuff they use in exorcisms when someone gets demon possessed."

"Right. Right. *Ceremonial objects* that help get me in the right spot. But if I keep working on my brain, I don't think I'll need them anymore, either."

"What are you saying, kid?" Roy asked, a tremor in his voice on the two-syllable word. For Tab, it was a welcome sound.

"I'm saying I might not ever be rid of you. I'm also saying you can't ever win. I have what I need to beat you. Over and over again. Thanks to Dr. Clifford. Thanks to my mom. Thanks to my brother. Thanks to my dad. I'm not alone. They might not see you, but they know you're there. They can help me fight you when I need them to. Not that I'll need them to do much."

"I'll keep coming back," Roy hissed. "Whenever you least expect it, I'll be whispering in your arrogant little shit ear. Telling you all the things you least want to know, all the things you and your family have done wrong, all the ways it's gonna all come back to get ya." He crawled up on his refreshed hands and knees and leaned in towards Tab, nose-to-nose. "You're gonna have to deal with me for the rest of your miserable little shit life."

"Maybe," Tab said, not breaking his gaze. "But it's not going to be fun for you anymore. I know who I am. I'm Tab. Child of Tim and Sandra Beard. Brother of Jeremy Beard. I'm nine. I'm an artist. Sometimes I'm going to make mistakes. I have good days and I have bad days. But I will never, ever not be a good person. Any time you come back for me, I'll be ready to send you away."

Roy's malicious grin faltered.

"You know it's true," Tab said. "I see your face. You know it, and you'd best remember it. If you want to continue to live in this world or move on to whatever's next, it's up to you. I'm warning you, though, you won't like where I can send you if you try to hurt me or my family anymore."

"You'll never get rid of me," Roy countered again, a song on repeat.

"I'm not trying to," Tab said. "But if you stay, you're staying the way *I* say."

Roy opened his mouth to rebut but could not find his tongue. He raised his phantom fingers to his lips, or where his lips should have been, and found them now gone as well. Tab had erased his mouth and had done so without stopping to watch what he was doing or falling into his trance.

He relished Roy's panic. The man with no eyes and no mouth could not scream at him. He could not protest what was happening to him any more than Tab could protest the bump on his temple or half his DNA originating from a rapist thug.

Roy scrambled to his hands and knees, looking like he was about to charge. Tab responded by erasing his legs, his arms, and his new hands. The ghost face-planted, his non-corporeal body without limbs. He lay grub-like on the floor of the hospital room.

"Whoa," Jeremy said, still peering from over the ledge of his bed at the events transpiring below. "Damn, Tab. You're stone cold!"

Tab grinned but did not look away from what he was doing. Next, he erased Roy all the way up to his neck, so nothing but the man's eyeless, mouthless head remained. Without the weight of the torso attached to it, the head cantilevered onto its neck and chin, giving Roy the appearance of a Halloween jack-o'-lantern left on the porch about two weeks too long.

The man's eye sockets pleaded with Tab to either stop erasing or to put him out of his misery and finish the job. It was impossible to tell which. Tab took those eye sockets next, not that Roy was going to miss them. He started to go ahead and erase the rest of the man from this plane, at least until Tab's anxiety betrayed him again and allowed the ghost to return. Then he had an idea.

"You still have ears, Roy," he said. "I know you can hear me. So listen. I know you'll be back. Fast if things stay the way they've been. But do yourself a favor and don't bother me when you do. Or else. I'll do this again. And again. And again. Every time.

"There will be times I get tired. You can't win them all. But I will keep fighting you. I will keep winning."

The transparent muscles in Roy's cheeks and forehead wriggled and twitched. He wanted to argue, Tab thought.

"God, do it already," Jeremy said.

So Tab did.

And Roy vanished.

For now.

CHAPTER THIRTY-SEVEN

Jeremy sat back on his bed, his eyes rimmed red and his face ghost white. He plummeted backwards and appeared to lose consciousness again. Sandra rushed to his side, dashing through the ghost of Tim Beard as she crossed the floor. She shuddered when she did. Tim, Tab noticed, reached out to her as if to give her a hug, but ended up hugging only the air in front of him. He had left his oldest son's body, having drained the boy of energy.

Tab could still see him, though. That was new. The ghost turned to him, seeing he could see, and smiled. "We're all exhausted now, I think," Tim said. "I should go, too."

"Will you ever come back?" Tab asked. Sandra, in the midst of pressing the button to call the nurse, glanced at him and then at the void to which he spoke. "Your dad's still here, isn't he?"

Tab nodded. "He is. He's saying goodbye."

"I love you, Tim Beard," Sandra said to thin air. "I always will. Thank you for looking out for us. But I promise, from here on out we're going to be okay. We're all going to be okay, no matter what happens. You can rest." She stretched out her hands, palms up. Tim took them, although Tab doubted either of them could feel the other.

He listened for the reply. "He said he loves you, too. He also says he's sorry for being so mad all the time at the end. And he said to tell you Facebook is shit? He said you'll know what that means." Sandra laughed. Genuinely, it seemed to Tab. It had been a while. A long silence fell between them. Finally, Tim waved, smiling as he vanished from sight.

"Is he still here?" Tears streamed down Sandra's face.

Tab shook his head. "He's gone. I don't know if it's for good or not. He didn't say."

Sandra nodded, dropping her hands to her sides. The door to Room 314 opened, after which two nurses rushed to Jeremy's side. One of them pried open his eyelids, one at a time, and shined a penlight into each pupil. Another checked his pulse and listened to his breaths.

"He fainted," the first nurse concluded. "Just too much stressful activity today is my bet." She checked his breathing, adjusting some of the cables connected to him to ensure that nothing was restricting his blood flow or oxygen. A moment later, he revived on his own.

"What happened?" he asked.

Sandra knelt by him and stroked the hair off his forehead. "You fainted, hon. That's all."

Jeremy's face bloomed pink again. His forehead was damp with sweat, but he otherwise appeared normal. Tired, though.

Sandra eyed the nurses. "Can we go soon? I think we all want to go home."

"I'll check with the doctor. I know they want to keep him overnight for observation. If he's doing well in the morning, they'll probably let him go."

To run up the insurance bill, Tab thought. Except that wasn't a Tab thought. That was a Roy thought. *Is he back already?* Tab searched his insides, scanning his body with his mind, seeking any hints of sensation that the bad man had returned. There were none.

After the sun trekked three hours above the eastern horizon, the Beards left Hollow River for the tiresome drive home. Sandra switched the air conditioner to its coldest setting, cranking the fan to High. She plunged her knuckles into her eyes now and then, rubbing at them to stay awake.

In the passenger's seat, Jeremy sat with his iPod Touch in his lap, its screen dark, the cord of his earbuds pooled around it. He propped his chin on his fist and stared out the window at the oncoming lane.

In the back seat, Tab snoozed. His head lolled with each bump and turn of Sandra's car. The composition notebook and half-pencil he'd discovered in the children's psych ward lay on the floorboard at his feet. The notebook was open to the page on which he'd drawn and erased Roy. The blank space surrounded by shapes of other figures with arrows pointing to them was filling in again.

The first thing to appear was an angry pair of empty eye sockets.

JULY 13, 2024

CHAPTER THIRTY-EIGHT

Tab tossed his their last hay bale onto the stack. They dusted their hands, enjoying the sweet aroma through their mask as it billowed off their gloves. Jeremy, who had not yet finished college but was home for the summer, occasionally ridiculed them for wearing the N95. Tab was not bothered. They had seen enough sinus infections and COVID deaths over the years to convince them that protecting the airways was an important step toward a healthier life.

"You're twenty-three, for God's sake. You don't have to worry about shit like that yet," their brother chided. "You don't even smoke!"

Tab responded with a simple shrug. An ounce of prevention was worth a pound of cure, especially if legitimate cures for most diseases of the respiratory system did not yet exist. Jeremy shook his head, tossed his own bale onto the stack, and eyed their mother.

Sandra sat at the edge of the loft, dangling her legs over it and gazing at the horizon as the sun disappeared beyond. The dust and chaff of the day's work coated her hair and clothes.

"Do you believe him?" Jeremy asked, mocking incredulity in his voice.

"Them," Sandra said without pause.

Jeremy smacked his forehead. "Right. *Them*. Sorry. I struggle with the whole pronoun thing. Sorry. Sorry, Tab! I forget you're a damn liberal now."

"What's that supposed to mean?"

"Well, you know. The hair. The pronouns. The makeup you wear sometimes when we're not throwing dead grass. Liberal."

"I'm not liberal or conservative," they replied, then drew a circle in the air around their own face. "This isn't a political statement. It's who I am, who I've always been. It just took a long time to figure it out."

"Well, on Fox—"

They waved it away. "Yeah, yeah. Are you kidding? I know you don't watch Fox. You might be a white man but you're not an *old* white man. You get all your bullshit from YouTube and Twitter."

"X."

"Fine. X. Look, gender is fluid. There are plenty of dude-bros and Karens, conservative *and* liberal, who refuse to understand that. Some of them are people you'd otherwise consider smart. But not everyone with a penis is an aggressive asshole who wants to fuck or fight everything, and not everyone with a vagina is a ball-buster or a fragile doll in need of your protection. You'll find plenty of people on every side of the political spectrum who still buy into those old stereotypes, though."

Tab waited, heart racing just a little too fast, for an argument, but none came. Jeremy returned in silence to hitching his final bale of hay for the stacks. Tab glanced at their mother, noting the wistful Mona Lisa smile on her lips. She got it.

All these years, all those times that Tab's older brother had tried to insult their masculinity. At times it was still capable of causing prickles of shame just beneath the surface of their skin. Grow up in a culture that consistently tells you that you are not who you are supposed to be…well, it's hard to put away those things even after you discover the truth about yourself and about humanity as a whole. Never mind that Tab didn't identify as either masculine or feminine. They wore a little makeup when they felt like it. They grew their hair long because they liked it that way.

Sometimes they had a "he" day: a little beard stubble, some wax to slick back the hair, turning up a cold bottle of beer on a rustic afternoon with a friend. Sometimes it was more of a "she" day: some makeup, providing an ear for a pal, dressing to the nines to take in a show. Most often, they were "they," and that was enough.

In spite of backlash from folks who didn't or were unwilling to understand, Tab felt a certain amount of freedom and security in being themselves. They could enjoy the masculine hormonal rush of accomplishment after fixing a running toilet or tossing a bale of hay *and* allow themselves to be vulnerable enough to tear up in front of strangers over movies like *Past Lives*.

In 2016, when Tab was fifteen years old, they'd figured out who they were. In secret at first, they began to connect online with others who identified as they did. Their true identity surfaced then, in the comfort and safety of their tribe. When the pandemic hit in 2020, Jeremy remained isolated in his college dorm while Tab locked down with their mother at the farm.

As days turned into weeks and then into months, they chose to come out to their mother. Only after careful conversations in which they attempted to engage Sandra about her political opinions and identify any latent phobias about the LGBTQIA+ community. When they felt safe, they had the talk.

Sandra, who claimed to be conservative despite everything that had happened to American democracy since 2017, accepted Tab's nonbinary self immediately. And that made it impossible for the more extreme right-winger lurking inside their brother to deny it. At least while their mother was still alive.

Speaking of not alive, Roy made fewer appearances these days. Tab learned about boundaries not long after Jeremy was discharged from the hospital. Dr. Clifford instructed them well on how to erect them and how to maintain them. Although Tab never opened up to him about who Roy really was, the doctor's lessons on combatting anxiety had a side effect of diminishing the ghost's ability to harass them.

Puberty seemed to have diminished Tab's art powers as well. At least for a while. Oh, they could still draw like the dickens. But their art had little effect on the real world while the pimples were popping and the hormones were raging. Looking back, Tab figured it was a good thing they hadn't been able to manipulate the external world in that way as a teen, before their rational adult mind emerged. Imagine the maudlin, overwrought results if they had!

It wasn't until they entered their twenties that they felt it resurge. Still, they were careful with it. Their ability had been useful to keep Roy at a distance, but under the wrong conditions it could cause as much harm to others as good.

Once, their mother had asked them why they didn't use that ability to change the world for the better: ensure the right people obtained power, or at least ensure that the wrong people didn't. Tab pointed out that what was right and good to them might not be right and good to everyone else. Interfering in other people's lives and decisions was not a role they wanted to play, nor was it a heroic or moral thing to do. Even almighty Superman, who had replaced Batman as Tab's favorite superhero, refused to play morality police in the comics from time to time. To deny others their choices and fates in the name of some perceived moral imperative felt too...well, authoritarian, for lack of a better word. Instead, Tab chose to make art when they wanted to and to use their abilities only when absolutely necessary.

Their work done for the day, Tab pulled loose their hair tie. Blonde curls cascaded from their shoulder-length ponytail, framing their face. They shook it, sending a magical aura of yellow dust billowing in all directions. Crouching with a grunt beside their mother, they dangled their legs out into space.

Sandra patted them on the knee. Crow's feet had invaded the corners of her eyes. The laugh lines that used to appear on each side of her mouth after a long, hearty guffaw had deepened into dry riverbeds framing thin and cracked lips.

When Sandra sighed these days, it was not a smooth sound, but ragged, as if something had caught in the back of her throat. She did so now, sounding choked. Tab had to resist the urge to clap her on the back. She'd had COVID twice since 2020. Her dry cough made it sound as though she'd never recovered from the second round. "Do you two care anything at all about keeping this place when I'm gone?" she asked, spreading her arms to specify the vast acreage of the Beard farm.

Jeremy joined them, concern in his eyes. He scraped his own mop of dark brown hair away from his forehead and sat on Sandra's opposite side, shooting Tab a "what is this all about?" side-eye in the process. Tab again replied with a shrug.

"I'm getting too old to keep running things here," she said without looking at either of them. "Too weak, too. All those things your dad wanted to do with this place, they're too much for one person, healthy or not. I was only the business end until he passed. The hands I hired years ago have all moved on from here. They either grew up or grew old or grew out, you know?" She sniffled. "And you two have your own lives you want to lead, don't you?"

Tab knew they did. They had their art. A number of their illustrations had been published in a popular horror anthology for kids a year or so before. One Hollow County librarian had invited them to a signing over in the Hollow River main branch, calling Tab the next Stephen Gammell. Tab didn't think so. They could do creepy, but they much preferred political satire and commentary, stuff the county commissioners and school boards seemed to enjoy trying to ban. Just because they chose not to use their power to manipulate others didn't mean they couldn't persuade them to change their minds on their own.

Jeremy still needed to complete his degree in media and entertainment with an internship he'd snagged at Channel 6. Tab grinned at the thought of their brother in front of television cameras, pretending to communicate with ghosts and demons. His custom-made Sta-Puft Marshmallow Man pillow, ratty with age, would no doubt ride along with him, part of his "I've always been into the paranormal" persona.

After all the years and everything they'd seen, Jeremy's paranormal investigation show aspirations endured. Hell, he'd even managed to wrangle an interview with a Channel 6 reporter, Afia Afton, in 2019. It was after he'd "investigated" the old Gordon place on a lark. A lot of what he'd seen and heard sounded made up to Tab, though. Except for the demonic dog-like creatures, of course. Those were real.

Now and then, looking out their bedroom window at dusk, Tab thought they could see those glowing red eyes, crouched in the distance behind thick rows of ragweed and dallisgrass. A blink, and they were gone again. If they had ever been there.

From somewhere, a lonesome, doleful howl permeated the summer dusk as if to confirm his thoughts. Tab shivered in spite of the heat. They had been a good kid, but those old doubts surfaced now and again. Had the demon dog intended to drag them to Hell that night in the midst of one of the most horrific flood events of their life? Had they been a bad kid up to that point? Were they really the good person now that their dad said they were back then?

And who were they to judge their brother? It's not like anyone would believe their own ghost story had they chosen to share it. Jeremy himself rarely acknowledged what they'd been through as kids. Tab found that odd, considering the older brother's preoccupation. If you were a ghost hunter, would you not want to share your history with ghosts? They never said so, but Tab thought Jeremy might have chosen to stay quiet about it for their sake. And that was fine.

"I don't think either of us would be able to keep this up the way you have and the way you and Dad did, Mom," Jeremy said. "Are you thinking about selling the place?"

She laughed. There was derisiveness in it. "We were thinking about selling it back when your dad was still alive. He was just about ready to sell your great aunt's old store and the property around it when he died. I never did hear anything back from the developer."

"He ghosted you."

She smiled at that. "Yeah. He ghosted us. A new one is interested. They want to subdivide it. Put up a bunch of McMansions to sit empty and be a nice tax write-off when the bottom falls out of the housing market again, I guess. Property value hit its peak early last year. Every time I get a Zillow email it's about how much the value has dropped. So I guess if I'm going to sell, it should be now."

"Sell it," her children said together, grinning at each other.

"Jinx," Jeremy said. "You owe me a Coke."

"Seriously, Mom," Tab said. "It's past time to let go of all this. You don't need the money anymore. Even if you did and the value keeps going down, what you earn from selling this place will outpace any income from keeping it running. If you can close at the right time, you might be able to move after the last cut this year. I guess you'd have to sell off the rest of the livestock first, though."

She nodded. "Yeah, that's what I keep telling myself. It's going to be a lot of work to wind this place down. It's hard to let go of your dad. This was the only place we ever lived together."

Both Tab and Jeremy wrapped an arm around her, Jeremy around her shoulders and Tab around her waist. "You're not letting go of him," Tab said. With their left hand, they fingered the bump on their temple. "It doesn't matter where you go or what you do with this farm, Mom. He's there. And he's here." Tab tapped their heart.

Sandra offered them a wan smile. "Yeah. You're right."

Together, the three Beards watched the remaining rays of sunlight disappear in the distance. The evening star twinkled brightly above where old Sol had trekked that day. They sat a while, until the floodlight affixed to the barn below their feet flickered to life in the mounting darkness. Their mother began to hum the tune to an old Eagles song, "The Last Resort."

Tab's bump itched and burned. An unexpected midsummer breeze attempted to cool it for them, but to no avail. Sandra coughed. The urge to clap their mother on the back surged again. It would not help. It would send her plummeting to the earth, possibly to her death. Tab would never follow through on it but felt a pang of guilt for having the thought in the first place. *Were* they a bad kid?

Not now, Roy. Not now.

They'd have to do some drawing after dinner that night. Just a little one they could trash and forget about for a time. Until it started to come back again, which it always did.

Then life would continue.

As it always did.

ACKNOWLEDGMENTS

Although most novels are birthed by individual authors, it takes a village to raise them into what you finally enjoy. *Tab's Terrible Third Eye* is the result of more than a year of drafts followed by weeks of beta reading, new drafts, more weeks of professional editing, and discussions with people who know things. Although I'll be the one who ends up getting the accolades (and admonishments) for this novel, what follows is a list of folks to whom I am indebted for their contributions during its development.

First up is my editor, Megan Harris. This is the second novel of mine she's tackled. She's a pro with an eye for detail and an ability to catch mistakes in both my grammar and my research. If you found any mistakes or awkwardness in this novel, you can be sure it is a result of my overriding her suggestions.

Next is Paula Rozelle Hanback, who illustrated and designed the cover for this novel as well as most of my previous work. She also provided the custom font that I used for the title, drop caps, chapter headings, and more. I loved the font so much that I ended up replacing the headings font on isaacthorne.com with it.

Third up is voice actor Tom Force, who narrated the audiobook edition of *Tab's Terrible Third Eye*. For the first time in the history of my work, an audiobook edition is being released at nearly the same time as the print and ebook editions. Tom's hypnotic performance brought Tab and all the other characters to life in a way that I could have only dreamt about.

Last but not least is the long list of beta readers who volunteered their time and energy to pore over one of this book's early drafts. More than forty people signed up for my beta readers list to be notified when new work is available. Of those, thirteen provided feedback. You'll find their influence most specifically in Tab's dialogue and behavior, Sandra's backstory, Jeremy's relationship with Tab, and Roy's menace. With gratitude, those beta readers are: Julie Beck, the poet Richard Bell, Janel Bernotas, Vickie Cox, Ashley Doran-Roth, Kate Forsman, Nicole Haugen, Kary Irle, Amanda Johns, Audrey Marmol, Edward Massey, Jim Phoenix, Stephanie Silvestri, and Lisa Westenbarger.

I made notes, relied on memory, and traveled back in email time to compile these names. If I have neglected to mention anyone, it is not intentional. Finally, I want to express my gratitude to you, dear reader, for picking up this novel and giving it a chance. Thank you.

—Isaac Thorne

ABOUT THE AUTHOR

Isaac Thorne is a perpetually starved writer who devours everything horror. He gets stranded in the hills of Middle Tennessee when it snows, but otherwise enjoys living there.

The audiobook edition of Isaac's 2019 novel *The Gordon Place* is the winner of the 2020 Independent Audiobook Awards in the Horror category. In a review of *The Gordon Place*, *Publishers Weekly* stated that "…this work proves Thorne to be a gifted storyteller."

Isaac's 2022 novel *Hell Spring* was a finalist in the Horror category for the 2023 Next Generation Indie Book Awards. *Tab's Terrible Third Eye* is his third novel.

When not writing, Isaac can be found running on a treadmill, reading, or streaming horror movies. He is also addicted to podcasts.

ALSO BY ISAAC THORNE

Novels
The Gordon Place
Hell Spring

Short Story Collections
Road Kills

PRAISE FOR 'HELL SPRING'

"...the mix of sorrow and shame powering these stories lends substance to the scenes of horror. The shocking moments deliver serious jolts." —Booklife Review by *Publishers Weekly*

"It is disorienting, grotesque, absurdly funny and oddly hot..." —Drew Rowsome, *My Gay Toronto*

"The small town and the store are compelling, claustrophobic backdrops to this drama, and the book's tension mounts at an exponential rate." —*Foreword Clarion Reviews*

PRAISE FOR 'THE GORDON PLACE'

"With the right amount of gore and a permeating sense of dread, this work proves Thorne to be a gifted storyteller." —*Publishers Weekly*

"...a thrilling throwback horror tale that tears through the pages like a hound from hell." —David Simms, *Scream Magazine*

"As comforting as sliding into a warm bloodbath. And just as soothing and nerve-jangling." —Drew Rowsome, *My Gay Toronto Magazine*

"Even the most strange and otherworldly scenes in the book are so well described that you feel like you're there in the midst of the action." —Yeti, *TN Horror News*

THANK YOU

Isaac Thorne and Lost Hollow Books appreciate the time you have devoted to this novel. If you like what you've read, please consider rating and reviewing this book on your platform of purchase or any other platform of your choosing. Ratings and reviews help books like these get discovered by readers like you.

You can find links to popular review sources and more at Isaac Thorne's landing page:

isaacthorne.contactin.bio

www.ingramcontent.com/pod-product-compliance
Lightning Source LLC
Chambersburg PA
CBHW021412150125
20375CB00016BA/34/J